THE
FOGHORN
ECHOES

ALSO BY DANNY RAMADAN

The Clothesline Swing

THE
FOGHORN
ECHOES

DANNY RAMADAN

CANONGATE

First published in Great Britain in 2022
by Canongate Books Ltd, 14 High Street, Edinburgh EH1 1TE

First published in the USA in 2022 by Viking, a division of
Penguin Random House Canada Ltd

canongate.co.uk

1

British Library Cataloguing-in-Publication Data
A catalogue record for this book is available on
request from the British Library

ISBN 978 1 83885 465 2
Export ISBN 978 1 83885 466 9

Book design by Jennifer Griffiths

Printed and bound in Great Britain by Clays Ltd, Elcograf S.p.A.

To those who took to the sea and those who the sea took.

O sea traveller, I'm here to bid my farewells
I burden winds with my love and send them after you.

But I fear the storms and the tides,
Instead my soul will travel with you: to deliver you, and to bring you back.

AMIL MUBARAK, *Lebanese poet*

2003

Children shouldn't know the horror of war, but Hussam was old enough by now. At first his parents barred him from the news while all of Damascus buzzed with tales from neighbouring Iraq: stories of mass graves and downed airplanes, of buildings as tall as mountains crumbling to dust, of invading Americans with blond hair and blue eyes. The cafés replaced the music channels on their television sets with an endless stream of news reports. Teachers substituted their physical education classes for military preparations sessions, teaching Hussam and his peers how to load a gun and how to build a functional gas mask. Wealthy neighbours sold their homes in haste and bought airplane tickets across the Mediterranean. Finally, when his mother needed his help setting up an emergency stash of canned fruits and pickled vegetables, she sat Hussam down and told him of the war.

"Every push by the Americans causes an attack by the Iraqis," she said. "No one will win."

He repeated what he'd learned in school. "Every action has an equal and opposite reaction."

Hussam became mesmerized by the war. After school, he ignored the calls of his friends to join them for a street football match and ran home instead. He unbuckled his school uniform belt as he climbed the stairs and kicked off his dusty boots at the gate of their one-bedroom apartment.

"No running in the house," his mother said. Hussam dodged her and rushed to the living room, turned up the volume on his father's old TV. He flipped the three Syrian channels for news segments on the American invasion with the same enthusiasm he'd once used to search for cartoons. Fascinated by fighter jets, combat tanks, and speeches from mustachioed military leaders, he mimicked the knee kicks of marching troops and the hand salutes of loyal soldiers to foreign flags of stripes and stars. Resting the wooden end of his mother's broom on his shoulder, he stomped like a guard, ready to jump into the hallway and snap his prized rifle at an elusive enemy.

In Hussam's fifteen years, he'd never visited Iraq. He knew of the country through his studies of regional history, aware that it was a capital of a long-lost Islamic empire. His father reminisced about the bygone glory of Islam, which had been shattered by what the old man considered unholy attacks on the one true Allah and His devoted people by the infidel West. At school, a boy from Iraq had recently joined Hussam's class. A refugee, he was told. A black-haired, short-tempered teenager with sun-kissed skin who spoke Arabic with a strange accent.

"Did you hear of the Iraqi man who shot down an Apache helicopter with his shotgun?" Hussam sat with three friends around a square plastic table; they each held thirteen playing cards tight to their chests and exchanged suspicious glances they'd learned from watching black-and-white westerns on rented VHS tapes. His mother set a tray of black honey-sweetened tea and a generous dish of mamoul on the table and poured the tea into golden-rimmed glass cups. It was a late May afternoon, and the streets of Damascus roared with the shamal winds, whipping dust and sand, tilting the trees into respectful bows.

If Hussam's father knew they were playing cards, he'd be raging mad. The exam season was only a month away, and they needed to focus on their studies. "Especially the son of Omar and his first wife," his father said, referring to Wassim, for he rarely could recall the names of Hussam's friends. Hussam's mother was more forgiving of his hobbies and allowed him to play the occasional card game, warning him in time of his father's return.

"I heard he shot it down with a single bullet," Wassim said, drawing a card. Wassim had never seen a military helicopter, only the ones that dropped colourful papers on the rooftops across his neighbourhood on national holidays, reminding people that the newly elected Syrian president was a progressive leader who supported the Iraqi brothers in their righteous war against the imperialist Americans. Whenever this happened, Wassim would hurry to the roof to sweep his pigeon cages so that none of the birds would peck at the sharp papers. He'd inherited thirty-three birds from his uncle, who'd died young of an unknown illness eighteen months earlier. Last summer, Wassim had built small birdcages on his family's rooftop using old wires and cheap wood. He printed his name in black marker on the feathers of the birds' inner wings and tied a ribbon to their feet before releasing them to the open skies. After a couple of hours of fluttering between clouds and darting through the maze of the old neighbourhood, the birds would return when Wassim whistled sharply and waved a flag made from an old T-shirt. He would count and examine the birds as he ushered them into the cages, surprised each time that all of them returned. He locked the deadbolts and hung the keys around his neck.

Wassim slammed a card on the table, initiating a new round. He parroted what he'd heard on his father's TV. "The Iraqi used his old shotgun to bring down the flying monster. He inherited the gun from his grandfather who used it to kill British invaders back in the 1920s." Wassim's voice was changing, becoming crisper and deeper than the piercing screams he and Hussam used to exchange while playing soldiers and thieves in their neighbourhood of Mazzeh.

Wassim raised his cards to his face, but Hussam could see his eyes, which were blue, unlike any he'd seen before. They contrasted his tanned face and crowned his high nose. Downy hair that hadn't blackened quite yet gathered on his upper lip, its colour similar to the soft fur Hussam noticed on Wassim's body last time they went to a swimming pool. It covered his forearms, rounded his chest muscles, and led to his belly button like an arrow pointing down. His clear skin looked hot to the touch.

Hussam, on the other hand, struggled with acne that he used all the old wives' tricks to combat, passed down to him from his knowledgeable mother. Weeks ago, on his fifteenth birthday, she'd poured cinnamon tea over a pot filled with honey and boiled it until all that was left was a golden slop. After plastering the hot sludge on her son's face as he screeched in pain, she held him still and blew on it until it cooled.

"This will make all the girls in the neighbourhood coo after you." She fanned his face, then skinned the mixture off. He groaned. "Your father wants to talk to you," she said when she'd finished her treatment. She handed him a wet towel for his agitated face and sent him to his parents' bedroom.

Hussam walked into the bedroom he was rarely allowed to visit. It was warm with his mother's crochet work interweaving colours and patterns into pillowcases and tablecloths. Photos under her vanity's glass documented Hussam's childhood, along with a black-and-white wedding photo in which she looked terrified and a recent photo of his father smoking argileh on the beach in Lattakia. His father sat on the side of the bed and tapped twice on the blue cover, inviting Hussam to sit next to him.

"Luqman the Wise was precious among the people of Allah." His father pulled out the Quran that rested on his bedside table. "And he passed his knowledge to his son in Ten Commandments not to be disobeyed."

Hussam rested his temple on his father's chest.

"O my son, do not associate anyone with Allah," his father recited from the holy book, his voice deep and rhythmic. "And We have enjoined upon man to care for his parents. Be grateful to Me and to your parents; to Me is the final arrival." Hussam heard the words breathed out of the lungs before they were uttered by the mouth. "O my son, indeed if sin should be the weight of a mustard seed and should be within a rock lost in the heavens or in the earth, Allah will bring it forth. Indeed, Allah is Subtle and Acquainted." Hussam caught a whiff of beard oil and the miswak his father brushed his teeth with. "And do not walk through the earth exultantly. Indeed, Allah does not like everyone self-deluded and boastful."

"Baba?" Hussam said.

"Son, it's time you stop calling me baba like children," the old man said. "You can call me Abu Hussam. I'm your father and you are my son, but you are a man now and we are two brothers."

Hussam's eyes filled with tears, but he was quickly admonished by his father.

"Men don't cry, son."

"Yes, Abu Hussam." Hussam sniffed.

Hussam snapped out of his memory when Wassim slapped the table with a winning card. "Here. This will show you all." The other boys protested, and one of them stood up and angrily flipped his cards on the table.

"You slaughtered us like sheep!"

Hussam always partnered at cards with Wassim; they understood each other's small winks and subtle finger gestures. They read each other's body language with ease. Between homework assignments and during breaks, they played together against other teams, winning every tournament, becoming notorious throughout the school.

The boys were supposed to have played cards that morning before class, but the Iraqi boy had brought photos he'd found under his father's mattress. He informed only a select group of friends about the treasure hidden in his backpack, tucked between the pages of an anatomy schoolbook. Hussam and Wassim gathered with the group in an empty classroom and watched in anticipation as the Iraqi boy unzipped his bag.

He pulled out three photos, one after another. With every photo, the boys gasped. The Iraqi boy handed the first one to Hussam. It was the size of his palm and clearly cut out of a magazine. The delicate paper showed a naked blond woman crawling on all fours. She strategically hid her nipples and slightly arched her back, centring her ass in the background. Hussam examined the photo, crowded by the other boys, then handed it to Wassim, who quickly passed it on. Next was a brunette with her hands on her breasts lying on a kitchen counter, her legs resting on the shoulders of a naked man. Hussam lingered on this photo. The man had a six-pack, a tribal tattoo on his biceps, and a hungry look in his eyes that seemed to pierce through the photo, as if he were staring at Hussam and ignoring the woman altogether. Hussam left a sweaty finger-print on his waist.

"Dude," one of the boys whispered. Hussam passed the photo on to Wassim, who held it in his palms like precious drinking water, then brought it close to his face and squinted. The last photo was of a couple sleeping naked on silky sheets. They held each other in a loving embrace that purposefully allowed a peek of the woman's breasts and between her thighs, while almost entirely hiding the man's body. The man's lips were parted in a permanent sigh, ready to be kissed.

"Look at the big knockers on that one," another boy said behind his ear.

The man looked peaceful, his arms extending to touch his lover, hair splashed on the pillow. The woman's hand rested on the man's chest, and her lips touched his ear, her back curved like a violin. Wassim held the photo with care, as if he worried it might melt in his hands.

Hussam's mother appeared in the doorway. "I think it's time to put the cards away," she said.

The boys gathered the cards and scoring sheet, and Hussam slipped them into a drawer he kept for his private things, tucked in a corner of his pullout bed in the living room. By the time his father walked through the door, the four of them appeared to be midway through their math assignments.

Hussam planted a kiss on the back of his father's hand and placed it softly against his forehead. He smelled of melting iron, greasy and smudged by a long day at his blacksmith workshop. He pulled his hand away with a softly whispered "Allah blesses you."

"My father is expecting you and your family this Friday," Wassim said respectfully to Hussam's father, who nodded.

Hussam wasn't fond of this family visit to Wassim's home across the street. Although he went there almost daily—to watch the pigeons, play a game of *Mortal Kombat 3* on Wassim's Nintendo 64 in his own private bedroom, or drink pop and eat expensive chocolate offered to him by Wassim's father's new, young wife—on Fridays the boys had to sit politely at the table with the grown-ups and be courteous not to interrupt their mundane chit-chat.

When Friday arrived, Hussam sat at the table in Wassim's family's guest room. He hooked a finger under his collar to loosen it around his neck. A vase filled with an intricate bouquet of flowers sat atop the expansive marble table, and the walls were covered with Quranic quotations printed on lavish fabrics. The curtains were majestically draped to enhance warmth. Hussam's family didn't have a special room for guests, so they entertained in their living room, where the couch turned into his bed and the table acted as both a dinner table and a study desk for him.

"Do you think they'll manage to invade Iraq?" Hussam's father asked the adults.

Earlier Hussam's father had instructed him to avoid eye contact with Wassim's father. "Respect is the only currency we have," he explained. "Call him Uncle Abu Wassim with a hushed voice." Hussam's father got many work opportunities through Uncle Abu Wassim, who owned a couple of shops in both Al-Hariqa and Souk Al-Khajah markets in the city, selling fabrics and leathers.

Uncle Abu Wassim had upgraded his home with furniture purchased at the markets on the Homs Highway known for their sophisticated woodwork and soft cushions. He even installed those foreign seated toilets to replace the old Arabian models that required one to squat. He was the first in the neighbourhood to buy a satellite receiver that caught over sixty international TV channels from neighbouring Arab countries.

Uncle Abu Wassim had been through three wives since the death of his first, and the current one had been with him for around five years, which was the regular expiration date for his wives. He usually divorced them, but never without providing enough money to assure them a comfortable life. He even bought a house for the wife who helped him raise his only child, Wassim, in the more prestigious area around Al-Shuhada square.

The two fathers had been friends since childhood, and although Uncle Abu Wassim made his fortune by expanding the family's merchant business, Hussam's father had wanted to build a life on his own terms after his Sunni parents rejected his pleas to marry an Alawite woman he met on a trip to the coastal city of Tartus. The love affair endured despite the families' disagreements, and Hussam's father left his family for the sake of his beloved wife. He bought her flowers every two weeks, and on Thursdays she made him his favourite dessert, a wonderfully creamy blancmange studded with orange peel. She planned for Hussam to play on the streets or visit Wassim every Thursday evening so that she and her husband could have the house to themselves.

"It's been weeks since anyone saw Saddam!" Uncle Abu Wassim said. "He's disappeared into his own dungeons."

Hussam avoided eye contact.

The two wives took to a corner and began whispering gossip before slipping out to the kitchen to prepare dinner. They first met when Abu Wassim brought his new bride home in a white Mercedes covered in floral arrangements, showcasing her to the guests and neighbours. When they walked through the gate of the building, Abu Wassim lifted her up so that she could slap the dough her mother made the night before onto the arch above.

"If the dough sticks," Hussam's mother told him, "the marriage will last." The night of the wedding, while she brushed her teeth before bed, Hussam's mother gasped when she looked out the bathroom window and saw that the dough had slipped to the ground. She rushed outside with a white scarf on her hair and stood on the tips of her toes to slap the dough back where it had left its mark. She pressed it with both hands to ensure it stayed and returned home, unseen by anyone but her son, knowing that she'd saved the marriage. The next morning, when she woke up, she looked out the window to see that the dough was still in place.

Since that day, Hussam's mother had taken the young woman under her wing. She was a nineteen-year-old beauty from a nearby village who knew nothing of the city. She didn't know how to navigate the streets to get to the meat souk or the farmers' market. She didn't know to visit Souk Al-Sitat to buy glamorous lingerie that would keep her man happy. Nor did she know how to cook a perfectly spiced yalanji. Hussam's mother taught the young woman how to negotiate better prices, find the right deals, and memorize the fruits and vegetables of each season to plan feasts accordingly. She helped her plan for her post-marriage life, too, advising her to ask for jewellery on birthdays and wedding anniversaries, fearing that her divorce was already written in the books on the night of her marriage.

Restless, Hussam interrupted the conversing men. "Can we play on the roof?"

From the kitchen, the young wife clucked her tongue and warned them not to play with the pigeons. Hussam's mother saved the boys from embarrassment as she walked in carrying a tray of coffee cups for the adults.

"Coffee before lunch?" she cheerfully said. "I'll read your cups to foresee your futures." Everyone welcomed the fortune telling, and the boys slipped from the room and raced up the staircase to the rooftop.

"Do you think we can see the war from here?" Hussam said. He stood with Wassim at the edge of the roof, looking up at the sky where the pigeons flew.

"Are you stupid?" Wassim said. "It's too far away."

Hussam argued that explosions from the air strikes—or the columns of smoke, at least—might be big enough to be seen from across the border.

Wassim gazed off at the horizon. "Maybe if we climbed on the birdcages, then to the top of the elevator shaft," he suggested.

They examined the pigeons' cages, cornered between the edge of the rooftop and the walls of the elevator engine. The shaft rested like a small cube placed neatly on the rooftop. They agreed that in order to climb the wall, they would need to balance on the stone corner of the perimeter wall, then rely on a metal rod on the side of the engine room to avoid a deadly slip to the ground, seven floors down. It would be an easy pull to end up on that small roof and have a better view of the city and possibly the surrounding countries.

"Let's do it," Wassim said, and moments later he pulled Hussam up onto the roof of the small shaft. The boys stood together, looking out over the city.

"How are we going to get down?" Hussam asked. A strong gust shuddered against him and wheezed through his clothes. It felt strong enough to carry them off into the sky like paper kites. He reached out and held Wassim's hand tightly. "I want to go down," he said.

"Don't be a chicken," Wassim said. He squeezed Hussam's hand and told him not to look down. They scanned the horizon for columns of smoke, falling helicopters, or red-and-blue rockets. They soon gave up and sat on the edge of the engine room roof, their feet dangling over the side.

The city opened its embrace to them. The heart of Damascus was marked by the Umayyad Mosque, decorated with intricate mosaics that glimmered under the sun. The mosque was crowded in by low-rises and tiny old homes that pushed one another across narrow alleyways barely wide enough for bikes and horse carriages, surrounded by taller buildings built by the Ottomans and the French back in their days of occupation. These were now circled by Soviet-inspired cubes of metal and cement, and finally, the tallest of buildings at the edges of the city. Damascus was a rippled city that ricocheted history back at its people, and every era was marked on its map.

Hussam looked down at his hand intertwined with Wassim's. He gazed into his friend's eyes; their blue glimmered like a quiet lake. Wassim's nose gloriously anchored his face, like the statues Hussam had seen in the National Museum of Historical Arts.

Wassim released his hand and now stretched his arm around Hussam's shoulder. His palm hung loose, and his fingers softly brushed Hussam's nipple. It was a move they'd watched in Hollywood romantic comedies. The budding lovers on the screen were usually in a movie theatre; the young man would pretend to yawn, then drop his arm over the woman's shoulder. Just like in the movies, Hussam dropped his head on Wassim's shoulder and cozied up to him. He felt Wassim squeeze him closer, his fingers hot on his skin.

In the past months, Wassim had woken up in a sweat many times after dreams in which he and Hussam shared a kiss. The dreams melted away like the flaky snow that came once a year in Damascus, too weak to turn the green city white, but the phantom kiss lingered on his lips.

He felt a shiver down his spine and looked down at Hussam. They locked eyes for a moment, and words died on their tongues.

Hussam took this as a sign. He leaned forward and kissed his friend on the lips. Wassim's feet kicked the air, as if electric jolts rushed through his veins. He pushed Hussam back and sounded as if he were gasping for air. They exchanged fearful looks, unable to produce a sound. Hussam blushed and avoided Wassim's eyes.

Wassim took another deep breath, as if preparing to dive underwater, and then he leaned back in. His lips met Hussam's softly, as though he were on his knees drinking from a desert's oasis.

They kissed for a long time. The sun must have dusked and dawned a thousand times; the moon, a glittering curve in the night sky, smiled at them. Wassim clutched at Hussam's hair and released it, then slid his hands up and down his back before resting them on his waist. Hussam's feet shook. His arms rested by his sides, as if in surrender to Wassim's new intensity.

Then came the echo of their names.

Hussam's father stood by the birdcages, looking up. His eyes were wide, and his face was a shade of red about to explode. He reached up and tried to grab them by the legs but Hussam and Wassim quickly pulled their feet up.

"I will kill you both today!" he shouted. He pointed to the ground and demanded they come down.

"Baba, it's not what—"

"Come down, you pieces of shit. I will break your skulls in half!"

Hussam gasped when his father started climbing toward them, cursing. Wassim slid backward behind him, and Hussam dragged his palms on the rough gravel of the rooftop, piercing his skin.

Hussam's father climbed the engine room and was almost on top of it when his foot slipped. He landed standing on top of the birdcages, which ached under his weight. Cursing under his breath, he attempted the climb once more and raised himself with both arms to the little exposed roof.

THE FOGHORN ECHOES   17

He was close enough now that his son could smell the iron
on his fingers and see the veins pulsing on his forehead. He
could see his cracked tooth and the silver watch on his hairy
wrist, a Father's Day gift.

Both Hussam and Wassim would be able to recall this moment
vividly for years to come. They would remember every twitch of
muscle in their bodies and every whip of fire in their brains. They
would forever remember whose foot kicked Hussam's father, the
sound the sole of Wassim's shoe made against the man's face. It
wasn't a strong kick, it wouldn't have harmed him, but it caused
him to lose his grip. Hussam, who moments before had tried to
pull away from his father's hand, reached out to him now as he
slipped from the metal rod he clung to. But Hussam barely managed to touch the tips of his fingers before his father lost his balance. With a gasp he fell to the pigeons' cages, smashing their
roofs and releasing the frightened inhabitants. His body rolled
and landed on the perimeter wall, surrounded by the flapping
wings of shivering birds, and for a second it rested there as if
deciding which side it would fall to. Then, as if in slow motion, he
slipped off the side of the building.

"Baba!"

They heard the body hit the ground with a muffled thud.
Hussam dangled from the engine room.

"Don't jump!" Wassim shouted, but Hussam released his
grip on the edge and fell into the broken birdcages. A nail as
long as a finger poked through the sole of his shoe into the arch
of his foot, but Hussam didn't feel it. He ran down the stairs,
screaming his father's name, a trail of blood behind him.

"Hussam!"

Hussam ignored him. He leapt down the stairs in threes and fours. His panting bounced off the walls and filled the staircase. "What have I done? What have I done?" he repeated in a whisper with every jump he took, until he reached the ground floor and sprinted to the building's glass gate.

The elevator behind him opened, and Wassim, covered in sweat, appeared between the sliding doors. "Hussam! Wait!" He rushed after Hussam, and the two ran into the huddle of men who had gathered, whispering the many names of Allah. Hussam weaseled his way through, pushing men out of the way and shouting unrecognizable words.

"Don't look, child." A man tried to shield Hussam's eyes with his palm. Hussam slapped the hand away and screamed for his father. The names of Hussam and his father were murmured around the boy, acknowledged by neighbours who'd borrowed a cup of sugar from them or shopkeepers who'd sold them a carton of eggs.

His body was splayed on the ground, a clean white bone stabbing out below the knee, one arm twisted unnaturally behind him, and his face was split with a stream of blood.

"Child, he is gone," a man behind him said.

Hussam began to murmur the Quranic lines his father had read him, tears curving around his lips. "Indeed, if sin should be the weight of a mustard seed and should be within a rock lost in the heavens or in the earth, Allah will bring it forth."

"Yes. Read him Quran, son," a man said. "That will help his soul rest."

Hussam was down on his knees now, hands covered in blood, attempting to put the cracked skull of his father back together, holding his father's red beard between his palms, pushing it back against his face.

Wassim placed his hand on Hussam's shoulder. For a moment, Hussam seemed not to notice, his eyes fixed on the broken glass of the silver watch. Then he looked up and locked eyes with Wassim.

"Don't touch me!" he said, but Wassim kept his grip tight.

"Hussam," Wassim whispered.

"I said don't touch me."

The men reciting the Quran around the body raised their voices, and an ambulance's siren wailed in the distance.

"Hussam, we have to be on the same page." Wassim pulled him up. "This was an accident."

"Fuck you!" Hussam shouted, but Wassim was quick to pull him in for an embrace. The men pushed them out of the way, opening the circle for the paramedics. Hussam tried to untangle himself, but Wassim only tightened his hold.

"No one can know what happened, Hussam," he said. "No one can know what we were doing before."

Hussam's shoulders tensed, and his back stiffened.

"I'll take care of you. I'll take care of this," Wassim whispered.

Surrounding windows opened, and the heads of men appeared, one after another, followed by the heads of women tightening their hijabs around their faces. The heads of Wassim's parents and Hussam's mother popped out of Wassim's penthouse. The women howled, and Wassim's father shouted in terror. Hussam, still in Wassim's embrace, looked up, his father's blood on his jeans and socks. All he could see were the birds, flying away with no one to whistle them back.

2014

VANCOUVER

My father stands in the corner of the club, angry, dark-featured, hard eyes and sharp fingers pointing at me. Our eyes lock as he flickers in the jolting beams of light like a broken neon sign. His face is never obstructed by the sea of shirtless bodies dancing to the pulsing beat. In one flash, my father smiles at me, and in the next, his face is streaked with blood. *I didn't kill you*, I hiss through clenched teeth, the words lost in the throb of the DJ's music.

I bob my head to the beat, and my fingers find the little baggie in my pocket. I look away from my father to the faces of my friends dancing in the crowd. Michael makes out with a random, pulling him close and grabbing his ass. He kisses him with opened eyes; their blue turns transparent in the black light and glows like a demon's. Our eyes meet, but his smile is half-blocked by the Random. I look away. Brian tries to take a selfie with all of us. He hates photos taken with the front-facing camera on his phone—so grainy and blurred—so he uses the back instead, clicking blindly on his screen before flipping the phone around to study his handiwork. He looks disappointed and wants to take another. The DJ slams the air with his fist as he spins another rendition of some unintelligible voice echoing syllables over and over. *Whoop, whoop, whoop.* The beat drops and everyone jumps, and as they land, the earth shakes and my father's ghost reappears under the spotlight. Shattered, broken, his tibia rocketed through the muscle and skin and clothes, pointing at me. The boys dance around him like wolves circling prey. I shudder. My hand squeezes the baggie, sweaty and slippery in my palm.

Again I see Wassim's foot hitting my father's face on that damned rooftop. The memory shakes as if electricity runs through my eyes. The music is muffled, the vocalist barely audible, the faces around me blurred. It's my feet kicking my father's face. It's Wassim's feet kicking my father's face. It's my feet kicking Wassim's face. It's his feet kicking me. My feet. His feet. My feet. His feet. It's both of us. *Whoop, whoop, whoop.*

My phone vibrates in my pocket. I ignore it. It vibrates again. I pull it out and see the blinding Skype blue and Arda's name under a photo I took of him: big smile, white teeth, the collar of his military uniform unbuttoned and showing his chest hair. "Cant," I text him. "Will call u later." He texts me a heart emoji. I look up and my father's ghost has gone. He won't return this time, I know it. The music fills the air. Beats meant to raise my heartbeat, and sounds meant to turn me on. It's computer-generated. *No actual musical instruments were used in the creation of this song.* I giggle at my own joke. I slam into someone. I'm alert. My naked upper body brushes against the soft hair of his chest. I smile my crooked smile. Narrow pupils, shifty eyes, an amused look on his face. He's high. The universe sends waves of sound back to Earth. I'm stoned, for sure. I've seen it on the news: the universe has been speaking to us and for millions of years we hadn't been able to hear it. *Whoop, whoop, whoop*, what a stupid sound it makes. It echoes like the bass in this DJ set. It's been speaking to us, and we couldn't hear it, because we're deaf to its song. Two black holes, I've seen it on the news, on opposite ends of the universe collapsed into each other millions of years ago and released the energy of a million billion suns into the dark, silent space around them. They crashed like two eggs rolling in a bowl, and the waves vibrated across the whole galaxy. They merged into a bottomless pit, eating at planets and aimless rocks. The sound of death got weaker and softer and sharper until it reached Earth. Scientists recorded it, I've seen it on the news, and they say it goes *whoop, whoop, whoop*. Such a dumb sound. These waves remain despite the years. They won't go away. My father's ghost is back, glimmering in the corner. I've failed at erasing him. I'm cursed forever. I'm doomed for death. *I avenged you*, I whisper, but he won't go away. One more hit and he'll be gone. One more round, another bloody red pill.

The boy strokes the hair on the back of my neck. "What's your name?"

"Hussam!"

"Hisham?"

"Hussam!"

"Ahmad?"

"What?"

"What?"

"Just call me Sam."

He's handsome. His hair is long and blond and it bounces when he jumps to the beat. He's younger than me, but that's okay, I'm in the mood for a twink. I can smell the spray-on tan giving his skin a colour he wouldn't dare stand in the sun long enough to achieve. He has two earrings and possibly a tongue piercing. Those are fun. With a finger, he traces the hairs on my chest down to my belly button and reaches the top of my shorts. I'm aroused. His nose is long, and his eyes are brown. Is he Pinocchio? A smile stretches on my face, and he slides a hand under the waistband of my shorts. Our lips touch for a brief moment, but I'd rather bite.

He pushes me back. "Oh, you're a rough one."

Brian is still trying to take that damn selfie. I frown. I don't want Ray to see me in this photo. Not another fight, please. I glare at Michael over Pinocchio's shoulder and he nods. He grabs Brian's phone and deletes the photos.

"Justin," Pinocchio whispers playfully in my ear. *Huh?* Who cares. Half the gay community in Vancouver are Justins. Pinocchio's fingers make their way through my pubic hair. He accidently feels the inside of my pocket and pulls his hand away quickly. "Oh, are these some party favours?"

I nod and gesture toward the bathroom sign.

"I have a boyfriend," he says.

"Bring him with."

He grabs the boyfriend's hand with a wink. The boyfriend, taller, sporting the build of a WWE wrestler, joins without question, flexing his arms when he sees me. Is he establishing dominance, like a gorilla in a zoo? He looks a bit like Randy Orton, with a hairier chest. I find it funny to picture Pinocchio and Randy Orton having sex. Not funny *haha*, funny *weird*.

The line for the men's is long, so we use the women's instead. Why they have a women's bathroom at a gay underground club is beyond me. We barge through the door, frightening a girl in sunglasses, and brush past her to crowd into a stall.

"Rude!" she shrieks.

I pull the baggie out and spread the white powder on the lid of the toilet tank. I use a loonie to divide it into lines.

"I only do oral." Randy Orton's voice doesn't fit his body. It's high-pitched and whiny.

"You don't say," Pinocchio jokes.

Randy Orton dips his finger into one of the lines and rubs it on his gums.

"Hey, watch it!" I snort my line, and it burns the inside of my skull, clearing my sinuses.

"Least you could share?" the girl outside says.

"Bitch, go away!" Pinocchio shouts back.

"Typical queens." She slams the door on her way out.

Pinocchio holds my hand and snorts his share. He giggles and leans forward, kissing his way down my neck and chest to my nipples.

"Where are you from?" Orton says from behind me.

"Syria."

"Oh my god, are you Aladdin?" Pinocchio mumbles as he slips down to his knees. I wonder if his nose would break if I kneed him in the face. Orton pulls me closer, and I rest my back on his chest. His beard tickles the back of my neck; it feels nice.

"Well," I say, "Aladdin is a fictional character from *The Arabian Nights*. So, no."

Pinocchio looks up and smirks, touching my dick through the fabric of my shorts. I tilt my head back and rest it on his boyfriend's shoulder. I can smell the heavy cologne he must have showered in. The ceiling of the bathroom is filthy. Yellow-bordered water stains and an air vent blocked with layers of dusty debris. There's somehow a used condom stuck up there. Pinocchio unbuttons his boyfriend's pants and pulls his meat out. His cock feels nice resting on the small of my back. The door of the bathroom keeps opening and closing, as if someone is checking on us. The music waves in and out rhythmically with the door's swinging. *Whoop, whoop, whoop.* My brain is finally empty. Pinocchio unbuttons my shorts.

"Sam, are you done?" Michael's voice comes from outside. The music rushes into my consciousness. I'm out of breath buttoning my shorts back up. Randy Orton sits on the toilet seat, his breath shallow. His flaccid cock hangs between his thick thighs like a party balloon drained of helium.

"Just a second," I call.

Michael sighs and the door slams shut again. Pinocchio wipes his mouth with his wrist and winks. I want to smack him. I slip out of the stall and stand in front of the dirty mirror, then I turn on the faucet, fill my cupped palms with cold water, and splash my face with it. My face feels like rubber.

"Why the hurry?" Pinocchio comes from behind and hugs my waist. "You can spend the night at our place." He prints kisses on my back.

I look in the mirror and smile. Exactly like I practised. "Are you boys looking for a throuple?"

He smiles without an answer. He turns back to the stall to check on Randy Orton, and my smile breaks into pieces. My nose melts in the running water, my eyeballs fall out of their sockets and circle the drain, and my hair slides down my back. My father's ghost blooms in the corner of the bathroom, as if manifested from the dirt and rot hidden behind the door. His eyes glow red. I need another hit. I take a deep breath, and it collects my facial features back together. I pull the baggie out of my pocket and see that the powder is almost all gone.

"Sam . . ."

Pinocchio's voice comes from inside the stall. Was he ever a real boy? I chuckle. In one breath, I take all the powder in.

"Sam, can you help? I think he's too wasted." This time, he's pissed at the inconvenience of having to carry his boyfriend home. I open the bathroom door and walk outside.

"Ready to go?" Michael has his hand down the Random's shorts. Brian is sitting in one of the few chairs in the corner, resting his head between his palms. The party is dying out. Michael questions me with his eyes. I smile that practised smile, and he lets me be. We head toward Brian, lift him by the shoulders, and walk to the coat check to collect our things.

"Is the Random coming with?" I ask Michael. He gives me a dirty look while tightening his arm around the Random's waist.

"Where's my phone?" Brian slurs.

Michael taps him twice on the cheek until he opens his eyes. He shows him the phone with the gigantic screen protector. Brian nods. He pulls himself away from our arms and staggers along. Did I do a hit with Brian earlier today? Yesterday? I can't remember. I put my T-shirt on. My jacket's in the car. Michael will drive. We spill onto Granville Street. Miraculously, it's not raining. The sky is still dark, but it's March and sunrise isn't until seven. There's a harsh breeze coming from the Strait. I'm not feeling well. Every streetlight is doubled, every shop sign is blurred, the ground feels like jelly under my feet.

"Can we get into the car?" Michael is pissed. "The keys, man. You have the keys."

I search my pockets. My exposed thighs are freezing.

"I don't have them." I slap both pockets. I slap my chest even though I know I have no pocket on my T-shirt. My neck feels like a bird's. It's so tight, it forces my face to jerk forward.

"The car's open," Brian says, chuckling. "The keys are still in his jacket, kids."

An unlocked car on Granville Street—we're lucky it's still there. I take shotgun. Brian gets in the back and instantly falls asleep. Michael pushes Brian's feet away, making space for the Random, then hops into the driver's seat and starts the car.

"You've had too much, haven't you?" Michael whispers to me.

The Random in the back looks out the window, dazed.

"Huh?" I stretch the smile on my face.

"Stop it with that weird expression. You look like a pissing dog." I let my face slowly relax. He examines me and sighs. "We talked about this, Sam."

"I'm okay."

There are two of everything around me and they're merging. I can see Michael driving, but in front of him is a silver plate of water dripping down the windshield. Michael's reflection leans forward through the water, and both Michael and his reflection meet—lip to lip, forehead to forehead.

"No one said don't have fun, babe." Michael stops at a traffic sign and squeezes my thigh. The warmth of his hand feels nice.

"You're twenty-six. We're not children anymore. Just be more responsible. We don't need *two* messes in this circle of friends."

Brian snores in the back seat. We giggle.

As we drive up Davie Street, Michael turns on the radio and we catch the tail end of a song he likes. He whistles along with the tune, taps his fingers on the steering wheel.

"It's raining," the Random says, as if he's discovered rain.

"Can you just take me home, please?" I sigh.

"Ray will be mad at you," Michael warns.

"Meh."

He drops me at Davie and Bute. The Random quickly jumps to the front seat. He doesn't say bye. Michael looks at me with sympathy. "I'll bring the car back tomorrow," he says.

The cold rain hits my face for a moment, then stops. Typical Vancouver weather. I walk through Jim Deva Plaza. A homeless man sleeps cradling a puppy inside the useless megaphone statue they've erected there. He has the face of my father. The puppy whines. *Whoop, whoop, whoop.* I descend to the beach. The chilly morning winds are unforgiving, but I'd rather be here than go home for now. At least until I gather myself. I jaywalk across Beach Avenue and take a right toward the Inukshuk. I sit on one of the benches there, pull my phone out, and Skype Arda.

"Hey stranger!" he says cheerfully.

"Move away from the window behind you. You look like a shadow."

He turns around and pulls a curtain to cover the window. It's four in the afternoon in Turkey, and the sun is still harsh. He stands for hours at his post guarding the refugee camp in

Gaziantep. He pixelates, but I can still see his dark eyes and thick black hair.

"Aren't you freezing?" he asks.

"Nah. I'm used to it," I lie. "Hold on." I place the phone on the bench facing me and pull a pack of cigarettes and a lighter from my jacket.

"Do you smoke now?"

"Dude. No!" I face the opened pack toward the camera. "These are joints."

He laughs hysterically, as if it's the best joke he's ever heard. His unrestrained laughter makes me laugh too. I put a joint between my lips, light it, and take a deep breath in.

"You grew up and only smoke weed now," he jokes. "Gone are the days when we fought over little pieces of brown hashish."

"Man, weed is so much better." I take another hit and then cough it out.

"Sounds like it."

"Here. Let me show you. Bring your face closer to the phone." I take a deep inhale and then blow the smoke over my screen. I hear him pulling air through his nostrils on the other side of the world. I cough again.

"Smells like blueberries." He giggles as he pulls back. He's in his own plastic tent in the refugee camp, sitting on a single bed with his military uniform hung up behind him.

"You're not on duty?"

"I am."

"You look like it!"

He explains that he was supposed to be on guard duty today at the camp's gate, but the truck carrying food and essentials hadn't shown up yet, so he escaped the hot sun. "You should come back and hang out with me here." He taps on the side of his bed. "I miss you next to me."

The wind picks up, but the memory of his skin pressed against my chest fills me with warmth. "I miss you too, buddy," I say, sniffing. I'm not going to cry on Skype.

"Are you okay, man? Is Ray bothering you?" Arda brings the camera closer to his face, as if to examine my features on his screen.

"Yeah. Yup. All is good." I quickly switch to the front camera, away from my face. "Look at how beautiful this beach is." The sky turns from black into aubergine. The ships line up against the horizon, and their dark blacks and reds reflect in long, melting trails in the water. Arda's face lights up with wonder.

"Whoa. That's one hell of a view."

"West End living is the best," I manage to say without breaking. I dry my eyes with my wrist. I switch the camera back to my face. "I can probably find a way to sponsor you to come here."

"You barely managed to get yourself there," he says. "Just focus on yourself, man, and build your life. Don't worry about me."

"All those Syrian boys in the camp are keeping you busy?"

"You know they can't resist a man in uniform."

We both laugh until our eyes tear. His face pixelates again, then a message appears on my screen stating that he has a bad connection. His laughter echoes while the screen freezes. *Whoop*, *whoop*, *whoop*. A white woman in yoga pants jogs past my bench, flashing me a dirty look. I stare at her blankly and pull a last inhale from my joint before I flick it in her direction. She mumbles something back.

"What did you say?" I shout after her. She hurries her step.

I look back at my screen. Arda's face is still frozen, so I click on the red circle and end the call. I text him that I'm cold. He sends me an eggplant emoji. I gather my jacket around my body and head toward home.

DAMASCUS

She spends her days crying in her bedroom on the second floor. I've learned to leave her to her sorrows. The crying echoes through the empty hallways of the old house, bounces off the dirty walls, but I mind my own business. I've seen her twice, floating through the house in her grey nightgown that hovers an inch or two above the ground. Her shoulders tilted forward as if guarding her rib cage, her head bowed allowing her wavy black hair to spill over her face, her feet relaxed with the tips of her toes barely touching the ground. I've seen her seep through tables and chairs, as ghosts do, while her tears glimmer under the early spring sun escaping through gaps in the heavily curtained windows. She is a guest of all hours. But she cares not for other stereotypical ghost behaviour, such as late-night appearances or scratches with long-nailed fingers. She holds no grudge, nor is she haunted by rings or undead demons. I assume she lived in this house until the day she died, years before I was born.

When she cried at night the first time, it had frightened me to the point that I'd considered leaving the safety of this abandoned house and returning to the busy streets of Damascus. I've seen enough horror movies to know not to look darkness in the eye after hearing an unexplained eerie noise. It was January when I first heard her, and it seemed as though it would snow all night. I knew I wouldn't find another warm shelter. The zig-zagging streets surrounding the house looked dreadful. The old homes, built in a time of prosperity, with long windows designed to bring in sunlight and arched gates curved to carry the names of hereditary owners, looked sleepy under their coats of snow. Men in hooded jackets hurried across the pavement. Ice splashed under car tires. Her crying reverberated through the house as if it shared her grief. I packed my small bag with what was left of my things and opened the front door, but the icy mountain winds slapped me in the face. Her voice suddenly muted, as if absorbed by the cold. I angled my body to avoid the gust, but my side ached still, from the heavy boot of the police officer who'd found me asleep under a park bench a week before. If I hadn't run fast enough to escape him, if I hadn't been lucky enough to jump a wall and find this house, I would have frozen to death outside.

I closed the door and went back inside. Her voice did not return that night.

Every night, I sleep on the dirty mattress I found in the house. I feel safe in the room I call mine. I found a small nursery nightlight in a closet upstairs, and it worked when I plugged it in the wall. I wondered who paid for electricity, but I was thankful for the little light. There was no heat in the house, but that little nightlight, designed to look like a tiny mausoleum with the light escaping from its open door, brings me warmth.

My father once told me about my mother. A Christian woman he claimed to have loved more than all his other wives.

She'd built a small shrine in her bedroom when she was hit with the sickness and spent her nights, unable to sleep, praying to the Virgin Mary to save her soul. My father maintained his love for her throughout her final days, back when I was four or five, even when she was losing her hair. He woke up every morning before she did and gathered the hair she shed on the pillows and hid it under the bed so she wouldn't see it when she woke. When she died he built her a mausoleum, like Christian people do, and refused to bury her the Islamic way, even when his family demanded it. He built her a huge shrine, mimicking the one she'd built in her own room. He ordered the shrine to be designed to look like a window, as if he would be able to see through into her soul. He ordered a replica of the Virgin Mary statue she had, but as tall as a young man, to stand by the window looking pensive. He promised on her deathbed to visit her and to take care of me. He visited her only once. He gathered all the hair that he'd hidden under the bed in a large wool bag, took it to her shrine, and tossed it inside through the window.

He married a new wife forty days after her death.

I went to see my father a couple of times before I found this abandoned home. I hid behind the police truck parked permanently on the corner of the Hariqa Souk Street, a makeshift kitchenette for the security guards. They'd gathered outside the truck on plastic chairs and made tea on a small electric heater hooked up to the engine. They paid me no attention while I gazed at my father's fabric shop from afar. Sometimes I saw him, but his schedule had no rhyme or reason since he'd become too old to stand behind counters and negotiate prices and fabric quality with bored women. I passed by the shop gate once, my hoodie hiding my face. He sat in the depth of the shop behind his old desk, smoking a cigarette and eyeing the women coming and going. He'd lost a lot of his grey hair and covered his balding head with a small white kufi skullcap that my mother had made him years before. The kufi's design was inspired by the mosaic of the Umayyad Mosque, intricate crochet details woven with stars and triangles; its yarn looked warm on his balding head. I ran away before I was seen.

"Wassim?"

I heard the call from behind me on that last trip. I didn't need to look to know it was Rima's voice. My shoulder tensed, and my head tilted to rest on it. My upper back rounded, and I quickly walked away. I must have looked like an insane person, lopsided and fast-stepped. I heard her footsteps behind me. Another pair of smaller footsteps followed her.

"Wassim! Wait! Come back!"

I elbowed the wall next to me and dragged my body against it as I hurried faster down the road. I felt the skin on my arm breaking. My head wanted to jerk back and look at her, but I didn't let it. I quickened my steps and rushed down the street until I came to a narrow road on my left. I slipped in and ran.

"Wassim!"

I only looked when I was at the last corner of the road before it zigzagged away from Rima's sight. She stood at the entry to the narrow street. She held the hand of a child, maybe five or six. She raised her hand, but I couldn't tell if she was calling me over or waving goodbye.

I dashed behind a horse carriage, grabbed a long cucumber

from a moving truck, and ran down a road toward the heart of Old Damascus.

I usually roam the house on sunny mornings guided by the soft light. When I first found this house, I thought it must be one of the homes I had heard about, abandoned by people who left the country during the war. People with money who'd found an easy route to Western countries on airplanes with first-class tickets. Others, coming from outside Damascus, found their route to the houses of the rich and occupied them without lease or deed. Houses with seven bedrooms and gold-rimmed windows now hosted seven families from seven different cities in Syria. Kitchens that had made only Cordon Bleu were now suffused with the oily smell of chicken melokhieh and zucchini stuffed with rice and tomatoes.

The day I found the house, I surveyed its two floors. Windows with dusty curtains that leaned aside as if permanently pulled back by an anxious onlooker. Walls with faded paint revealing the stone and wood panels beneath it. A large wooden front door opening up toward a garden that surrounded the house like a bracelet on an old woman's wrist. A large fence protecting it from the world outside, with an adorned metal gate big enough to allow a car in. I figured it wouldn't hurt to try. I knocked on the door and then hid, waiting for someone to come out. But no one did. I peered through the windows and saw furniture covered in white sheets, a circle of conversing ghosts. I twisted the doorknob, and to my surprise, the door opened.

Over the course of my first week here, I pulled all the dusty sheets off the heavy antique furniture. One of the cushions worked perfectly as a pillow, and a small table with brown flowers drawn on it and one squeaky leg became my bedside table. The sheets, layered one over the other, provided me with a good cover at night. I whipped them clean of dust for hours, coughing the whole time and coating myself in their grit.

There was running water in the ground-floor bathroom, but it was cold and there was no soap. The door didn't close, but that didn't matter since I was alone. I took off my boots. My big toe was blue because a hole in my sock had cut off the circulation. Was this frostbite? Would I lose this toe? I removed the hoodie Hussam had given me a couple years ago. Underneath I wore three T-shirts for warmth; I took them off one after the other. I took off my jeans, noticing how loose the waist was on my diminished size. My side ached as I took off my underwear. Naked, I observed myself in a mirror for the first time in three months. My skin was smudged and dirty, and my armpit hair grew long enough for me to see even when my arms hung loose. I smelled like a carcass. The blue bruise on my side had grown to cover the left side of my body. It was painful to the touch. I stepped into the bathtub and stood defenceless, letting the water run, hoping it would get warmer. It didn't. I jumped toward the stream like an attacking animal, muting my own shrieks as the icy water splashed my skin. My teeth chattering, I frantically rubbed myself with my hands. Satisfied that all the dust had ended up in the muddy pool of water gathering at my feet, I turned the water off and stood clutching my body. That's when I realized that I didn't have a towel. I sighed and dried myself with my dirty clothes.

I decided I'd take another shower in May, when the weather is warmer.

By my second week there, the ghost was weeping for hours every night. Sometimes she hushed her own cries, as if afraid they might lead me to her. Other times she cried with confidence, like a lone wolf howling.

On the third week I witnessed her re-enacting her own death. Her sobs were louder than usual, and I gathered the courage to slowly climb the stairs, my hand on the rotten and splintering bannister. I peeked inside the bedroom I assumed was hers, one I'd avoided so far. She sat in front of a vanity with a large silver mirror that did not reflect her, applying invisible makeup to her shadow of a face.

I breathed quietly. She adjusted makeup on her cheeks with an unseen brush and held her fingers together in a steady move to draw lips—with what I assumed was a daring red—before she circled her hands around her head as if tightening a hijab. She then stood, looked around her room, and walked in my direction.

I cowered in a corner as she walked past me to the bannister, leaned head-first over the railing, and plunged down the staircase. I gasped and rushed forward to grab her, but my fingers could feel only the cold of her nonmaterial. Her body dipped through the floor as if disappearing under the water's surface, with a flash of light and a loud snap. I ran down the stairs, not sure what to do other than kneel by the spot where she had submerged. I saw a dent between the dusty tiles on the floor, marked with the red of blood that no one had attempted to wash away. Before I could wonder if I'd ever see her again, I heard her weeping in her bedroom, returned to her afterlife, unharmed by her own death.

I wondered why she would pick falling. There are many kinds of death. There are bad deaths: sudden, tragic, and brutal. There are accidental deaths: as common as a car crash or as spectacular as being eaten by a shark. There are peaceful deaths: a slumber that becomes endless at an old age, or a final rest after a battle with cancer. Falling, however, carries a message about the person who died. It tells a story of their final moment and reduces their lives to the crumble of their bodies.

After many dreadful nights, I realized that her crying was innocuous; contrary to what the ghosts I'd seen in movies would have me believe, she meant me no harm. A month ago, I learned to ignore her and pull a pillow over my head to block out the noise. It had become annoying, possibly rude.

But tonight, I decide I've had enough.

"Don't cry." I send my voice into the dark corners of the house. "I can tell you a joke if you stop crying."

I assume my words fall on deaf ears. I hear her, but can she hear me? Is she aware of my presence? Is she as frightened by my company as I am by hers? After all, it was I who invaded her secluded space. I'm surprised to hear a gasp of air before she floats through the wall, leaving a trail of white glitter behind her. She enters my room and stands in the opposite corner, shivering in and out of my sight like a blurry mirage. I still can't see her face, but her grey nightgown, waving as if she's swimming in the thickness of air, is strangely calming. She stands in silence, waiting for me to fulfill my promise of entertainment.

This is the first time the two of us have stood face to face in the same room.

"All the people from Homs gathered at the doors of their city," I say. "They were fuelled by the drums of war."

I'd always hated that my mother city was the butt of jokes told across Syria and Lebanon. Homsi people were seen as simple-minded, easily distracted, prone to being conned. I had a distaste for Aleppo, as many of those jokes were created and populated by the people of the economic capital. When the war in Syria started a couple of years ago, Homs was the first city to be destroyed; its buildings were piles on the ground, its people were images of death on TV channels. That's when the jokes stopped being funny.

The only clear memory I have of my mother was when we visited Homs together. I was three, maybe four, and my father drove us there. I sat in the back seat, playing with a purple horse he'd got me for my birthday. My mother asked my father if we could take our lunch at the Krak des Chevaliers castle on the way, suggesting we order the food to go and spend the afternoon on the sunny roof of the citadel, overlooking the valley of Lebanon and taking in the late spring sun. We walked the empty halls of Krak des Chevaliers, built in the time of the Crusaders, garnished with narrow windows for archers and deep unfenced wells in the ground. The walls were so thick that it was blindingly dark in certain parts, and I murmured to my mother, tightening my grip on her hand, that she shouldn't be afraid. "I'll protect you," I said, and both of my parents laughed, walking me toward the light.

"They've had it with the people of Aleppo," I tell the ghost. "Those fuckers should stop making jokes about how simple-minded Homsi people are." I hear a short chuckle from afar, where she floats, intently listening.

"The council of all of Homs made a clever decision: they would melt all their metal and get all their gunpowder and make the biggest cannon known to man, place it at the doors of the city, and shoot it in the direction of Aleppo, destroying it forever." Finally, I can see her face. Framed by her long black hair, it's small and round with dimples on her cheeks. Her eyes are wide and dark, and her nose is petite. She has full lips that have lost their colour but must have been rosy red back when she was alive.

"All the people of Homs gathered on that glorious day, standing behind the magnificent cannon they made together," I say. Her forehead is wide and justified, her chin small and rounded, and her neck long like a royal anchor to the majestic ship of her face.

"They stood behind the cannon and celebrated with food, wine, and song. They were ready to destroy their mortal enemies, to burn that city down." She is the first person to hear my voice in the last three months, since I managed to find my way back to Damascus. The woman who'd slipped a ten-pounder into my hand, the little girl who'd shared half of her sandwich, and the man who'd tried to persuade me to get into his car—none of them heard me speak. I looked at them with dark eyes and kept my voice to myself.

"Their mayor carried a torch, stood on the top of the cannon, and lit its fuse."

She hovers above the ground as she moves toward me. *This is not a horror movie*, I repeat to myself, *this is not a horror movie*. There is no well-planned soundtrack to accompany this movement, no sudden loud noise to make me jump out of my seat. Just a ghost moving toward me with her nightgown flowing behind her like a princess standing on a seashore rock. She shimmers through my bedside table. I sit down on my mattress, looking up at her, and she smiles. It's a cold, elegiac smile. She's a monochromatic shadow, a statue like the Virgin Mary guarding my mother's grave. Her robe is carefully made with knots and sequins and layers of velvet. I can't tell the colour it used to be, but I assume it's a happy yellow or a soulful purple. She's an older woman, or used to be, before her death, or possibly she's only showing me the age she wants me to see. She's almost human in her movement, like a gentle soul walking around her wonderful home without a care in the world, a woman of patience and lushness. Every once in a while she glitches, as if pulled away by a calling from the beyond that she resists.

I pause when she gets closer. I stumble on my words but quickly find my footing.

"The big cannon, designed by the fools of Homs, backfired, destroying the whole city, burning down its gardens and levelling its buildings. The city's beautiful minarets smashed to the ground, and its bakeries, known for the sweetest desserts in all of the land, exploded with yeast as the fire baked all of their dough."

She sits next to me. Her colours manifest across her figure, as if she's a water jar someone has dropped paintbrushes into. She solidifies next to me and her shoulders fill out her robe. Her right arm snuggles to my left; it feels like an itch. Her face lightens up, skin the colour of olive oil, eyes brown and lips red, flecked with stardust like the wings of a butterfly. She rests her back on the wall behind us. Her legs stretch in front of her like those of a playful child, the once ghostly shadow of her limbs now pulsing veins and delicate skin. Her hair changes from grey to chestnut brown. She appears to be in her late forties, a woman of status and grace. Her lips move as if she's talking, but I can't hear a sound. She looks confused and gently presses and readjusts her throat like it's an old radio that needs tuning. Her lips move again, but I barely hear a hiss.

Her face becomes gloomy, and the colours escape it. Her sadness returns her to her ghostly shape. I place my hand on her shoulder but my fingers pass through her like jelly. Tears gather in her eyes, glimmering in the orange glow of my nightlight.

"The mayor," I say, reminding her of the joke. "The mayor sitting on top of the cannon is the only soul to survive the destruction of Homs." Indeed, her colours stop fading; she halts her own tears and stares at me with anticipation. "He looked back onto his own city before him, ruined, destroyed, erased by his own doing, and whispered to himself"—I pause—"'If this is what happened here, imagine all the destruction we caused Aleppo.'"

For a moment I think she didn't get the joke, but then a smile cracks on her face. Her giggle is the sound of bells, her laughter is an angelic echoing, untamed by the dusty world she belongs to.

I laugh as well, loudly and uncontrolled. It takes us a minute to catch our breath. She's back to her human colours, alive and beating like a bird's heart.

"I'm Wassim." I smile. "What's your name?"

She looks at me, a woman from another time. "Kalila," she says. Her voice breaks a bit, but she coughs twice, and it comes out clear now. "A joy to meet you, Wassim."

We sit in silence. She's named after one of the storytelling jackals in *Kalila and Dimna*, the Indian book of fables about talking animals and jungle lion kings. She rests closer to me and sighs, as if in relief, that she can finally talk to someone else. "How long have you been . . ."

"Dead? A while, a long while."

VANCOUVER

Ray asks me to take off my sunglasses. "We're indoors, Sam," he scolds.

The elevator rises fast to the twentieth floor of the Telus Garden building, and I'm in a full suit. I fucking hate heights. Why don't they have mirrors in elevators anymore? I remove my sunglasses and see my reflection in the silver walls; my eyes are red balls like an owl's.

"You were smoking weed again, weren't you?" Ray says.

I pull the eyedrops from my jacket pocket, where I keep them for emergencies such as this, and squirt a generous amount into each eye.

"Are you *trying* to embarrass me?"

Ray's tone is getting higher, his voice thinner. I blink twice, and my vision becomes clearer. Everything around me is brighter. I look back at Ray, and his skin glows. He's shorter than me—a fact he's very conscious of, and insists that all the shoes I buy have a thin heel. At his age, he shouldn't be as aggressive at the gym. His skin stretches over his muscles, leaving scar-like lines on his arms. The T-shirt he wears under his expensive blazer looks awkward on him, like he's trying to be hip.

"I paid two hundred dollars a plate to come to this fund-raiser," Ray hisses. "These are my friends, Sam, and you need to show them some respect."

I sigh, and he takes that as agreement. He styles his hair too smoothly back, and it's stuck to his skull. Today's dye job worked well at hiding all the greys, but patches of brown stain his forehead. He showered earlier—I can smell the shampoo on him—but the dye takes a couple of days to disappear off the skin. He never seems to notice.

"Just be present today," he insists as he adjusts my jacket on my shoulders. The elevator dings. "We'll talk about this after."

"Okay, okay, I'm sorry. I'll behave." The elevator whisks us with a final sturdy move, and I catch myself before I release a short scream. I fucking hate heights.

A young woman with a lanyard around her neck waits for us in the hall. She offers a prim smile and leads us up the stairs to the coat check. Ray exchanges pleasantries with her about the weather. These people love to talk about the weather: analyze it, report on it, compare it to the weather of last year's March, insist that they never saw as much rain as this year's, hope for a better summer.

"But it's good for the trees," she says. She excuses herself and rushes back when the elevator dings again.

"Raymond Robinson, you son of a bitch, long time no see." A man with equally dyed hair approaches Ray.

They hug and tap on each other's shoulders twice. Ray smiles at the man, who has a well-groomed moustache and wears a tight floral-print shirt with a rainbow bow tie. He has one of those smiles that makes me uncomfortable. Most smiles make me uncomfortable. I turn away to inspect the hall. It's large, with floor-to-ceiling windows, surrounded by a patio that's closed today. The rain knocks politely against the glass. The view feels claustrophobic, with the dark clouds gathering low, making the otherwise open horizon feel like a prison.

"You brought your hunky boyfriend with you too," Moustache Man says.

I extend my hand for a handshake, but he pulls me in for a hug. His face is an inch away from mine. I can tell he wants to give me a kiss like the one he just gave Ray, so I turn my head to look out the window. I get dizzy just imagining how high I am.

"Long time no see, young man," he says as if we've known each other for years.

"Sam, you met Andrew at my last birthday."

Suddenly I remember: I felt just as uncomfortable hugging him then. I use my palms like a barrier between us and gently push him away. It takes a moment of awkward laughter before he gets the message. Two more men join us. Ray pulls my hand to him and tangles his fingers within mine as if to mark his territory.

The men converse, their mouths machine guns spitting words like bullets, and I can't follow. It must be the weed. I take a deep breath and exhale loudly.

"Are you okay, cutie?" Moustache Man asks. I've already forgotten his name. He must be a John or a Michael or a Bradley.

"Oh, I'm perfectly fine."

He smiles and winks aggressively. "What a cute accent your boyfriend has, Ray." He doesn't acknowledge me anymore. He talks to Ray, who's filled with pride over his accented boyfriend.

"Excuse me." I attempt to leave the circle, but Ray's hand stiffens around mine. I'm stuck here for show and tell. Ray talks about me in the third person whenever he wants to show off. I'm an arabesque table he bought while visiting Morocco, a Cuban cigar he paid too much for when he was told virgins rolled it on their thighs, an African mask of dubious authenticity belonging to a tribe whose name he can't pronounce.

"He dazzled me from the first time we met on Facebook. I felt like a teenage stalker going through his photos." Ray giggles, and his friends laugh. "He said the most earnest things." Ray continues to share our electronic courtship story from back when I was in Turkey. He adds layers of new material with every telling, and each time he tells this story, the new version becomes the truth. Once he claimed that I couldn't speak much English when we talked for the first time. I was always fluent in English, but I didn't correct him. Now I can't even remember if I could conjugate a verb back when I was in Turkey. "I moved heaven and earth to get the government to bring him here." I try to pull my hand from his, but his grip is tight. "I told them he's my refugee, and I'll sponsor him no matter what it takes."

"I need to go to the bathroom," I whisper to Ray. He's taken by the admiration in his friends' eyes. I pull harder, and we're almost playing tug-of-war now. "Let go!" I mutter, loud enough for everyone to hear, and their laughter subsides. Ray's nails dig into my palm. The tips of my fingers turn red. "I need to go to the bathroom," I say, almost pleading. Ray returns my hand and I walk away, leaving an awkward silence behind. The ghost of my father stands in the corner, right by a small rainbow flag. I tell him I've done my best. He shakes his head in disagreement.

I take a deep breath and rush toward the bathroom. I woke up at 5:19 this morning, which is not great, especially because I got into bed at 4:22. I blame the crows. Apparently it's the season of their return to Vancouver. They hoarsely shout outside our window, they caw and rattle and feverishly blame one another for their ugly song. Today, I wanted to open the window and scream "Shut up!" but Ray was asleep, and the sleep of a tyrant is as holy as worship.

Maybe I still have jet lag. Ten months in and it hasn't gone away. I tried over-the-counter sleeping pills, prescription sleeping pills, melatonin, and a slew of other drugs. I tried running around the block for thirty minutes before going to bed, I tried having sex before going to sleep, I tried drinking warm milk and even camomile tea. Still, my biological clock wants me to stay up. I stopped fixating on it. It doesn't help that I go to the clubs at least three times a week and stay out until the early morning hours.

The bathroom's music is upbeat. Of course: the serenity of pissing to the tempo of lounge music. I don't like to use the urinals, so I step into a stall and slam the door behind me. My piss goes everywhere, and somehow that brings me joy. I imagine Moustache Man walking in after me and having to clean the stall before he can use it. Fuck him. As I'm peeing, I reach into my pocket for the little Ziploc bag with two pills inside. Just touching the pills brings me comfort. Maybe I'll pop them after I wash my hands. I finish and zip up my pants. I don't flush. Fuck you, Moustache Man. At the sink I try to get the soap to fill my palms, repeatedly waving my hand under the automatic dispenser. No dice. I'm invisible.

In the mirror, I see the reflection of a man in one of the stalls. He extends his leg and flushes the toilet with the sole of his shoe before turning back and drying his hands. He locks eyes with me and smiles. He's not white, and I'm embarrassed that I didn't flush. He looks about my age or older, tall, with soft features, a well-groomed beard, and a large nose. His sharp eyes shine like a Damascene sword he sheathes with his long eye-lashes when he blinks.

"Are you okay?" The man's voice is soft, and it echoes.

I'm in a tunnel and his face is the light at the end of it. My father duplicates. His ghosts become copies of themselves, and they surround me. They encircle me like a fence around a prison, their faces barbed wire and their eyes searchlights. I look at myself in the mirror and see my father's eyes, my father's nose. He blessed me with his thick beard and proud forehead and then cursed me with his ghost.

Then it's Wassim's face in the mirror. "Hussam," he begs. He smashes his fist on the mirror and it cracks and branches with fractures. They glimmer like waves of a moonless sea. I jump back and gasp, and Wassim's face breaks into pieces and disappears.

The bathroom music slows down, as if someone placed a heavy finger on a turntable. My father is everywhere; he is everyone. I'm sorry. Fuck. I'm sorry. I didn't want to keep the secret. I didn't mean for him to fall down and his face just disappeared into dark water and he fell so far away and I didn't even reach for him. I just watched. I stood there and watched.

"Hey, hey, okay. Take a deep breath," the man instructs. He pushes through the ghosts and extends his hand. "Can I touch you?" he asks, and I nod, shaking. He puts a palm on my shoulder.

"I want you to take a deep breath and hold it in. Follow my count-ing," he speaks slowly. His thumb touches the root of my neck, while the rest of his hand rests on my T-shirt. An inch of his skin touches mine. I struggle not to break down in tears. "In and two and three and four, hold and two and three and four, out and two and three and four." His hand squeezes my shoulder rhythmically.

I shiver, then I slowly recall what it feels like to take the air into my lungs. The ghosts of my father are brushed away like dust sparkling in the light of the bathroom. The music returns to normal. I look at the mirror, and its solid silver reflects only us.

"In and two and three and four."

The man is too close to me and I flick his arm away with a swift twitch. He takes a step back.

"I'm okay," I say to him. "I just didn't have enough sleep."

He gives me more space. His teeth shine; one of them is crooked, as if he was in a fight and was left with a badge of honour. "Yeah. Sleeping is hard sometimes," he says.

"The damn crows are gathering outside my window every morning!"

"It's such a cliché." He washes his hands. "We come from across the world and then complain about the crows like true Vancouverites."

I splash water on my face, then slap it softly with my palms.

He hands me a paper towel. "I'm Dawood," he says. "What's your name?"

"Hussam."

"Hussam! What a glorious name! Like an Arabian sword." Other than when speaking to Arda on Skype, it's the first time in months I've heard my name pronounced correctly.

"You speak Arabic?"

"*Shway shway*," he says, indicating his limitations. "Just the right amount to be able to communicate. My parents emigrated from Syria in the seventies, but I was born here."

His face looks familiar. I could have met a distant cousin of his back in Damascus. He could have been a student in the same classes at university, or one of the men who walked with me in the protests. He could have been one of the people wearing yellow life jackets on the boat.

"I'm Syrian, too. I came here ten months ago." He walks out of the bathroom with me. I don't know whether I want him to keep walking by my side or to leave me alone. "You should welcome me to this new home," I mumble.

"Huh?"

"I mean, everyone welcomes me when they realize I'm a refugee."

"That's ridiculous!" He stops walking. "You're not a refugee anymore. Are you? You arrived here and you have a permanent residence. Yes?"

I'm confused. Ray deals with this. "I think so?"

"You're home. This is your home. You don't need anyone to welcome you to your own home." He grabs my face between his palms and forces my head up. Our eyes meet. Our lips are inches away, and I almost want to kiss him. "You're home, kiddo," he says.

"Hi there." Ray inserts himself between us and slides an arm around my waist. Dawood's hands slip away from my face. "I see you met a new friend."

"Dawood, this is my boyfriend, Ray. Ray, this is Dawood. We . . . uhhh."

"We bonded over the lack of soap in the bathroom dispenser."
We all fake-laugh. Ray pulls me closer, holding on to me like a
child afraid of getting lost in a crowd. "Nice to meet you, *De'aod*.
What a handsome man you are," Ray says. "Where are you from?"

"Vancouver."

"No, I mean, where are you really from?"

Dawood's face tenses, and he smiles politely. "I was born in
Burnaby, actually—so technically I guess I'm from Burnaby."

There's a moment of silence between them, as if they're
challenging each other to a duel. Ray did not anticipate the
battle of niceties. "I mean"—he digs himself a bigger hole—
"where are your parents from?"

"Right. Okay. I think I'm going to go back to the hall now."
Dawood smiles at me. "Take care of yourself, Hussam. It was
lovely meeting you."

"Wait," I say, and both Ray and Dawood look at me. "Can I
have your phone number?"

Ray's arm tightens around my waist.

"You silly thing, no one cares for phone numbers anymore."
Dawood chuckles. "Here, give me your phone."

I unlock my phone and hand it to him. He navigates it with
the tips of his fingers until he finds Instagram.

"You little Insta-gay." He smirks while scrolling through
my photos, then taps the search field and types his name.
"Here. This way you can always find me." He clicks on the little
blue Follow button and hands the phone back to me. He waves
goodbye and walks off.

The second Dawood turns the corner, Ray lets go of me.
"We talked about this, Sam," he barks. "You can't embarrass me

in front of my friends. You can hook up at the clubs but don't bring your boy toys to these events."

I sigh and wonder if I should break up with him. Would Michael or Brian host me until I found a place to live? "I wasn't hooking up with anybody. We talked about bathroom soap and crows. Nothing to report here."

Ray's about to say something else when Moustache Man saves me from the lecture. "Excuse me, boys." He walks by. "The speakers will start soon. I'll just duck into the washroom."

Ray sighs. "We'll talk about this later. I just want the best for you, Sam." He sounds tired, as though I'm now the child he parents. He drags me out to the event hall.

All I want now is my bed. No going out tonight. No hooking up. No Grindr photos or texts from Brian and Michael. No crows. Just me and my bed tonight. I don't even want Ray in there. He sleeps like a starfish, his arms and legs extended.

A young server in a suit offers us a platter. "Our hors d'oeuvre today is crab and shrimp puff."

"What's in it?"

"Kewpie mayo and furikake," Server Boy says with a smile. He's Black and has flirtatious eyes. Have we fucked? I take a puff. It tastes like garbage, but Ray's watching so I can't spit it out.

"Do you like it?" Ray snaps his fingers at Server Boy, who quickly leans the plate toward him. I accept his offer of a napkin, and our fingers touch for a second too long. We haven't fucked. We might fuck later, though. I turn around and spit the puff into my napkin. "It's delicious," I say. "I loved it."

Server Boy holds back a laugh. "Just let me know if you need anything else."

Oh, we're definitely fucking. He'll twitch between my arms as I squeeze his chest. His legs will wrap around my waist. Suddenly I'm no longer tired. I don't want my bed; it smells of Ray's heavy cologne, and we pull the bedsheets between us all night long.

"The speeches are starting," Ray tells Moustache Man, who is just coming back from the bathroom.

"I stepped in a puddle of piss." The yellow line on the sole of his white shoe fills me with joy. "Some asshole can't aim, apparently."

A woman with a large smile steps up to the microphone onstage, welcoming us and thanking Telus Garden for hosting the event. She flashes her teeth at everyone in the room. "We would like to begin by acknowledging that we are fortunate to be able to gather on the unceded territory of the Coast Salish people," she says, sounding pleased with herself, "the land of the Musqueam, Squamish, and T-T-Tsleil-Waututh." She laughs nervously and looks out at the audience. Someone nods. It sounds rehearsed, but not rehearsed enough. There is awkward applause. The lady keeps talking, saying something about the importance of something, then something about the lack of support for another. Server Boy looks at me. I will bite his nipples, dig my head into his armpits and lick his curly black hair. I will place my hand on his throat and put some weight on it. His eyes will roll into his skull in ecstasy.

"Without further ado, I'd like to introduce the recipient of the Rainbow Success Award 2014," the woman says with a melodramatic flourish. "We're proud that we're bringing diversity and inclusion into our awards, and we think this recipient embodies these values we hold dear. Please welcome artist Dawood Makki."

The crowd parts for Dawood to join the woman on the stage. He offers her a hug and she departs the podium.

"Isn't that your new friend?" Ray says.

"Shush." I bring my finger to my lips.

Dawood allows a meaningful pause. "Thank you so much for hosting me here tonight, and for your generous and support- ive award," he says. He pronounces the words in perfect English, with clear huffing of the p's and rounding of the g's. I envy his lack of accent. I want to sound just like him, capable of fooling those around me with my English. I want them to think that I was born here too. "I truly believe in the power of a community coming together to support artists and creatives. When the community comes together to stand by your side, you feel seen and heard and acknowledged."

Moustache Man is looking at Dawood with intent. I wonder what Moustache Man ever needed from his community.

"I also believe in the accountability of a community as it stands in front of a mirror and recognizes its systemic impact on the minorities within it, be it the folks identifying with the queer, trans, and the two-spirit communities, the POC com- munity, and those identifying within the intersectionalities of such communities."

I don't understand a word he says, but it feels as if he's recit- ing poetry.

Dawood thanks those on the board of Rainbow Success before stepping off the stage, swallowed by applause. He locks eyes with me and nods.

Once all the speeches are over, I find him, now surrounded by a group of men. He answers their questions in short sentences and polite hums. I join the circle and stand by him. Ray is quick to appear at my side.

"I've had a friend who benefited greatly from the counselling program you started," one of the men says. "Focusing counselling on gay men and providing support through counsellors who identify within the community is such a needed service."

"I appreciate you saying that," Dawood says.

A drag queen is introduced on the stage and a loud Gaga song plays. The men turn their attention to the lip-syncing queen in an elaborate red gown. Dawood looks back at her and snaps his fingers. She sees him from afar and cheers for him.

"Great speech, man," Ray says to Dawood, placing a hand on the small of his back.

"Thank you—Ray, is it?" Dawood takes a step away from the touch.

Ray instead grabs me around the waist. "Yes. Sam's boyfriend."

I smile gingerly. Dawood is confused, then he gets the nickname. "Sam! A great name. Like Uncle Sam?"

"I don't know who that is," I say, and both Dawood and Ray chuckle.

"Don't worry about it." Dawood is genuine. "It's a silly joke."

"So, what are you up to tonight, Dawood?" Ray says. "We're really *hungry* and are about to go out to eat, if you want to join us." He pulls me closer to him meaningfully, and I can feel his breath on my neck. "Sam has a killer appetite, if you know what I mean." Understanding appears on Dawood's face. He looks at me, and I don't know if he can read my discomfort. I grin politely and Ray rests his head on my shoulder.

"I'm not *hungry*," Dawood says, "but you folks enjoy the

night. I'm sure many here will be interested in joining you for dinner." He waves his hand at the two of us and walks away.

"What a tease," Ray mutters. I push him off me, head for the exit. "Where are you going?" he asks.

"I don't know. I really don't know." I walk out the door and toward the elevator.

"What's your number, sir?" the woman behind the coat check counter asks. Shit, the little card is with Ray.

"It's that red one right there." I point to my jacket.

"I'm sorry, sir, we can only give you the jacket if you have the card," she states firmly.

I look out the windows behind her. The wind has picked up, and it's pouring rain. Fuck.

"I've seen him with that jacket, Susan." Server Boy has taken off his blazer and is carrying it on one arm. "I'm sure we can make an exception tonight."

Susan slips the jacket from its hanger and hands it to me. I refuse to thank her. I turn away and walk with Server Boy to the elevator.

"My car's down in the parking garage if you want me to drop you somewhere." He presses the elevator button. *Hard nipples, wet armpit hair, red throat.* The elevator dings, and we step inside. The second the door closes I pull him in for a kiss, biting his bottom lip. He pushes his tongue rhythmically against mine. I squeeze his nipple through the fabric of his button-down, and he gasps. I growl in his ear like a wounded wolf. The elevator dings again and we separate. We cross the parking lot in quick steps.

"I'm David, by the way."

I know I'll forget his name by the time we exit to West Georgia.

DAMASCUS

I hear them on the radio saying that it never happened. The announcer's deep voice repeats that it's a conspiracy planted maliciously by the West with its imperial tendencies. "No chemical weapons were used in Syria," he reassures.

Weeks ago I explored the attic, where I found the radio hiding among locked chests, old dusty jars, and moth-eaten clothes. It's made of wood and metal and has multiple large knobs that control its needles and volume; some were rusty and others were missing, leaving me with feeble audio from a single station I can't switch away from. It didn't work when I first plugged it in. I had to slap its top until it lit up with a flickering yellow light that dimmed with every word the announcer said.

The announcer introduces an expert on conspiracies spread by news networks. They spend the next hour discussing how the chemical weapons attacks in Kafr Zita never actually happened. "These so-called victims are paid actors, filmed professionally in studio sets in Qatar built to look like the town of Kafr Zita," the guest says confidently to the announcer's murmurs of agreement.

I stare at the ceiling, lying on my makeshift bed, bored. I make out shapes and faces in the cracks and fractures. Hussam and I used to do that with clouds. We'd lie on the unpaved rooftop hiding from the striking sun in the shadow of the elevator shaft, our hair mixing with the pebbles under our heads. Some of the clouds were sheep, others were faces of cats or bodies of dogs. Once, we saw a giraffe; we'd never actually seen a giraffe in real life, but a cloud giraffe was the next best thing.

I see no faces or sheep in the cracks of these walls. Only a detached layer of paint hangs by a tiny resisting pit. Maybe I'll clean it if I find a broom. Or a ladder. The things I'd do if I could find a ladder. The spiderwebs I'd remove, the corners with mysterious black gunk I'd clean, the burnt-out bulbs in the high-ceilinged bathroom I'd replace. I would make this house a home. But I'm a man without a ladder.

The announcer and the guest bid their goodbyes to the audience, proud of the work they do to expose the imperialist conspiracies of the Western-controlled media. A song from the eighties comes on. Their catalogue hasn't been updated in years.

I hear the chants from the streets. A pro-regime slogan: *God, Syria, and the president.* They repeat it like a mantra, their voices hoarse, broken like the howls of crazed dogs. The chant gets louder. I struggle with the window lock before it snaps open, and I lean out to hear the hymn. Their steps reverberate as if they tap-dance on the asphalt. Over the fence, tips of Syrian flags wave. Maybe I should join them.

"I wouldn't do that if I were you," Kalila says behind my back.

I jump. "You have got to stop scaring me like that!"

"I'm a ghost. Force of habit."

Kalila is friendlier now. She's learned to control her own form and appear less grey and more flesh-and-blood. I've yet to learn how not to have a small heart attack whenever she materializes.

The chants get closer. The leaders of the march appear through the metal gate. I hide behind the wall while Kalila stands at the window in full view, unafraid. They chant against the lies of the West. The president never used chemical weapons, they insist.

"I'm curious to see them."

"It won't be safe," she warns.

"I'll watch them from the garden." I'm already walking to the front gate. I step outside and cross the garden to the fence, climb up it. The marchers all wear identical white T-shirts with a grey-scale portrait of the president on their chests. A sea of white-and-red caps. There is an endless stream of them, and buses appear in the distance, pouring more of them into the streets.

Kalila waves me in from the window, but I ignore her. I slide down the other side and land on the ground, catching the eyes of a small huddle of chanters. I hide behind a thin tree and watch them. They're mostly young. High school kids, peppered with some older men with big bellies and walkie-talkies whispering things to one another. I'm blinded by a reflected light coming from a rooftop. I look up. Someone in a military uniform stands watching. He brings a device to his face and speaks into it. The marchers continue their walk, but the small huddle that noticed me stops.

"Who are you?" one of them shouts from across the street.

"He's not wearing the T-shirt," another says. "He just jumped that wall."

The third says something, but his voice drowns in the chants of marchers.

"I'm just watching," I yell back.

They walk toward me. I feel an urge to run, but I hold my place. They get closer, examining my outfit from afar. One of them pulls a walkie-talkie out and speaks into it. The reflected light blinds me again.

"Run, you idiot, run," Kalila whispers in my ear. I look back but she's nowhere to be seen. My heart races, and I begin to walk backward as the gang gets still closer. "Now, Wassim. Run!"

I give my feet to the wind. I hear their steps hitting the ground behind me. People at the tail end of the march watch with curiosity. A couple more walkie-talkies. I take a hard left around the fence of the house. I glimpse them still running after me. One of them shouts at me to stop.

"Here. Jump now," Kalila says. The fence is shorter at this end. I run toward it and with one jump I'm halfway up. I manage to flip to the other side before they turn the corner.

"Sit down. Be quiet."

I squat. I hear them passing on the other side. I attempt to stand but an unseen force keeps me close to the ground.

"Stay down, fool."

I hear running steps beyond the fence, then a calm returns to the streets. The chants, now repetitive and almost sinister, mellow and disappear. Kalila appears beside me, squatting as well.

"I told you not to go," she says.

They singled me out. I stood out like rotten seaweed in an ocean of perfect coral reef. This city's people hate me. They chewed me up and spat out my bones. I can't even watch them from afar. I had no time to see anything in them; how did they have the time to see anything in me? I was judged and deemed inappropriate and persecuted into disappearance.

"I'm more of a ghost than you are."

Kalila stands up and walks to the door. She seeps through it, and I follow her. "You will always be safe here," she says. She walks into my bedroom and sits down on the mattress, leaving enough space for me to sit next to her. I drop my body down, bringing my knees to my chest and resting my head on them.

"They'll never accept who I am, and what I did." A tear slides down my nose and drops on my dirty T-shirt.

"You don't want to be accepted by them. They're blinded by the regime's propaganda. They believe anything they hear. They're a literal herd walking the streets of Damascus."

I look up. She's blurry, like a reflection in a moving stream.

"These are not the people you would feel safe around anyway," she says. "You'll find your people soon enough."

For weeks I'd feared that if I left the house, it wouldn't be here when I came back. Or it would be taken over by some other drifter looking for a warm place for the night—someone too strong for me to push, too big for me to kick. I couldn't imagine someone else sleeping in my makeshift bed; it's mine. But hunger is God in the eyes of the abandoned, and so, two days after the march, I leave the house in search of food.

I roam the streets of Al-Jisr Al-Abyad, avoiding the dry river street where checkpoints are stationed. I walk by a shawarma place, and the smell makes me realize how hungry I truly am. Chicken rotates over an open flame. Pita bread sandwiches toast on the panini press, the garlic dip bubbling on the hot surface.

The cook ignores me while he offers his services to paying customers, each walking away with their sandwich wrapped in newspaper, the pages insisting that Kafr Zita was not targeted with chemical weapons and praising the pro-regime march. He turns away, hands on his waist, arms tilted back. The show is over.

I soon find myself on the corner between the American embassy and the American cultural centre. They were abandoned months before; all Americans had left the country when the protests started in 2011. Guards stand at every corner protecting the empty white buildings. The American flag, which used to wave at those looking at it from afar, is nowhere to be seen. Lower windows and gates hide behind the grey walls and the barbed wire atop them. One of the guards eyes me suspiciously, and I hurry away.

My feet drag me to the shop where I used to buy coffee back in the day.

"That coffee shop opened before your grandfather was even born," my father used to say. "Turkish coffee is both the quality of the beans and the spirit of the seller."

I walk by the entrance and take the smell of coffee into my lungs. I haven't had Turkish coffee in months. I miss the bitter taste on my tongue.

"Hey, kid."

The shop owner stands at the door. His hairline has receded since I last saw him, and a few extra wrinkles have appeared around his eyes. He still wears the same outfit: black sherwal pants, a clean white shirt, and a traditional waistcoat garnished with golden branches.

"Aren't you the son of Abu Wassim?"

I turn away. "I think you've mistaken me for someone else."

He pauses. He waves me over, but I don't move.

"Come here and let me take a good look at you," he demands, but I walk away. "Wait!" I don't look back. I take the first alleyway to my right and sprint.

Ten minutes of running leads me back to the shawarma place. The cook notices me again. Sweaty armpits and hurried breath. He ushers me over. Like a stray cat, I get as close to the man as possible with enough room for me to run if I need to. He hands me a shawarma sandwich, explaining that someone had ordered six and he'd made one extra by mistake. I jump into his circle of reach, grab the sandwich, and jump back. He asks how old I am.

"Twenty-six," I say between bites. The hot oil and melted fat burn my tongue and the insides of my cheeks, but I quickly swallow. He tells me to wait and goes inside, returning with a bag of canned food.

"These are shiners. Cans that lost their labels. I don't know anymore if they're pickles or chicken or cat food. You can have them."

I snatch the bag out of his hand and run off.

"See? There is goodness in people still," Kalila says when I get home. "You can still find your own people in this city."

For the third day in a row, yet another pro-regime march passes by. Quickly this time, and with only a few leaders with megaphones, it fades away and the streets return to the people. Kalila follows me to the window. Passersby walk fast. They look up often, possibly fearing jets dropping bombs or tear gas or chemical weapons. "The people are fearful of the regime, the

THE FOGHORN ECHOES   69

Americans, the Israelis, even one another." She hovers through the room and finds a chair to sit on.

"I highly doubt it would make a difference to me after I die to know who killed me." I smirk.

She falls silent. I follow her gaze to the crack on the floor outside my room, at the centre of the hall. She flickers like a campfire.

"I'm sorry you're—"

"Don't be. I'm comfortable in my afterlife." She flutters like a mirage and my heart skips a beat. I'm thankful she was there to save me from my foolishness a couple days ago.

"Do you, like, hear a calling from the beyond?" I ask her. "Maybe you should go to the light?"

She chuckles. "You watch too many movies, my friend."

"I used to go with Hussam to the American cultural centre to learn basic English," I say, wanting to change the topic. "Back when we were students."

"Who is Hussam?"

"I'll tell you all about him."

Hussam lived with us for years after his father's death. Before returning to her village, his mother had asked my father to keep him in Damascus for his studies, and my father welcomed the idea. He moved into my room a week after the funeral. We barely spoke for the first month. I walked in a few times and found him lying on his bed staring at the ceiling. I wondered if he'd gone insane. He woke up many a night screaming in fear, bringing my stepmother to the room. She'd cover her head with a scarf to offer him a glass of water and a quick reading from the Quran.

"This boy needs to toughen up," she'd say, then she'd offer him the biggest piece of the cake or the last of each grape cluster and leave marshmallows for him in a jar in the kitchen.

"My father thought that Hussam needed something to occupy him," I tell Kalila. "He paid for him to join the basketball team and enrolled him in swimming classes."

The only thing that caught Hussam's attention was the English class. We went three times a week, twice for formal lessons in the afternoon and once on Friday evenings for conversational lessons. In the evening classes, Hussam sat across from me and next to Nazeem, a Turkish student. Nazeem had moved to Damascus to learn both Arabic and English. He was a bit older than us, with green eyes and brown hair and a smile large enough to crack mirrors.

Every Friday, Nazeem waited for us at the centre's gate, sometimes with chocolate, sometimes with a pack of cigarettes he shared with Hussam but not with me. Hussam still didn't talk to me, but he was talking to Nazeem—the two of them picked up English faster than me, conversing easily and correcting each other's grammar and pronunciation. Once, Nazeem invited Hussam to his rented apartment in the old city, but I interrupted the conversation and switched the subject before Hussam could give an answer.

The English teacher tasked us with a debate. He appointed Hussam and Nazeem as debate captains, and they spent a week talking over the phone preparing for their assignment. The two of them conversed in English as I sat across the living room biting my fingernails.

"He's getting so much better," my stepmother said one day, bringing us slices of watermelon on a platter. I couldn't tell if she was talking about Hussam's grief or his English. She got used to wearing a hijab in her own home because of his presence. Hussam became a second son to my father, and might be here forever, unlike her. Her fate of a fast divorce was delayed by the death of Hussam's father, but that was almost a year ago. My father was already asking around for a good matchmaker.

I half listened to Hussam's phone conversation with Nazeem, limited by what little English forced itself inside my thick skull. Then I saw it; he smiled. It was the first time I'd seen him smile since his father's death. It was a smile he'd smiled at me before, and he gave it away to a stranger on the phone. In that moment I hated Nazeem. I felt as though he'd stolen something from me, something I couldn't recall but cared for all the same.

"Wassim, are you gay?" Kalila interrupts my story.

"No!" I say, a bit louder than intended.

"Listen, kid," she says, rocking her feet back and forth under her seat, "after you die, nobody cares who you loved in this life."

"I am not gay." I try to hold on to a pause, but she gives me a knowing smile.

"It's not like I'm going to go around telling anyone," she says. "I will literally take your secret to the grave."

I smile too. "Well, if you tell anyone, you're dead to me," I say.

We laugh, and I tear up a bit. Suddenly hunger grows like a mushroom inside me. I could open a can of tuna, but I don't want to run out too quickly.

"Are you okay?"

"I'm just hungry."

"What happened to Nazeem?"

I hadn't known that it was Nazeem's birthday the day of the debate, but apparently Hussam had. He didn't come with me to class. He told me, in his short sentences and matter-of-fact tone, that we would meet at the centre. I got there early and sat in the tree-covered pathway waiting for him. When he finally arrived, he wasn't alone. He walked in with Nazeem, talking cheerfully and holding hands the way we used to.

"And what of it?" Kalila said. "You know that's common among Damascene men."

"You didn't see them, Kalila," I say. "Their fingers were seesawing."

It felt as if they'd joined in squeezing my Adam's apple between their palms. Nazeem had a stuffed giraffe under his armpit. The plush toy had a bow tie around its neck, with a birthday card hung from it.

"Where were you?" I asked Hussam.

"We'll be late," he said, ignoring my question. We went inside.

I barely heard the debate. I sat at the back of the classroom and looked at the two tables in the centre, where Hussam and Nazeem sat. They negotiated the terms of the debate and the rules of conversation. The American teacher did not interrupt. As the debate got heated, the two boys looked different. With every word they exchanged, it seemed as though they were getting closer, as if the tables between them had evaporated. Nazeem's hand on Hussam's wrist. Hussam's hand on Nazeem's chest. The two sets of lips coming closer, the four ears getting redder. So close they could smell each other.

"Okay, that's enough," the teacher announced. Nazeem had won the debate. Hussam stood and shook hands with his friend. They held hands for a long moment.

I couldn't sleep that night. Nazeem's cologne wafted from Hussam's bed. With every breath Hussam took, I thought of Nazeem's lungs filling with air. I felt Nazeem's tongue down my throat; I felt his hand deep inside my chest. I opened my eyes to the darkness of the room around me. My eyes adjusted, and I saw the posters over Hussam's bed. He had posters of American singers, whereas I had posters of local football players.

Beyond the walls of our room, my father must have fallen asleep next to his soon-to-be ex-wife. The television set was off. Water dripped from an untightened faucet. Hussam's breathing was steady; his body was resting. He hadn't had a nightmare in almost a month. Did he dream of Nazeem's embrace? His red lips? His green eyes filling with tears of joy as they touched? I felt an urge to scream at him. I was the one who had saved us. I was the one who had kept our secret. I carry it to this day like a stone in my gut. I feel it today like I felt it back then: heavy and metallic. It tastes like dirt.

I slipped out of bed and walked over to Hussam. In the dark, he looked innocent, but I knew. He must have done it. He must have broken our unspoken promise. His kiss branded my skin. It tasted like jasmine flowers. It ached like a cracked rib. I shook him awake.

His eyes opened wide. "What? What's going on?"

My lips pressed upon his. He shivered. He grasped my shoulder and squeezed it. He tried to push me away, but his resistance was weak. He wanted this. He lowered his hand and allowed me closer, and our lips mingled together like two lost lovers embracing after a year of solitude. His lips parted to let my tongue in. I leaned on him. He pulled me in and I fell into the bed. Hot air exhaled from his lungs and I inhaled it. His air was mine, his face was my kingdom. His eyes were shut tight as if he were swinging, like a pendulum, between joy and pain. My fingers found his nipples and squeezed; he arched his neck and took a deep breath.

"*Shush.*" I tilted my head down and gently bit his nipple, feeling it get hard. He slipped his hands under my T-shirt and found my shoulder blades, drawing me in closer. My naked torso pressed against his as the shirt rolled up between us; he pulled it off and threw it by the bed. He knew what he was doing. Did Nazeem teach him? How did he know where the pleasure lay in my body? How did he know what would make me ache? He grew against my hip. I slipped a hand under his shorts and touched his penis, held it firmly. He produced a short gasp, and I placed my hand on his mouth. Now his eyes were wide open.

He untied my pants and pushed them down with his foot. I was naked in his bed. I pushed the covers away and pulled his penis out of his shorts. His hands pushed the waistband down, and the two of us were finally naked together. Two bodies hungrily touching each other. I hesitated, then dipped my head down and took him in my mouth. At first it felt weird, but by the time I came up for air I only wanted more. He watched me with sharp eyes. I went up again and kissed him.

I remember flashes. His arms squeezed my back closer. His face between my thighs. His eyes softened. He smelled my armpits. The taste of him in my mouth. He tickled my belly with his tongue. His arm hair against my side. He said nothing through it all. He bit my left shoulder. I remember the wetness between our legs. The tip of his tongue in the loop of my ear.

"I promise I won't hurt you," I whispered as he locked his legs around my waist. He was dry, but I used my spit and then pushed myself inside him. He covered his mouth with both hands. His eyes rolled back at first, and then he looked at me as if he were begging. I couldn't tell if he wanted me to stop or to go further. I pushed one more time. His legs pulled me closer to his body. I was inside him and around him. A tear rolled down his cheek.

"Are you okay?" I whispered.

He pulled my face closer with both hands and kissed me. I embraced him and pushed his body to fit under mine. A burst of light grew within me. It felt both liberating and imprisoning.

"I'm about to come."

He nodded. I sensed the release inside him. He stretched his mouth open, droplets of sweat hung on his forehead, and his cheeks turned red. I wanted to fall asleep in his bed. His pillow felt softer than mine. His beard, young, still forming, scratched the back of my hand. I slowly pulled myself out. He moaned.

"Are you okay?"

"I think so."

I reached down and found him still hard, then brought him to climax with my hands. I kissed him and freed myself from his body. He didn't resist. I walked across to my bed, pulled my pants on. Half an hour later, he asked me if I was awake. His breathing was still heavy.

"Yeah."

"I didn't kiss Nazeem."

"Huh?"

"I went to his house yesterday. He wanted to kiss me. I didn't kiss him."

"Why not?"

"I don't know. But I didn't kiss him."

"Good."

After a pause I heard his voice, raspy and deep, asking me what we do now.

"Go to sleep," I said.

The sunset sends rays of light through the window. They hit Kalila's ghost and pass through her. She leaves no shadows on the wall. Sunspots dance on the floor like a rosebud that broke into pieces and blew into the room.

"Why did you sleep with him that night?" Kalila asks, her voice slow and inviting.

"He is mine, that boy is mine," I reply, steadily. "I earned him. He belongs to me."

She stands at my side, and we look out the window together. I reach down to take her hand, but I drift through her body. My fingers feel cold and stiff.

"Thank you for saving me the other day," I say.

"That's what I'm here for."

Out the window the dark clouds are gathering, promising a late spring rain. The chants return. The repetitive noise permeates the walls, entrapping us, and we pray for rain together. We stand on our toes, looking through the window to the skies, and we notice, right before it merges into the others around it, a frightened little giraffe cloud.

VANCOUVER

My phone buzzes in the gym shorts I just took off, the screen lighting up through the fabric. It vibrates against the wooden bench in the Y's locker room. I check to make sure it won't fall to the ceramic floor. I can't go back to Ray with a cracked screen and ask for a new phone. He just got me this one. The buzzing stops, and I examine my naked body in the mirror. There are half a dozen other men in the locker room in various stages of undress. Brian is in the showers. I can hear him singing, interrupted by the water filling his mouth. He is shamelessly off-key.

My chest is pumped and my arms are large, but my face looks tired. Black bags under my eyes, messy hair. The scar on my side is no longer visible. Indoor tanning and the hair on my torso help keep it hidden. Only the trained eye can see it, small and mouth-shaped. When I look at it in the mirror, it smiles; when I look down at myself, it frowns. It's the wicked smile of the Syrian regime agent who placed the hot edge of the knife on my side and sliced it. He told me that I'd never leave that basement unless I said what he wanted me to say.

"What do you want me to say?" I begged him. "I'll say anything." He said I knew exactly what I should be saying. I didn't understand. I clenched my teeth while the knife caressed my torso. The gap in his smile from a missing incisor a dark cave with snakes and spiders and bats.

A man in red underwear checks me out. He flexes his pecs at me, left, then right, then both together. As he takes selfies in the mirror, his smile grows like the Cheshire Cat's. A waxing crescent.

The ghost of my father hides behind the lockers, a black shadow pulsating at the edges with eyes sparking yellow. He moves like electricity across the room.

In the mirror, my body melts away like paint in murky water. I blink repeatedly, trying to focus.

"Look at you!" Brian walks by me with a towel around his waist, steam rising off him. He smirks and slaps my butt with a wet hand. "Never thought I'd see the day when you walk around naked in a change room."

My phone buzzes again.

"Someone's popular today." Brian drops his towel and digs stuff out of his locker. He scratches his balls, then pulls his underwear out. He sniffs them and retracts, scrunching his nose, before shrugging and pulling them on anyway. The first time we came to the YMCA together, I'd insisted on changing in a stall and he laughed at me, pointing out the men changing around us, unapologetically on display.

I snap the waistband of my underwear and grab the phone out of my shorts. It's a Grindr notification. Selfie Guy. In his profile photo, he's wearing a green Speedo that hugs his junk and enhances the green in his eyes. His chest hair is trimmed, and his shoulders are round as baseballs. His smile is inviting and mischievous, as if the man taking the photo just told an endearing silly joke. Maybe he's sent me a greeting or a sweet compliment. I open the message window to find a dick pic.

"Look at that," Brian says over my shoulder. He takes my phone and zooms in. Selfie Guy passes our lockers and nods in my direction. Brian waves slyly.

"You get all these hot men texting you," Brian says. I shush him but he keeps at it. "You should go say hi."

I snatch my phone back and type a quick "woof" before hitting Send. "It's because they all have this Arabian Night fantasy on their bucket list."

"So what? You're in an open relationship. You get to play and go back home to your sugar daddy."

"I don't like it when you call Ray that."

"Okay. Your glucose benefactor."

"You're an ass."

"All I'm saying is, if hot men want you, who gives a fuck why."

Another shirtless man walks by our lockers. He and Brian exchange a quick but meaningful look. Brian watches as he walks toward the sauna and pauses outside its wooden door. They both smile as the man slips inside. Brian checks the time on his phone, then starts to undress.

"I guess you'll be enjoying a quick sauna session," I say, tying my shoes.

"That's what the YMCA is for, my friend." Brian crams all his stuff back into his locker, picks his towel off the floor, and wraps it around his waist. "Talk to the guy, go have fun. The day is still young," he says, loud enough for the whole room to hear. A chuckle comes from afar. Brian opens the sauna door, then turns back to me. "Love you. Mean it."

My phone buzzes in my hand. Selfie Guy has sent me a stream of photos. On a hike with three other guys, their faces blurred; at a club with a purple strobe lighting his body; in a sombrero at a beach. He's shirtless in all of them. I send him three photos from my gallery, each taken in a bathroom mirror at home or at the gym. Two PG-13 offerings, and one with a towel strategically hiding my junk while revealing my ass. I slide my phone into my back pocket and walk out of the locker room and out of the building. It's sunny outside. They call it Fool's Spring. I pull out the aviator sunglasses Ray bought me last week.

"Woof yourself."

Selfie Guy stands in the sun in a tank top and shorts, his gym bag on his back. His tank ripples in the breeze, his sculpted upper body visible through the custom widened armholes.

"Aren't you cold?"

"I know a couple of ways to warm up."

I get closer. His lips are thin; I wonder how they'll feel against my larger ones. He's a ginger, with facial hair that's dense along his jawline and creeps up his cheeks in patches. He likely has twenty thousand followers on Instagram.

I give him my practised bedroom eyes. "I'm sure you're creative that way."

"Well, with your help, anything is possible." He extends his hand. "I'm Robert."

"Sam."

"Nice to meet you, Sam. Do you live nearby?"

"Yeah. Around here." I gesture toward Davie Street, then pull a pack of cigarettes out of my pocket and offer him one. "You?"

"Dude, we just finished working out." He hesitates, but takes one. "Davie and Richards."

I light my cigarette, holding it between my teeth. I try to light his, but the wind blows my flame out. I get restless, and smoke from my own cigarette fills my nose. He reaches over to steady my hands. I try the lighter one more time. I can't see if it caught flame or not.

"Here. Let me do this." He pulls the cigarette from my mouth and holds the lit end to the tip of his, sucking the air till the flame catches. He chuckles, smoke coming out of his nose like a dragon. He places the cigarette back between my lips.

We walk together toward Davie. I pay attention to the way I walk: tall posture, head tilted and shoulders back, chest fully presented, glutes tight and back straight. Selfie Guy is taller than me. He probably has zero percent body fat. He's mastered the art of looking effortlessly handsome. I wish my body reacted to my commands the way his clearly does. I wish I could ask my body to clean the dirty laundry in my head, to swallow the scar on my waist, and lose the small layer of fat off my belly.

"I liked those photos you sent," I tell him when I find nothing else to say. He exhales smoke. "I didn't have time to examine that first one. My friend Brian was admiring it."

"Yeah. I heard him." He laughs. "Oh my god. You're blushing, you little thing." He puts a heavy arm around my shoulder and pulls me in closer; I find myself dipped into his armpit, my temple against his chest. It feels nice, so I don't resist. The smell of the Y's cheap shower gel mixed with his deodorant fills my nose. He's tall enough that I barely reach his shoulders, and his chiselled face looms over me, tempting me to touch it. We walk in this intertwined formation, and people part ways on the sidewalk to let us stay together.

"Oh, you guys are so cute," a woman walking her dog says. I'm about to correct her but Robert speaks first.

"Thank you. This good man is one hell of a catch."

I'm not a good man. I'm debris after the fall of a good boy. I'm the skeleton of a building, with exposed columns and dark burned spots and broken furniture.

"Hey." Robert pinches my ass. "I hope I didn't cross a line. I just find you really cute."

"No. I just—" I keep my eyes on the pavement. "No one's ever said I'm a good catch before."

"Sam, I've been admiring you at the Y for weeks."

We stand in a sunspot. He looks as though he's about to propose to me, and it's crazy but if he did I'd say yes. I see myself making him coffee in the morning, his naked body in clean white sheets in our sunny bedroom. Snuggling up to him in a movie theatre while watching a romantic comedy and eating popcorn from the same bag. Twinkling my nose against his in an engagement photo. He'd introduce me to his family, and I'd clean his apartment every Tuesday and grill him chicken and make him pasta with alfredo sauce. For dessert, I'd mix tahini and date syrup in a small dish, and remove the leaves from a head of lettuce one by one, teaching him to dip the firm end of the lettuce leaf into the mix before munching on it. He'd drip some on his naked chest and I'd lick it clean.

I kiss him.

I taste the cigarette as he digs into my mouth with his tongue. He holds my waist with both arms and pulls me in so firmly my back cracks. My nails scratch his shoulder blade. His dick grows against my belly button.

"Whoa. That was something," he says. His palm rests on my butt and squeezes. "Nice bum, kiddo." He guides me back to walking. "What do you do for a living, Sam?"

"Well," I say. I'm still catching my breath. "I studied English literature back in Damascus. But that doesn't get me any jobs here."

"Oh, you're from abroad?" As if he couldn't tell from my skin colour or accent.

"Yeah. I'm Syrian."

"Oh, is that in Europe?" I give him a dirty look. "I'm joking! It's a joke."

I can't tell for certain, but I laugh nonetheless. This is not a deal-breaker. I can show him where Syria is on Google Maps. We walk hand in hand until we reach Burrard and Davie. We stop and look at each other. He scratches the back of his neck, his biceps large and round with a tribal tattoo designed to hug it. "Do you want to come over and have some coffee?" he asks.

I hate coffee. "Yes. I would like that very much."

He beams. We cross Burrard toward Richards, still holding hands. There's warmth growing inside my chest, a little flame thawing icy veins. We pass by a storefront and I check my reflection in the window. My hair is still a mess, and the circles under my eyes are even more pronounced in the darkened glass. What does Robert see in me, after all? He'll soon realize that he's completely out of my league.

"I look like a zombie," I mumble.

"Oh, you silly goose." He pinches my butt again. "You look like a prince."

For the first time in forever, I believe a compliment. The brown of my skin and the honey in my eyes shine under the sun. My beard is perfectly trimmed, and my arms are warm, my toenails clipped.

We finally reach Robert's building and in the elevator he kisses the base of my neck, tickling me. He laughs when I push him slightly away, refusing to give in. When we get to his apartment, I intentionally step in with my right foot first for good luck.

It's a bachelor with a twin bed against the back wall and a small open kitchen in the corner. There are dirty dishes in the sink, and two wine glasses stained with remnants of red in their bottoms. He has multiple cacti lining the windowsill, three nude pictures of himself on the walls. He smiles to the camera shyly in one, hides his cock with both hands in another, and in the third has an American flag draped over his shoulders.

"Are you American?"

"No. Why do you ask?"

"No reason."

I take my jacket off but find no place to hang it. I leave it on the floor on top of my shoes.

"Welcome to my humble abode," he says theatrically. He turns large speakers on and streams a club tune, then grabs the two wine glasses and places them carelessly in the sink. After he clicks the buttons of the coffee maker, the sound of beans grinding fills the room.

"You take it black?" he asks.

"A bit of cream."

He opens his fridge. It's empty but for two bottles of white wine, a dozen beers, and some takeout leftovers.

"Sorry. It has to be black."

"No worries."

The machine churns and coffee begins to drizzle out into the cup.

"What do you do for a living?" I ask.

"I'm a model. I moonlight as a bartender sometimes."

"With a body like yours, you must be getting a lot of tips."

"Stop it." He smirks.

He hands me my coffee and sits next to me, leaning back and lifting his arm as an invitation to cuddle. He locks his arm around my chest.

I sip the bitter coffee. We sit without speaking while the music fills the room. I try to ignore it even as the beat gets more intense. His skin is soft like a pillow, yet his body is hard like a rock. I could stay like this forever.

He takes the coffee cup from my hands and puts it on the table. "Come here, you sexy thing." He pulls me up and bites my shoulder through my shirt, then squeezes my nipple. Ouch. He inserts a knee between me and the back of the sofa, and I'm in his lap. Now he squeezes both nipples. It still hurts, but I don't complain. When we start to kiss, he bites my lower lip a bit too hard for my liking. He tries to pull my shirt off.

"Hold on. Let's talk for a bit," I say, but my head is already inside my shirt. I lift my arms and the shirt pops over my head. He removes his tank top, pushing me to the other side of the sofa. He mounts me and digs into my lips for more kissing.

He's rough in his movements and demanding in his actions. I used to be an active participant in my hookups, but for the first time, my body is a toy in someone else's hands. Some giant who pushes me around and bends me whichever way he wants. The thought excites me, and my dick grows against the tough fabric of my jeans. His chest is large, his arms bulge with veins, and his back is rounded as if he's sucking his belly in. The tip of his dick peeks out from the waistband of his shorts. He bites my neck and chest and armpits. He pulls himself up, stands tall on the sofa, his head almost touching the ceiling, and slides his shorts down. He presents his cock as if he's a chef revealing a dish. Then he kneels down and sits on my chest.

Before I can protest, he slaps my face with his dick.

"I—"

He pushes his meat inside my mouth. He holds my head with both hands and rhythmically pulls me forward and back. My saliva drips onto my chest, a bubbly line of it stuck on his balls.

"That's a good boy." He stabs my face with his dick. My arms are stuck under his thighs. His weight holds my body down. I kick two fluffy throw pillows off the sofa. "You like that, don't you."

I can lie and say that I like it. Maybe I should just go with it. Maybe if he likes having sex with me, he'll ask me to go on a date. I relax my jaw and I let him slide all the way in. He pulls my head toward his groin and holds me there, refusing to let me retreat. My gag reflex kicks in. I open my mouth and produce a begging noise. He pulls out.

"Hey, you okay? I thought you were enjoying it."

"Yeah. I am," I lie. "You're just too big."

He smiles as he sits on my chest, his cock pointing at my face. When he tilts his hips, I free my arms and start stroking his dick. I hope he comes fast so that we can get back to cuddling. He fumbles for my belt buckle and undoes my jeans. If I'd expected to have sex this morning, I'd have worn a jockstrap. I pull down both the jeans and my boring underwear in one motion. Still holding eye contact, he grabs my dick. I'm flaccid.

"You're into this, right?"

"It's normal. Sometimes I lose my erection."

He gives up on my dick, moves his hands up my body, and stumbles upon my scar. He draws its line with the tip of his nail. I prepare to lie and say it's from a bike accident, but he doesn't ask. He stands and pulls me up by the hand, leads me to the twin bed in the back corner. Maybe I should ask to leave right now? Maybe I could suggest we meet in the evening over sushi or burgers? Maybe we can go see a movie together? A comedy about straight white people falling in love, or a horror movie, so that I can scream and burrow into his chest like a teenage girl. His firm hand pushes me face down on the mattress, and he holds my face against the pillows. I don't protest. He climbs on top of me again and rests his body against mine, his cock cradled between my ass cheeks.

"You're a really handsome man," he whispers in my ear before biting it. I flinch from the pain and wonder if he broke skin. I tell myself that this is sexy. He's taking control of my body; he'll take me on a good ride. My cock begins to stiffen, impeded only by the bedding underneath me. He licks my upper back and works his way slowly to my ass. "You have a sexy hairy bum, you little devil," he says. His tongue feels good enough to relax me a bit. Then he jams one of his fingers up my ass. I arch my back and tell him to go easy.

"All you bottoms want me to go easy," he says. He opens his nightstand drawer and pulls out a jar of Boy Butter. I watch as he digs two fingers in. Seconds later, I feel them inside of me.

"Easy," I say. "That hurts."

He pushes deeper.

"I don't think I'm ready to be fucked," I say, but I don't think he hears me. "Robert," I repeat, louder this time, "I don't think I'm ready to be fucked."

"I think you are. I can feel it." He adds a third finger in. I lay there passively waiting for him to stop. Maybe I should just let him fuck me. He has a nice cock and I'll probably enjoy it. He seemed like a good guy; maybe this is part of the act. He plays tough and strong, but he's the same person who moments ago cuddled me and whispered sweet nothings in my ear. If this is how he gets excited, maybe I should just let him do it. I relax myself. He feels it.

"That's a good boy."

He dips his hand back in the Boy Butter. I hear the slippery sounds of him massaging his meat. I feel the wetness of the cream on my lower back. He pulls a small dark bottle out of the nightstand and screws it open. I hear him inhale behind me. He puts the bottle to my nose, and I stop breathing. Poppers make me woozy.

He can tell I'm not breathing it in. "Don't act like you don't want to." He spanks my ass, and I take a deep inhale. Blood rushes to my brain and my vision gets tighter, my breathing heavier. Poppers make everything brighter. There's a fire burning inside me and I want Robert to ease it, to penetrate me with all his might.

I arch my back and lift my ass up, and I hear him gasp in pleasure. He slaps my ass again, a little too hard. He pushes his cock inside, and his pain invades my body. I hear a sound similar to tearing fabric. I push myself up, and now all of him is inside. He grabs my hair and pins my head to the pillow. "See, you wanted it after all."

Sweat gathers on my forehead as he thrusts in and out. He pulls my hair tighter, and I gulp deep breaths through my mouth. The dark bottle reappears in front of my face. I suck the chemical smell in and it opens my insides. He pounds me, and it feels like I'm watching a porno on double the speed. Everything is moving faster; everything feels hazy. I just need a moment to breathe. I see my reflection in his dark television screen, and I'm bent down as Robert slams himself inside of me. He grips my hair as if taming a wild horse. I catch his eyes, but he's not looking at me; he's looking at his own reflection. He smiles to himself, moves his hips for himself. He's transfixed by his own body as he fucks my ass.

The poppers wear off. They never last longer than a minute or two. I suddenly feel the pain of him inside, and I shake my head, releasing my hair from his grip. I dig my face into the pillow and moan in pain.

"That's it."

His cock is a dagger stabbing my insides. My mouth is dry. I want him to stop. I want to scream and push him off me. He's stronger than me, but I'm strong too. I can push him off against the wall and free myself. I can punch him in the face if I have to. I look up, and I see the ghost of my father, his arms crossed. He walks toward me and covers my mouth with his palm. He has a wicked smile on his shattered face, and his fingers smell like poppers. I deserve this pain. I should just let this man do whatever the fuck he wants with my body. I groan with closed lips.

"Motherfucker!"

We notice it at the same time. The familiar sharp smell fills the room instantly. Robert curses before he pulls himself out. I told him I wasn't ready. He didn't hear me.

"Man, I thought you were clean." He pushes himself off me and I soon hear the water running in the bathroom. I look down and I see a patch of brown on his sheets.

"I told you I wasn't—"

"Shit, man, just go." His voice comes from behind the door.

"But I wanted to—"

He opens the door and pops his head out. "Listen, dude. You should go." In his wet hand, a roll of toilet paper. He throws it at me. He slams the bathroom door again, and I'm face-down naked in a stranger's bed. An ache rushes up my spine. I touch myself, and I see bits of red and brown on the tips of my fingers. I slide off the bed, avoiding the dirty patch, and clean myself up with the toilet paper. I leave the dirty tissue on the coffee table. I wash my hands in the kitchen sink over his dirty dishes, then I get dressed and walk into the hall barefoot, put my shoes on while I wait for the elevator. When it opens, I'm greeted by my reflection in its mirror. I pull a comb out of my gym bag and finally fix my unruly hair. I grin, and my teeth are covered in blood. He must have jammed his dick in there so hard that my gums are bleeding. I see a tear in the corner of my eye and wipe it with the sleeve of my jacket.

I text Michael. "Hey can we talk?" I wait for the talking bubble to appear on my screen. I sigh and exit through the lobby while tapping on the Skype app.

"Hey! Hussam!" Arda answers. His face is too close to the screen.

"Hey, wait a second." I pull my headphones out of my gym bag and connect them. "Can we talk?"

"Yeah." He hesitates. "I mean, you okay?" I see my own face in the app. My eyes are red, and there's a hickey on the side of my neck. Who leaves hickeys anymore? I put my sunglasses on.

"I'm fine." I avoid people walking up Davie Street. Some of them stare at me as I speak in Arabic. "I just haven't talked to you in a while."

"It's like eleven at night, and I was about to go to sleep, so—"

"Eleven? Since when do you—" I pause. He's pixelated, but I can see a reflection in the dark window behind him. There's a shirtless man in the room with him.

"Hussam. What's wrong?" he asks.

"I'm losing you," I lie. "What did you say?"

"Can you hear me now?"

"I can't hear you. Hello?" I click the red dot and end the call. He tries me moments later, but I let it ring. I need to sit down. My back aches. Maybe I'm bleeding. I insert my hand between my pant legs and check for wetness, and a woman looks at me weird. I cross Burrard, but I feel like I can't take another step without falling on my face. I reach a bus stop and sit on the bench. Sitting hurts. What did that dude do to me? My phone buzzes.

"Hey! Let's go out tonight!" Michael writes back, ignoring my original text. I leave him on read. I'm four blocks away from home. I cradle my head between my palms and shake.

"Hey, are you all right?" asks a woman waiting for the bus.

"Mind your business," I snap at her. She takes a step back and looks away.

I scroll my phone. I call Ray, and he picks up on the first ring.

"Sam! Where are you? You went to the gym hours ago."

"Can you come and get me? I'm at Burrard and Davie."

"What's wrong? Why can't you walk home? Are you okay?"

"Can you just—"

"I'll be there in two minutes," he says. I hear the car keys jingle. "Do you want me to stay on the phone with you?"

"No."

"Okay. Just stay there."

"Okay."

"Love you."

I pause. He says it all the time; the words lose flavour like chewing gum. But the way he just said it was different. He said it as if he meant it. His voice thinned with worry and hushed with care. He stretched the *you*, as if to provide reassurance. He wasn't just describing how he felt; he wanted me to feel that his love is engulfing and available. It felt unquestionable, almost eternal. He breathed it out so easily, like a fact of life, as if he was confirming that the sun rises in the east.

"I love you, too," I say. To my ear, it sounds like a question. As if I'm asking myself if I actually do. I hear him open the car door before he hangs up.

When I love someone, is that love mine to hold or his to receive? Loving Wassim was an everlasting burning coal I held in my hands, bouncing it between my palms hoping it would cool down. Then I pushed him, and he was gone. Is that how love should be? A constant breaking and reshaping of my own heart until it's a mess of bloodied muscle and tissue? Loving Arda was a cold wet cloth pressed against the burns of my past. It wasn't meant to heal; it was meant to sustain and soothe. It was mine to receive. I gave Arda the touch of my skin, and he stabilized me, like an ER doctor applying pressure against bullet wounds until the surgeons come in with their sterilized gloves. I told Ray I loved him a week after I met him on social media. Was it love when I knew I didn't want him to touch me? Was it love when all I wanted was to find a route out of a place that destroyed me? I got tired of fighting the beasts of my past, and I just wanted peace. Ray looked good for his age. His balcony overlooked English Bay with a direct view of annual Pride parades. His shirts were white. I never bought white clothes before I came to Vancouver; they would get dirty too fast, and my ability to launder them was limited. Is it love that I had for Ray, or envy? I wanted what he had: the apartment, the shirts, the city that celebrated Pride. I thought I deserved these things, too. Turns out it was all true: his world is easier than mine, always has been, always will be. Now, he has me too, and his world is perfect from the outside. His world is perfect to him.

"Hey." He parks by the bus stop, and I get in. "What happened to you?"

"I don't want to talk about it."

He drives in silence for a moment. I look out the window at the people going in and out of Starbucks on the corner. "You've got to talk to me, Sam," he says. "Just tell me what happened. I'm worried about you."

If he noticed the hickey, he's not saying anything. "I just want to go home."

"You can talk to me, Sam. You can tell me anything," he lulls.

I push my sunglasses up and rub my eyes with my palms. Tears wet the edge of my sleeve.

"I don't know if I can do this anymore. I'm falling apart," I say. My voice breaks. "There's darkness inside, and it's swallowing me."

"I don't understand," he says.

"I didn't want him to fuck me."

"Who?"

"I'm sorry. I shouldn't tell you this."

He parks the car in our spot and turns off the engine. "Don't worry. Just tell me what happened."

I tell him about Selfie Guy. How he held me down by the back of the neck like a dog he was taming. I tell him I might be bleeding. I keep some details to myself. I don't tell him about the accident at the end. About how Robert's fingers dug deep into my back, and how I still feel them there.

"Did he use protection?" Ray asks after a pause.

"What?"

"Did he use a condom?"

"Yes," I lie.

"That's good. That's good to hear," he murmurs. He removes his driving glasses, places them inside their case, and throws them in the glove compartment. Silence fills the car. The other gay couple who live on our floor drive by and park a couple spots down. Ray fakes a smile and waves. I hide my eyes behind my sunglasses.

"I don't know why I can't just stop," I say. "This side of the world is open and easy, but it speaks in codes and I don't know how to decipher it." I'm reluctant, but it feels good to speak.

"I'm scared, Ray. I'm frightened all the time. I thought I could leave it all behind, but I brought my fears with me. This life scares me. I just want to run from it, too."

"Maybe you're just addicted to running, Sam," he says. "The only way you know how to survive is to escape."

The gay couple walk toward the building carrying groceries, their laughter echoing through the parking garage. One opens the door and holds it with his back, and the other slips in.

Ray breaks the silence. "We should close up our relationship for a while. Focus on us for a bit until you feel better."

"You think so?"

He leans forward and embraces me over the gearshift. At first I resist, but his chest feels warm. I relax in his arms. "Let's just be the two of us," he says, "just for a bit."

I nod. My tears wet his T-shirt.

"I'll take care of you, Sam," he says. "I promised you that since day one. You're my responsibility, and I'll do whatever I can to protect you. You don't need to run from me."

His arm presses on my side, his skin rough against mine. Tears feel like a flood within my head, and I pour them out. I want to open the car door and run until I'm winded, but I have nowhere else to go.

"Yeah. Let it out. It's okay."

"I'm sorry," I say between the tears.

"You don't need to be sorry. You'll be fine." He pauses. "We'll be fine."

He pulls tissues out of a box in the back seat and hands them to me. "Come on," he says. "Let's go home. I'll put some ice on your neck."

DAMASCUS

Kalila's past remains a mystery. She listens to me talk about my history but never shares her own. She appears when she pleases and disappears mid-sentence. She morphs from her grey-scale into living colour, or she floats around the house uninterrupted by my calling her name. She has stopped crying, which comes as a relief. She hasn't re-enacted her death again, which spares me the cold shivers down my spine. I do wonder sometimes if she lives on the same plane as me, with the same rules of conversation. Is she ever going to tell me her story like a classic narrative, starting from the day she was born and ending with the day of her death? Her presence used to unnerve me, but now it brings me comfort, quieting the loneliness and guilt I'm destined to live with.

But I doubt she's a woman of classic narratives.

I sometimes wake up to find her floating in my bedroom. I suppose one can't be bothered to knock when walking through walls is an option. I don't want to anger her; she might kick me out of her home. I'm thankful that I haven't had to sleep on the streets for months now. The bruise on my side heals slowly, but its dull ache reminds me of what awaits me outside.

The night before, I'd brought down some boxes from the attic and left them in the living room. I hoped I would see Kalila this morning, but she's nowhere to be found. However, it seems that one of the boxes was moved in the night. By her? She wouldn't tell me if I asked. It's locked, but I pry it open to find yellowed papers and contracts with faded ink. In the bottom of the box, there's an old photo album. Black-and-white photos of children standing politely next to one another, the corners bending and cracking like the fine lines on an old man's skin. Photos of fez-wearing men with curled moustaches large enough for a bird to perch on each side. And then, in the middle of the album, right where the spine of the book breaks, Kalila's wedding photo. It was taken back in a time when the bride and groom did not smile for the camera. She gave a profile view of her dress, her hand rested on the shoulder of a suited man that I assume is her husband.

On the other side of the page, I find a wedding invitation.

The honourable Shareef family and the honourable Mamlook family invite you to the blessed day of the wedding of their son, Mohammed Shareef, and the daughter of the Mamlook family. Please join us for the celebrations on June 18, 1965, at 7 p.m. at the Al-Sharq Club's Weddings Hall.

Children and maids are invited to stay home.

"My name was not to be mentioned on my own wedding invitation," Kalila says.

"We talked about you jumping me, Kalila."

She smiles. She likes her metaphysical form and the freedom it provides her. She moves like the drift of her dress, mesmerizing and hushed. She is playful with her afterlife, living her death with a wicked mischievousness.

"My family didn't want my name to be stained on the tongues of people," she adds. "It was hidden from all except for my family and his."

"You were married to this guy until you passed?"

She ignores my question with a smirk. She is a mistress of meaningful smiles. She knows that in her current state, no one can force her to answer questions she doesn't care for.

"Tell me about your wedding day."

Her father and Mohammed's were close friends and neighbouring merchants who had decided, before she was born, that she would marry Mohammed. She was seventeen when she learned of her fate to marry a man twice her age whom she'd only met on formal occasions. She protested, but her complaints were ignored. In late April of 1965, she was informed that the men of both families were to gather and read Al-Fatiha—the opening sura of the Quran, a blessing for the new partnership.

On Al-Fatiha day, she cracked the door to her family's guest quarters to watch the men, her father and Mohammed at the centre, raise their palms to the sky and mumble the short verses, then shake hands.

She'd asked her mother to intervene. "I want to finish high school," she begged. "My grades could get me into Damascus University. I could be a nurse, or even a doctor." She'd heard of Sabat Islambooly, the first female Syrian doctor, who graduated in 1890 from the Woman's Medical College of Pennsylvania and came back to Syria to practise medicine. Women had been graduating in medicine from Damascus University since 1911. Kalila's mother mocked her, saying that these women ended up spinsters. "What good is a framed degree for a spinster?" her mother asked.

Frustrated, she sidled up to her father as he drank tea one afternoon. She reminded him that she was his only heir, and that she needed to learn more about the world and its ways. She sweet-talked him into listening and mustered the courage to ask him to cancel the wedding. She cooed her words and stretched her loving sentences. She touched his forearm and kissed the back of his hand.

"Don't be silly," he said.

"Baba, please," she pleaded, "I don't want to get married."

"Don't be silly." And that was the end of the conversation.

In early May, Kalila was informed that it was time for her father to sign the book of her marriage. A man from the Islamic court of Damascus came to their home to meet with her father and her future husband, and a festive gathering of close relatives was called into session.

The man from the Islamic court walked into the house wearing a long brown jacket and a white skullcap. He carried a large well-used governmental archive book. Kalila slammed the door open in front of her family and her future husband. She begged the government official to convince her father to wait until she finished school.

Her father stood in the corner of their guest room, embarrassed, and the government official turned around and left. Mohammed shook hands with Kalila's father, and they agreed to talk later. Mohammed gave her a sideways glance as he left. Her distant family talked about the scene she made for years.

Kalila expected her father to slap her that day. She expected her mother to shout and scream. But weeks went by, and no one brought up the incident again. She thought she'd been successful in her mission, until the morning of the eighteenth of May. On that sunny day, her father asked her to dress up modestly and put a headscarf on.

"Please don't take her," her mother begged, but he insisted. She relented and brought Kalila a long blue niqab that her grandmother used to wear. Kalila didn't know where she was going, but her father had given his orders. She'd never seen him in a traditional Damascene outfit before: a red-dotted white headscarf and a long black vest covering a white shirt.

"Why are we wearing these outfits, Baba?" she asked. He opened the door and ushered her out without a response.

They lived on the outskirts of Qassa'a, right on Al-Zaynabia street, on the border of the Christian neighbourhood. She loved walking with her father. He used to walk with her down the street to Bab Al-Salam, then along the Straight Street. He would tell her the stories of the saints and prophets who'd walked on this historic road, whose steps still echoed on its stones, their handprints kissed by pilgrims of all religions.

But on that day, he wasn't in the mood for storytelling. They walked by the antique shops and the lantern makers in silence. She struggled to see the world around her from underneath the niqab, given that it was the first and last time she ever wore one. She kept tripping on its skirt, and it felt heavy on her shoulders.

They were not alone in their mysterious quest. Everyone else on the street walked in the same direction. The streets were getting busier, and the coffee shops and healthy cocktail venues were closed. Soon they left the doomed streets of Hariqa with its tiled roads and hurried along the hot asphalt of the Al-Bath street.

She asked her father to slow down. They'd walked this street a million times before, but never this fast. He told her to hurry up and never let go of his hand. They walked together through the crowd toward Al-Marjeh Square.

It was mostly men around her. The streets that used to be filled with cars and horse carriages were empty. There were a couple of roadblocks with parked cars behind them, monitored by two or three bored police officers surveying the crowds with little interest.

"Where are we going, Baba?" she asked again.

The crowd kept getting thicker. She already felt suffocated by the niqab on her shoulders, as if she were walking inside a tent. Still, many men looked at her. They whispered that this was no place for a woman, this was not a day for a woman. She tugged on her father's hand but he jerked back. He firmly pushed men out of their way.

At Al-Marjeh Square she was the only woman in sight, surrounded by thousands of men. "Baba, why did you bring me here?" she asked. Her voice was frightened enough for her father to stop, turn, and look her in the eyes.

"I brought you here to see," he told her.

They reached the front of the crowd. Metal barriers created an empty circle in the square's centre. She'd never seen this many people gathered in one place before. Television cameras were installed everywhere, and windows were shut.

The clear waters of Barada River were running along two sides of the square and hidden underneath the streets that formed a plate atop it. In the middle of that plate rose a tall obelisk erected to commemorate the martyrs of Damascus, with a stone replica of Old Damascus crowning it. In the 1800s there was a central prison in the middle of the square, but by then, prisons in Syria were unknown buildings that no one could find on a map.

"Look!" her father instructed her.

In the middle of the square, right underneath the martyrs' obelisk, was a wooden stage. The crowd waited patiently. Was there going to be a play? A speech? She couldn't tell. Four men with their faces covered in black shawls stood around the stage, protected from the crowds by dozens of police officers who shouted obscenities at the gathered men, forcing them to stay in the designated areas.

The crowd opened from one side, and Kalila saw a black windowless truck driving toward the stage. When it slowed down, the four masked men hurried to the only door in the back, and the crowd cheered as a man was pushed out.

"Baba, why are we here?" she asked again. She had finally figured out what was happening around her.

The man wore a red prison uniform. His wrists were cuffed in front of him, with a chain attaching to his waist like a belt. He was carried by the shoulders and forced to stand up, and the crowd hollered in anger. Kalila, her eyes wide like saucers, took in every detail with both curiosity and horror. The man was barefoot, and his feet were large and swollen. They looked like two oversized tomatoes about to burst under the weight of his body. "They prefer feet whipping," one of the men near her said. "It kept him alive while they extracted information." Kalila looked back and saw that the man speaking had his young son with him. The boy watched on with crystalline eyes.

Her father gathered her under his arm, and they watched as the officers dragged the man to the wooden platform. He was tall, with black hair and a crooked nose. His fingernails were bloody, and some were missing. The four guards held the struggling man up to the jeers of the crowd. Someone behind Kalila threw a rotten tomato and it landed unceremoniously dozens of feet away from the platform. A police officer shouted not to throw things. "This is official business!" he yelled, nudging his baton.

A noose was rolled down the platform like a lizard's tongue and hung there swinging. The prisoner was slowly led toward it, eyes now covered with a black scarf. Kalila could see his mouth, trembling with words she couldn't hear.

The man was pushed to stand on top of a stool under the noose, and one of the four men tightened the noose around his neck.

"People of Syria," a disembodied voice boomed, bringing silence to the square, "hear the justified end to those who wanted to harm us."

The voice was coming from large speakers installed around the square, but no one could see who was speaking. Was it live or recorded? Kalila couldn't tell. "In the name of the Arab people of Syria, the military court has ruled in its seating on the eighteenth of May, 1965, that Eliyahu Ben-Shaul Cohen is to be executed for crimes he committed against the people of Syria and the occupied territories of Palestine, and for spying on Syria on behalf of the Zionist enemy."

The voice narrated the smart and conniving ways the Syrian intelligence forces managed to arrest the Israeli man, Eli Cohen, by monitoring radio frequencies to narrow down the source of his communication with Tel Aviv and breaking into his house in the early morning hours, catching him in the act.

Louder cheers came from the crowd, and Kalila could no longer hear the voice. People threw their arms in the air. Kalila cowered deeper into her father's embrace, and he tightened his arm around her.

She didn't realize the speech was over until she saw one of the four guards place his foot on the base of the stool Eli Cohen stood on. The guard held his stance for moments of anticipation, then kicked with all his might.

The man hanging by the noose was airborne, and the square went completely silent.

His neck, Kalila could tell, did not snap. His feet thrust in all directions, and his back tensed. He tried to pull his hands up to grab at the noose, but they were chained to his waist. His jolting made his body swing back and forth, and the officers around him had to dodge his feet. For three minutes this went on, his jerking kicks slowly losing conviction until his legs finally settled and his head rested on his shoulder. A stream of piss dwelled on his foot before dripping from his toes.

The crowd shouted, and Kalila's father pulled her away from the dead man and his observers. Beyond the square, the streets were almost empty, except for a few police officers standing at their posts, trying to see the execution past the crowd.

They walked home the way they had come, along streets Kalila had never seen so empty. They walked quickly, and she panted, but she just wanted to get home.

"We're in for difficult times." Her father squeezed her hand. "You and your mother will have no one when I'm gone."

She nodded and ran up their building's stairs. When her mother opened the door, Kalila didn't even take off her niqab; she threw herself on her mother and cried.

Two weeks later, she stood in the corner of their guest room. The same guests from before gathered again; the same groom showed up at the door, and the same government official, with his brown jacket and old archive book, arrived on time. He found Kalila in a modest dress and headscarf and gave her a questioning eye. She nodded.

The official sat between her father and her future husband. The old man dropped a white handkerchief over the men's hands, and they shook. He asked Mohammed if he wanted to take the daughter of the Mamlook family as his wife, and Mohammed said yes. He asked her father if he wanted to give his daughter to Mohammed, and he said yes.

The government official announced them husband and father-in-law, and the women released a loud zalghouta, a celebratory ululation Kalila always heard at weddings and upon the arrival of new baby boys.

Kalila tells me that her name was hidden from her, as if it were a treasure she was unworthy of. She'd never see it on a diploma and would lose it soon when people started calling her

Um Ahmad instead of Kalila. Mohammed told her that their first-born would be called Ahmad, and she would be called his mother.

"My name wasn't even on the funeral announcement when I died." The notice that went up in their neighbourhood named her father, who'd died by then, her mourning husband, and all of her male cousins.

Soon, other death announcements were posted on top of hers. She was forgotten by everyone but her withering mother, she tells me, and she flickers away.

"Kalila?" I'm surprised by her sudden departure. I run into the living room, search the kitchen. I climb the stairs and call her name again, but she's nowhere. I stand at the bottom of the staircase, where her head hit the floor the night of her death. The curtains on the windows wave at me, and the chilly spring breeze seeps into the empty home. I attempt to close the windows, but they're stuck. The faces of the men and women of Damascus outside appear like ghosts between the cracks of the fence, and I fear them seeing me. What if Rima and the child passed by the house and saw me inside? What if she recognized me as she did back in the market?

I had learned Rima's name a week before our wedding. My father told me that I would marry her, and I nodded. I did not protest as Kalila had. I did not try to save the moments of tenderness with Hussam. I needed no convincing.

"A woman is what you need to straighten you up," my father said. I too held my palms up and mumbled Al-Fatiha in Rima's father's house. When another old man with a long brown jacket and a white skullcap walked into our home with the Damascus Islamic court archive book, I signed my name as instructed. I held my sweaty hand to her father's. Both hands disappeared under the white handkerchief, and we were announced married.

Maybe I should go and find Rima. Maybe I should own up to the woman who carries my name and looks after my child. Maybe if I kneel at her feet and beg for forgiveness, she would take me back in.

"Kalila!" my voice begs. "Please don't leave me alone."

I wait for her to appear in front of me. I jolt around, jumping on both feet, hoping to see her appear behind me.

"Kalila," I whisper.

I find myself haunted by memories of Rima and my child. They stand at every opened door. The tips of their shoes peek out from under every curtain. They reach out for me and beg me to return. Rima had lost her name and become my wife and then the mother of my child. What fate did I place upon this naive woman, to be known for the rest of her life as the one whose husband escaped her for another man? What shame must she carry until the end of her days?

I rush outside to the gate. I hold the knob with both hands. I try to twist it open but it won't give. Is it stuck, or am I not putting enough force into it? I twist it again, and it trembles between my fingers. I pull as hard as I can, and the door opens. The breeze picks up and hits me in the face. I take a couple of steps back. People walk the streets. They carry plastic bags filled with vegetables and fruit and balance cardboard egg trays on one hand. A family—a father, a mother, and two children—hold hands as they pass. An explosion booms in the distance, but they pay it no mind. When they disappear, I retreat inside and close the door. I lock it twice.

VANCOUVER

Ray wants me to get a haircut. I haven't left home in weeks. I rarely shower. He says that if I spend one more night smoking weed, watching porn, and jerking off, he'll lose his mind. "It's time you get over this funk, Sam," he says. I told Michael and Brian I was sick with the flu, and I ghosted Arda's Skype calls.

I'd given up applying for jobs after sending my resumé to dozens of postings I found on LinkedIn and not hearing shit. The WorkBC social worker suggested I change my name on the resumé. Ray wants me to take his last name. *Sam Robinson*. It sounds made up, like a character in a daytime soap.

"What do you want to do with your life, Sam?" the social worker had asked. I shrugged. She wanted me to come back and take a Myers-Briggs personality test, which would help her figure out who I was and what jobs would fit me best. I never returned.

Ray doesn't care for WorkBC, because he makes enough money for the both of us. Today the tank top he bought me online arrived, and he asked me to put it on.

"We're going to Junction," he says.

"I don't want to go to Junction."

"For fuck's sake, would you just shave?"

He picks up my phone, dials Michael, and hands it back to me. Michael just landed at Vancouver airport after a three-day pairing. He needs to go home to change out of his WestJet uniform, then he'll meet us at Junction. "I'll plan with Brian," he says. "We're going to have a good time tonight."

A couple of hours later, I stand in line outside the club, pretending I'm not cold.

"It's so nice out," Michael says.

"So much nicer than last month," I lie.

"Look. At. Her." Brian points to a guy wearing baggy overalls. The guy walks alone eating a donair he must have gotten from the nearby Greek restaurant. One side of his head is shaved, and the other has long, pink hair that looks slapped on. Is he wearing mascara?

"She forgot to look in the mirror before she left home," Michael quips.

"She doesn't own a mirror, honey," Brian says.

They wait for me to say something witty, something nasty.

"I think every time she looks in any mirror, it cracks." The three of us giggle, and Pink Hair looks back at the long line of eyes examining him. He hurries his step.

"Boys. Boys. Let's be nice," Ray says, but he also chuckles.

A twink at the end of the line waves at me. He stands with a much larger muscle man.

"Do you know that guy?" Ray asks.

"I dunno. Maybe we fucked."

"Slutty, slutty, slutty," Brian singsongs.

"Not anymore I'm not," I reply, making sure Ray hears. "I'm monogamous now."

Brian and Michael give me a look.

"Sam! Haven't seen you in a while." Fuck. I don't know who you are, kid. I'm sorry that your face looks exactly like the face of every twenty-something twink in this city. I'm sorry that you're indistinguishable from all the other gays in your age group. I'm sorry that you were probably such a lousy fuck that I can't remember you. I'm sorry but I honestly can't—

It's Pinocchio! Oh, I remember you.

"Oh hey, cutie," I say. Pinocchio gives me a hug that I awkwardly return. Ray keeps his eyes on the situation. We all stand in a circle silently. I shuffle my feet. Is he going to leave me alone now?

"We haven't heard from you," Pinocchio says. "We were hoping you'd come over to watch a movie or something."

I feel Ray's hand grip mine tighter. "This is my boyfriend, Ray. This is Michael, and that's Brian." I pause. Ah, shit. "What's your name again?"

Pinocchio rolls his eyes and walks off in a huff, rejoining Randy Orton at the back of the line. Whatever, dude. You can take your interchangeable boyfriend and find a third somewhere else. You can go off and live your twenty-first-century fantasy of polyamory, but what we had was sex. Plain, dumb animal sex, and nothing more.

"The line is moving," Michael announces.

I smell weed wafting from a cluster of smokers. I have three joints in my backpack; Ray called his dealer and got us some this morning. Brian asked me to keep his coke in my bag, and I agreed, but I don't want to do blow anymore.

"ID?" the bouncer asks. I pull my card out and hand it to him. Suddenly it's my father's ghost examining my permanent resident card with hollow eyes. They sink inside his skull, dropping deep enough to fall down his throat and peer at me from within his opened chest. I shiver and blink. The bouncer hands back the card, and I get stamped on my wrist.

The club isn't yet full. A few people stand by the bar, and three or four tables are gathered around the stage. The DJ plays random songs from the late 2000s, and there's one boy, maybe nineteen, dancing alone on the dance floor. He looks high. Michael takes me by the elbow and we walk to the bar while Brian and Ray find a table by the stage.

"Why did you bring Ray?" Michael whispers, and I explain that he invited himself. "Club is church, Sam. There needs to be a separation between church and state."

"Let it go."

"Man, you need to have some space for yourself. He can't be around you twenty-four-seven," he insists.

"Four vodka sodas, please," Michael orders without asking me. If homosexuality is a country, vodka soda is our national drink. The bartender, a cute shirtless bear, pours a calculated amount of vodka in each glass, then fills them with soda.

We walk back to our table. The young dancer is still at it. He even thinks he's good. A group of girls at the table opposite us cheer him on loudly. One wears a bride's veil. I already regret leaving home.

A tall woman takes the stage holding a mic. When the light hits her face, I realize that this is not a woman.

"Five-minute warning, everyone. The show is about to start." The DJ lowers the volume for her. "We have a great show for you tonight with some of your favourite local talents, so get your drinks and tip your waiters and come back for us." She's wearing a blond wavy wig, maybe two or three stitched together, and her face is covered with a layer of heavy makeup. Her eyebrows are drawn halfway up her forehead. She has a short red dress on, with stockings and high heels, and a rubber replica of woman's breasts around her neck like a child's bib.

"Is it drag night?" I whisper to Ray, who hmms a yes. "You should've told me!"

"Meh, it's just for like an hour." Brian's eyes are glued to his phone. "Then we dance."

Ray squeezes my forearm. "Lighten up, honey."

The drag queen talks to the DJ, air-kisses men she knows, laughs at a joke someone tells her. She walks comfortably in heels. The lights dim and the music stops. The dancing twink continues to sway to a beat of his own. A spotlight hits the stage where the queen in the red dress stands. She mouths something while fidgeting with the mic. "Girl, turn this mi— oh, here we go.

"Good evening, everyone," she announces like a circus ring-leader, "and welcome to Girls' Night Out, our weekly drag show here at Junction." The crowd breaks into a roar of applause. "My name is Blair Bitch Project, and I will be your hostess tonight." She notices the dancing twink. "Someone's having a good night." The crowd thunders in laughter. She walks to the dancer and taps him on the shoulder. The spotlight doesn't follow the queen. It stays on the stage, where my father stands with brain matter gliding down his forehead.

"Honey, didn't your mama tell you never to share a stage with a drag queen? It's not a good look."

The women who earlier cheered on the dancer now scream in unison, as if they'd practised. It sounds like the roar of a dinosaur.

"What do we have here? A bachelorette party? Welcome to the Village!" Blair turns to the audience. "They're here all the time. We should ask them to pay rent."

My friends laugh. I don't see what's so entertaining. Why can't Junction just hire a couple of go-go boys and play music all night? "I'm going outside to smoke," I say. "Wanna come?"

"The show's just started," Ray says. Brian is on his phone, consumed by Grindr. But Michael gives me an understanding look.

"I need a joint to relax," I tell him. "Do you want to partake?"

"Maybe after Blair's done?" Michael says. He taps my forearm twice, and I fidget in my seat.

Blair manages to bring the dancing twink to a full stop and then pushes him to a seat. "Honey, she's a mess tonight." The crowd erupts into more laughter. "We have a great show for you. My dear sisters Scarlet Silk and Rachel Minority are back-stage getting ready." The spotlight follows her around. "But first I thought I'd start you off with some Britney!"

The music starts, and my company ignores me to watch the stage. Blair dances seductively to the opening of "I Wanna Go," and when the lyrics begin, she unhinges her jaw and mouths the words exaggeratedly. At a musical interlude, she poses in front of the audience and crudely mimes masturbation. The audience laughs and cheers, and some of them approach the queen with bills in their hands. She insists that one of them, a handsome man she seems to know, insert the ten dollars between her fake boobs. He does so while laughing, and they air-kiss.

Suddenly the whole club goes silent and dark. Everyone disappears in a flash of light, and I'm alone. The spotlight focuses on my father's ghost. He stands at centre stage, eyes closed. The music returns, but it's jittery and shaky. My father's ghost lifts his arms and slow dances with an imaginary partner. It's a twisted ballroom dance. He swings left and right while the spotlight follows him around. He takes a final sway before stopping in front of my seat. His eyelids open to reveal empty sockets, and black blood pours out of them.

I inhale so loudly, Michael hears it. I'm back in the lit club with the dancing queen and the roaring audience.

"Are you okay?" Michael asks.

I unzip my backpack, pull out one of the joints. "Yup. Just need some fresh air." Ray eyes me as I leave the table, then focuses back on the show. I push through the crowd toward the exit. I show the stamp on my wrist to the security guard and walk into the little smoking garden outside. It's really cold. I should have brought a sweater or a jacket.

The line to the club is still long, but it's full of new faces, except for the very front where Pinocchio and Randy Orton are waiting. They give me dirty looks.

I shield myself from the chilling breeze and ready the joint in my mouth. I tap both shorts pockets to locate my lighter. It's not in my right, and it's not in my left. I am out of pockets. This day cannot get any fucking worse.

"Here." A hand presents me with a lighter on an opened palm. These are some long nails.

She's taller than me, but that can be attributed to the six-inch heels she wears. She wears a wig of long, untamed grey hair that has a silvery sheen in the streetlights. Her outfit, a power suit, is made of dark blue leather that hugs her body, curving with her legs and tightening around her waist. Her butt is large, with hips arched down the lower half. There's a hint of glitter on her cheeks, over her olive-oil-brown skin. Her lips are painted royal blue, and she wears three sets of eyelashes, one on top of the other.

There is something both repulsive and attractive about her. I can't take my eyes off the beauty she's created, and yet I can't stop myself from seeing the man underneath it. My hand freezes in midair, inches away from her open palm.

"You can take it, I don't bite." She sounds amused. "Unless you ask nicely."

I accept the lighter.

"Attaboy. Took you long enough."

"Thank you," I mumble, the joint between my teeth. I inhale, and the smoke calms my insides like icy water spilled over burned skin. Remedies. I live through intermissions between remedies. My life a long haul of pushing through darkness interrupted by short bursts of light.

"Whoa, dude. Easy there." She is not wearing bib boobs like the other one. She uses makeup to draw an illusion of a female chest that's made visible by the cut of the power suit. Two half-moons powdered and lined and artistically rendered with shadows and highlights to look three-dimensional.

"Hey, my eyes are up here."

"Sorry."

She grins and extends her hand. "Can I have my lighter back?"

Her fingers are adorned with two rings, and her wrist is encircled by a beautiful golden chain. If I saw this woman on

the street, I'd admire her outfit. She perfectly matched everything to go together but allowed for the odd clash here and
there to break up the beauty. The most beautiful things are a
bit broken. I hand her the lighter.

"Now, be a gentleman and give me a hit."

The request feels like an invitation to continue standing
together, but I don't want to talk to her anymore. I don't want
to talk to most people anymore. I just need some alone time. A
moment when I'm in a room alone with no human or animal
around me. No drag queens, no ghosts. Nothing.

"Sure." I hand her the joint.

After inhaling she holds her breath, and slowly, like a wise
dragon, releases the smoke through her nostrils.

"Ah, that was nice. Thank you." She hands me back the joint,
and I notice the light print of her blue lipstick on it. It's not even
a third burned. Such a waste to throw it away. I put it back in my
mouth, trying to avoid the lipstick print, and take a hit.

"Aren't you cold? You poor soul." Her voice sounds familiar.

I look at her and gather myself. "Nah. The weather is lovely.
It's better than last month." I fake a smile. She smirks.

"Oh, you're not joking." She does a double take. "You
adapted well to Canada."

"Huh?"

"Nothing. Good on you for looking at this from a positive
point of view."

"Aren't *you* cold?"

"The foam protects me." She circles a finger over her hip
and butt.

"Those are foam?" I ask.

"You can touch them if you like," she says nonchalantly.

I hand the joint back to her for another hit, then regret it. Force of habit. I place my hand on her butt. It feels like I'm squeezing a pillow.

"Okay there, cowboy," she says. "You're handsome, but you should buy me dinner first."

I laugh in spite of myself. This guy's all right for a drag queen. Maybe one day he'll abandon the whole drag thing. Maybe we could even be friends.

"Well, thanks for the top-up, stranger," she says, "but I gotta go in and do my thing."

She leans in, presenting her face. I awkwardly try to print a kiss on her cheek, but she pulls away. "You silly thing," she says as she walks away, "only air kisses for a drag queen. Don't ruin our makeup." She blows a kiss, and I smile at the cheesiness of it all. "It was nice to run into you again, Hussam." She disappears through the club's door. It's a moment too late for her to see my shocked reaction.

I try to follow her, but I'm stopped by the security guard, who checks the stamp on my wrist before letting me through. The club is now three times as busy as it was when we got here an hour ago. Dawood walks through the crowd and waves at people. I push through the drunk gay men and the lost straight women trying to catch up. By the time I'm by our table, she's disappeared backstage.

Michael looks up. "Hey, you've been gone awhile." Ray's across the dance floor talking to the dancing twink. Brian's already making out with someone.

"What happened to the show?"

"It's intermission," Michael says. "They'll be back."

Blair Bitch Project reappears from behind the curtain. She now wears a long, brown wig pulled back into a braid, a pair of grey shorts, and a green push-up bra. There's a toy gun on each hip, pointing down to her thigh-high boots. She waits for the crowd to come to a complete silence.

"If a drag queen is on stage, you bitches better listen," she says into the mic in a British accent. Everyone laughs at her Lara Croft impersonation. She walks around, telling jokes, insulting people, and collecting tips. People cheer whenever she gets closer to them.

Blair singles out Brian, who's still making out with his new random. "Ladies and gentlemen, here we see a prime example of a desperate homosexual in his natural habitat."

Brian stops and looks at Blair, confused.

"Oh, don't stop on my behalf, child," Blair says, and everyone laughs.

Brian flips the finger at the queen and goes back to making out with the random. Everyone laughs at my friend, and the queen laughs, too. This irritates me. Who is she to fuck with my friend? Who the fuck does she think she is, other than a man in a wig?

"What did you do with your junk, dude?" I shout, and the whole club goes silent. Michael holds me by the elbow and pulls me back a bit, but I snatch my arm away. "No, really, it's a legit question." Ray, from across the dance floor, gives me a mortified look.

Blair doesn't miss a beat. "I don't see how this is any of your business, darling. Some might think I stuffed it up your ass, but you couldn't pay me enough to get near you."

The crowd laughs, delighted. I want to charge the stage and shut this drag queen up.

Michael holds me back. "This is no place for a fight," he whispers. "We don't want to get banned."

Ray leaves the dancer and comes back to the table. He stands between the queen and me. "Here, fantastic show." He pulls his wallet out and tips the queen, smiling.

Blair accepts the twenty and walks back to centre stage; she yells "Hit it!" and the DJ plays "Holding Out for a Hero." She lip-syncs to the song with ferocity. She flips upside down. She dances and kicks. She drops on the floor, splitting her legs apart, and landing on her back. The crowd cheers for her and sings along.

"Can you try not to make a scene for once?" Ray hisses in my ear.

I snap his face off my shoulder with a shrug. "I didn't want to come anyways."

The song ends, and Blair stands in the spotlight, taking in the applause and tucking the tips she's gathered into her bra.

"And now, ladies and gents, we welcome to the stage a queen after my own heart," she says theatrically. "*Literally* after my own heart. This bitch has been wanting to kill me for decades." The crowd laughs.

"Bitch!" We hear Dawood's voice coming from behind the curtain.

"JK, Miss Thing, JK," Blair replies. "We welcome to the stage a diamond in the queer community, a lovely human with so much to give all of us. The one, the only, Rachel Minority!"

The lights dim, and a familiar beat starts. There's a soft whistle of a nay, a daf vibrating gently, a qanun touched with a shy hand, a violin played with a broken heart. They build up together like a choir. Just as they're about to hit a high note, they retreat back to a slower pace. I know this song, it's Warda's "Batwanes Beek." The beats come to a close, and we hear clapping on the audio track, recorded off the radio almost fifty years ago. The applause generates more applause in the crowd, and the curtain is lifted. Dawood emerges from the darkness and walks onto the stage.

The spotlight shines on her. Is it Dawood? I can't tell anymore. She stands in the centre, with a flowing brown wig that falls all the way to the curve of her back. She wears a belly dancer's veil adorned with diamonds and pearls, and her fire-red lipstick shines through it. Her large earrings look like chandeliers. Through the mesh of her pants, I see a tattoo of a flower growing among thorns and almost breaking through the skin of her leg. When the light hits, I realize she's wearing a skin-coloured corset around her waist to give herself the female hourglass shape.

She belly-dances to the beat of the song, keeping the crowd engaged with her swift movements, her controlled core, and her sensual body language. They all watch her, silent and mesmerized. Even Brian and his random stop making out to look at the stage.

Warda sings the lyrics, and Rachel lip-syncs to them, slowly revealing her face from behind her veil. I know this is a recording, but Rachel makes me feel as if she's conjured the spirit of Warda and brought her to Vancouver. At first I'm protective of my Syrianness. Is it okay for a gay man dressed in a wig to do something so Syrian? But it feels impossibly right. I can't help but appreciate the beauty of this woman in front of me, to see her as the illusion she creates. The illusion is not a veil upon her face anymore; it's her truth, and I believe it. She is him, she is a Syrian man, and a gay Canadian, and she timidly dances on that tightrope.

Warda sings about loving souls, and Rachel dances my way. She stands in front of my table, winks and sways for me. The crowd and Ray and Michael and Brian all disappear. The club lights dim and the furniture evaporates. The world around me fades until all that's left is me and Rachel, and I'm watching her as if she's a fairy of fire dancing between my palms. She extends her hand and touches my cheek.

When I was seven, my mama played this song on her small radio in the kitchen. She held the wooden spoon like a microphone and sang along, red sauce dripping onto her apron with the purple flower on its pocket. She rounded her chest and jerked her hips, unaware that I was watching her. She finally noticed me standing at the kitchen door, holding on to its frame.

Grabbing me from under the armpits, she lifted me up in the air and sang the song as she twirled. Her laugh stretches from the depth of my forgotten memory all the way to the surface of this dance floor. My hands shake. My shoulders, usually gathered like a tight knot, relax. There's warmth around me, and it tickles my skin and softens the goosebumps on my forearms. It engulfs me like the sunny days of Damascus. I smell my mama's jasmine perfume. She touches my face. She tells me that I will grow up to be the prince of men.

Tears stream down my cheeks.

"Are you okay?" Rachel mouths. She's taken away by a fan offering her a tip. The song ends, and Rachel bows like a ballerina. She gives me a last worried look before she disappears behind the curtain.

"We need to go," I tell the boys.

Ray rolls his eyes. "Sam, would you please—"

"Now. We need to go now."

I sling my backpack over my shoulder and leave the table, push through the crowd that's still cheering for Rachel. Each face morphs into the face of my father. The ghosts snatch at my clothes and pull. I'm drowning in a sea of hands with stretched fingers, and each finger has its own hand with its own stretched fingers. I bend down. I hear Ray and Michael calling my name. I zigzag toward the bathroom, cutting in line.

"Hey!" Randy Orton shouts. I push the door open. There are two men at the urinals and one at the sinks, washing his hands. I pull my bag open and frantically dig into it for the baggie of coke Brian hid there.

"Sam! What's going on?" Michael calls from outside. I lean against the door, blocking it. The men in the bathroom eye me warily. I open the baggie and inhale half of the white glimmering powder.

"Whoa, man. Not in public," says the man at the sink.

"Fuck off."

I hear my own crisp voice. Each of my limbs burns with white fire that heals and fixes. When Abraham was thrown to fire by his people, God ordered the fire not to harm him. I am Abraham. I am a prophet whose people abandoned him. I am the prince of all men. I am the sun. I glow hot enough to sanitize the dirty bathroom around me. My heart pumps blood strong enough to erupt from my eyes like two volcanoes. I slam the bathroom door open and walk out. Randy Orton is still here, in my way. I shove past him.

"Watch where you're going!" he yells.

His features rearrange into my father's face. He opens his mouth and spits out yellow teeth with rotten roots and bloody nerve endings. I look up, and he smiles at me with a toothless mouth.

"You fucking piece of shit." I punch my father's ghost in the face. The ghost falls back into the arms of two men in line, who bounce him right up, and it's Randy Orton. Dazed, he holds his jaw.

I have no time to apologize. He delivers a swift hook to my chin. I'm lifted off the ground.

"Sam!" Michael kneels next to me.

"Stop." Ray jumps between us and looks up at Orton. "He's high. Just stop."

Randy Orton stands over me. I slide back on my palms, anticipating a kick. A bouncer breaks into the circle.

"He started it, man," Randy Orton says. Pinocchio appears behind him and hands him tissues to press against his lip.

The bouncer stoops beside me. "I just need to leave!" I beg the guard. I turn to Ray. "Can we just leave?"

Michael and Brian take my arms and help me stand, wobbly at first, then steadier. I hurry my steps toward the exit.

"Fuck. What was that about?" Michael asks when we're outside. He studies my face. "You're gonna have a black eye tomorrow. Shit, man." He brushes chalky dust off my beard and moustache. "You have coke all over your face."

His hand smells nice. Zesty like an orange.

Ray catches up. "What the fuck, Sam? What's wrong with you?"

"Easy on the kid," Michael says. He glows like a blue giant. He floats in the streetlights.

We walk. There are stars in my eyes. They expand. They eat at one another. I'm torn between each of their gravity fields and I stretch like a rubber band. I'm thinner and smaller. I am taller than buildings. I fly. I glimmer like glitter. I am alone walking on clouds made of black ooze and rotten tobacco. I pushed him off and he died. I killed him. His face slipped between my fingers as if it was made of sand. The jury is out, and it's off to the guillotine for me. I'm a headless man. My veins are roller coasters for my red blood cells. They are crowded by white powder. I'm hollow.

This is my capital punishment. I evaporate out of my own body. I disintegrate. I disappear.

DAMASCUS

I haven't stolen food in weeks. I haven't seen Kalila for an eternity. My days are dull and endless and even the sounds of war—explosions, machine-gun fire, bullets whizzing by, ambulances wailing—are background noise I rarely notice. I call Kalila's name, but she doesn't appear.

I have nothing to do but listen to the radio. The news is always celebrating the amazing advances of our great Syrian Arab Military against terrorists. I listen to the names of towns I've never heard of being liberated over and over again. Syrian soldiers killed insert-number-here terrorists in such-and-such town. I check the kitchen, the bathroom, and the attic for Kalila. I barge into rooms with doors I can open, and I kneel by the locked ones to peer through the gap beneath. I leave dusty footprints on carpets. I wish I was able to conjure her. I wish I could call upon her spirit with a Ouija board.

The people of Damascus pass by outside as if the Syrian apocalypse hadn't already happened. A girl in a pink dress talks excitedly to her bored mother. A loud thunder ripples across a cloudless sky, but neither mother nor daughter look up. The girl and I lock eyes. She waves at me; I hide behind the curtain. The girl tugs on her mother's sleeve and points at my window, but the mother doesn't look up.

Why are these people not hiding, sheltered from Armageddon like me? Some have never had their sense of safety betrayed by the world, and it shows. They've never had to dig deep inside themselves and build a well into which to scream their secrets and then close the lid. They never had to gather themselves deep within their bodies until their own hands and feet were foreign to them, their hearts beating for a body they no longer occupied. They never had to find comfort after having every string of attachment to the world cut. I had my secrets. I screamed them down my own well, and I closed its lid. But the field of my body flowered with a million stalks of wheat. They all drank the waters of my secluded life, and they all sang a hush-hush song.

"If you come back, I'll tell you another joke," I say into the empty hall. In times of war, ghosts can simply float away; they don't need passports to cross borders or boats to sail through seas. Maybe Kalila now haunts the camps in Lebanon or the mud buildings on the outskirts of Istanbul. Maybe she seeped into a plane and got herself a first-class ticket to Canada or the US.

"What joke?" she says behind my back.

"Finally," I say. "I thought you wouldn't return."

She looks fragile, like an autumn leaf, yellowed and easy to crunch.

"Tell me," she says. She starts fading again.

"Once there was a man who went to a doctor because he was suffering from depression," I say, and she floats closer. I see a sparkle in her eyes. "'Doctor,' he said, 'I'm so sad all the time I can barely sleep.'" I mimic the voice of a sad man, and I can't tell if it's any different from my own. "'Nightmares haunt me, and dreams of death fill my brain.'"

"'Listen,' the doctor replied, 'you'll be fine. I have some great news for you. Yousef, a world-renowned comedian, is in town. He has brought laughter to the hearts of millions. He has made women weep with joy and men yell in amusement. He's the funniest man alive, and he's full of surprises that would clear your heart from all of this misery.'"

I up my tone, then lower it with anticipation. "The man stood and cried. He shouted in agony, falling to his knees." I pause for effect. "'You don't understand, Doctor. *I* am Yousef the Comedian.'"

"That wasn't funny," she says. Her colours fade, and she vibrates as if briefly pulled into another dimension.

"I'm sorry," I say. "I can try another one."

I reach out and attempt to pull her in, but my hands drift through her and she disappears with a final glimpse of light.

"Please come back!" I call out. "I know you can hear me." I don't want to be left alone in this home. It feels bigger, as if it's growing. All the old heavy furniture crowds me. I fear I'll be crushed under its weight.

"Kalila!"

I sit down and cup my face between my palms. My loneliness eats at me like a monster growing from within. I'm out of breath. My heart pounds against my chest. My tongue is dry, and when I try to stand, I feel weak in the knees. I stumble to the kitchen and hold the faucet between my shaking fingers. I can't control them enough to turn the tap and pour myself some water. Every inch of my body aches. I fall to the kitchen floor, breathing heavily as though I've been running.

"Kalila, I'm not okay." The base of my skull tenses, as if the muscles of my upper back are trying to pull my head in and hide it between my shoulder blades. My back arches like a bridge, and my limbs feel numb.

Three years ago, a doctor had called this an attack. I sat in his office with Rima, waiting for him to explain. An attack of what? Did my body recruit an army and attempt to invade? Is there a civil war breaking out within me? Are my insides a stray dog that's been kicked one too many times and now bites the hand that feeds it? We both waited, but he never explained. Rima asked all the questions.

"What do you mean by an attack?"

"It means that he had an attack. Some people have them."

"Is it his brain? His spine? His back? Maybe it's his stomach? He always gets indigestion when I make him pasta."

"No. It's an attack."

The doctor pulled a card out of a Rolodex and handed it to me. It bore the name of a specialist in psychology and a nearby address. I threw the card back at him. "Are you calling me crazy?"

"We did an EKG and all the bloodwork. There's nothing wrong with you physically." He avoided eye contact. "There's nothing wrong with seeing a psychologist when you need one."

I stormed out, and Rima followed. She asked me to slow down, but I didn't want to. She held her round belly and told me that fast walking was not good for the baby. I waited, and we got into the elevator together.

"There's nothing wrong with seeing a psychologist when you need one," she repeated.

Rima was born in a little cluster of houses on the outskirts of the city to a family with too many daughters and not enough sons. She never finished high school, nor did she care for it. She was raised to become someone's wife and was cursed to be mine. And not once did she question her fate to marry me at nineteen.

She held the specialist's card. "These attacks started months ago, Wassim. Maybe you need to see someone." She caressed her belly. "We're young, and we have the world on our shoulders. Sometimes you need to put that weight down to be able to breathe."

She leaned on the elevator wall. "Mohammed Omar is kicking," she said, guiding my hand over her clothes to the spot. I felt his tiny feet at the heel of my palm as the doors of the elevator opened.

We exited through the emergency wing, its dimly lit corridors filled with patients reaching out for nurses who weren't there.

"Isn't your father coming to pick us up?" Rima should have figured out by then that my father avoided me like a stranger on a bus. He did so with intention. He answered my questions with close-ended sentences and had a coughing fit whenever I tried to engage him in a longer conversation. He refused to let me make his coffee in the morning, saying that he preferred it differently. With milk, with cardamom, with a blond roast or in golden glasses he didn't like me to touch. He knew how to avoid me, ever since he kicked Hussam out in the middle of the night. Ever since he walked in on us naked in bed a year ago.

Hussam and I had gotten reckless. We'd stopped waiting until everyone was asleep before we excused ourselves and went to our room. We turned the radio on, thinking that it would hide our lovemaking. We said we were playing video games or studying for university. Everyone knew we were close. Everyone praised us for our friendship. We winked to each other across the room. We spoke to each other in whispers during dinners and lunches. We played footsie under the kitchen table. We held hands on our way to Mushroom Park. We smoked hashish while talking shit about everyone we knew. We kissed goodnight every night. We murmured loving words to each other. We went to university on the same bus, and we planned our classes so that we could always have lunch together. He studied English literature, and I studied geography. We agreed we would be teachers in the same high school. We agreed that we would be lovers until the end of time.

"But what do we tell your father when he wants to find us wives?" Hussam was naked in my arms in my bed. The cassette player, loudly playing Metallica's "Nothing Else Matters," almost made it difficult for us to hear each other.

"We'll move to a different city for work and live together." I kissed him. "We'll be gone so long they'll forget about us." I knew that was a lie. The day would come when my father would want me to marry a woman. Hussam knew, too. By then, my father had already divorced his wife, given her an apartment of her own on the city's outskirts, and found himself a younger and prettier woman to marry. She was due to arrive in a couple of weeks, when the wedding planning was over and the books were signed for her marriage. We both knew it was a matter of time before my father wanted me to marry, move out, and bring him grandchildren.

THE FOGHORN ECHOES   131

"Maybe we can find two lesbians who are in a relationship," Hussam suggested that night. "I can marry one and you can marry the other. We can live next door to one another."

"I'll go to the supermarket and order us two lesbians right away."

"Don't mock me," he whined, and I laughed. It had been a long day, and we were both tired. He fell asleep with his head on my chest. I dozed on and off for a while, thinking that I should turn off the lights.

"What the fuck are you doing?" My father stood in the doorway.

I jumped out of bed and grabbed the cover to hide my body. Hussam pulled the pillow over his head and screamed.

My father gave Hussam twenty minutes to pack his bags and get out. Hussam snatched up some clothes and his government ID card and rushed out the door. In the morning, my father called a matchmaker to find me a wife.

Hussam returned two days later and begged my father for forgiveness. He'd slept on the cold streets and had been mugged. The muggers left him with a black eye and a broken dignity, and he brought both back home with him. He cried in our living room and promised my father that it had happened only once. He said I was like a brother to him. Hussam tried to call his mother back in her village, but she was already remarried and had nowhere for him to live. I stood in the corner, ashamed. My father gave Hussam some money and told him that he wouldn't cover his university expenses anymore. He said that he needed to find a place to live away from our family.

"I'm not doing this for you. It's for the memory of your father."

Hussam locked eyes with me, but I averted my gaze. He nodded and left. Two weeks later, I stood in front of a hundred family friends in a black suit, getting married to Rima. All I knew about her then was that her face was round and white, like a full moon. It was supposed to be my father's wedding. He'd booked the most expensive hall in Damascus and hired the most dazzling belly dancer. But he told his new bride that it was only fair to marry his son first and promised her a get-away wedding in Thailand or Malaysia.

"You're lucky no one else was in the house that night," my father told me over dinner the night before my wedding. "I'll break your skull in half if you ever bring this up."

On the day of my wedding, Hussam stood at the far end of the hall watching the belly dancer dancing around me and Rima. When it was time for the dabkeh and all the male guests gathered in a circle for the wedding dance, Hussam took my hand and led me in. With every step he took, he squeezed my hand once. My father inserted himself between us, giving us both dirty looks.

My father herded Rima and me into my bedroom after the wedding. "The newlyweds need their privacy," he said. He'd planned to spend the night in a hotel. "I'll come back tomorrow with a hearty breakfast." We listened to his steps as he headed to the gate and closed it, loud enough for us to know we were alone. It was the first time in my life I was alone with a strange woman.

My father had ordered a new king-size bed to replace the twin beds Hussam and I used to occupy. Draped in cotton sheets and a silk comforter, it looked uninviting. It was too grand an upgrade. Still in her wedding gown, Rima sat at its foot, her head

lowered and her hands clasped in her lap. I walked to my side of
the room, untied my shoes, unbuckled my belt, and removed the
golden watch a distant uncle had given me for the wedding.

We sat quietly for a long time. The room filled with the
heavy perfume she wore. Her dress rustled. Finally, I looked at
her once more, and we locked eyes.

"Hi," she whispered.

"Hello."

"Do you want me to take off my scarf?" She pointed to her
face. Her hair was hidden under a heavy white hijab.

I nodded.

She unveiled a mane of long, black silky hair that cascaded
over her shoulders like a waterfall. Suddenly her face was now a
red moon. She quickly pulled the hijab back over her hair.

"It's okay. You can leave it uncovered," I said.

She hesitated, then pulled the scarf off her shoulders and
dropped it to the floor. She was my wife and I was within my
right to see her hair, which she hid from all other men not
directly linked to her by blood. Her dress, zipped all the way
up her back, must have been suffocating.

"Do you need help taking off your gown?"

"No." She almost shouted it. "I mean—" She lowered her
voice. "Yeah, if you don't mind."

She stood and gathered her hair over her shoulder. I reached for
the zipper at the back of her neck and tried not to touch her skin
with my fingers, but the zipper was stuck. "I'm sorry." I pulled
harder. I felt the hot skin of her shoulders on the tips of my cold
fingers. "It won't—" The zipper finally gave, and it slid all the way
down to her waist in one swift move, revealing her bra hook.

She quickly faced me. She gathered the dress around her chest with both hands and avoided my eyes. She hesitated again. "Would you mind turning around?"

I nodded and turned away. I looked at the empty wall where my football posters used to be. Squares and rectangles of cleaner paint marked their coordinates. I heard the crinkling of the dress as she disrobed and a click that let me know she'd taken off her bra. The covers on the bed lifted.

"You can look now."

She was already under the comforter, holding its edge with both hands and pulling it up to her neck. She had pearls in her hair that were clustered like jasmine flowers. Her lashes were long and lined with kohl. The silk comforter outlined her body in ways I had never seen before. I was both captivated and repelled by her presence in my room. She felt like an invading spirit who'd weaseled herself in, both a privilege and a curse. I looked away from her. She wasn't him. She wasn't the man I had loved for years. My father could have moved the earth and the sky, but he couldn't remove the smell of Hussam from my skin. My man's touch ached like a fresh tattoo. His mouth burned like the first sip of black tea. I gave Rima my back and removed my clothes slowly down to my underwear. I sat on the edge of the bed and took off my socks.

"Could you turn off the lights?"

I flicked the switch and found my way back to bed in the dark, slipped in next to her. She breathed heavily. Moments later, her hand searched under the covers for mine. We held hands. My knuckles grazed her breast. I snapped my hand back as if I'd touched a scorpion.

"I'm sorry," she whispered in the dark. "My mother told me that men like to—" She paused. "I'm sorry."

"No. Don't worry." I turned to my side so that we were facing each other. I could see the borders of her face illuminated by the streetlight outside the window. Her eyes were closed. She looked peaceful and endless. Like the opening of a tunnel to new roads. Was I betraying Hussam? Was he standing outside our window right then, looking up as the lights went off? Would Rima tell my father that I didn't touch her on our wedding night? Would she know what I really was? Would she tell the whole neighbourhood after asking for an annulment? Did I have any other choice back then, other than to touch her? Other than to be her husband in real life after I'd signed the marriage papers?

I caressed her face. "Is this okay?" I asked.

"Yes."

I moved my hand down her neck. "Is this okay?"

"Yes."

I pulled her closer to me. "Is this okay?"

"Yes."

We kissed. Her body curved within mine, her hair in my eyes. Her back was smooth, and my hand followed its curve downward. I wasn't ready, but I didn't think she knew what that meant. She passively allowed her body to be toyed with. Her eyes were tightly shut and her lips quivered. "Are you okay?" I asked.

"I am okay." She sounded like she was about to cry.

I stopped. "Why are you crying?" I asked.

"I don't know." She rested her head on my chest and wept.

Her hair under my hands smelled like blueberries. She felt small, almost breakable. I told her it was okay to cry.

"But it's our wedding night." Her voice was calmer.

"It's okay." I felt a tear down my own face.

Her stiff neck rested on my upper arm, and her legs cuddled mine. The feeling that she found safety in me excited me. I felt myself grow against her body, and she felt it too. She looked up and kissed me.

In that moment, between the waves of our bodies merging and breaking, while we whispered sighs and hushed aches to each other, I felt her morphing. She was almost him and I was almost me. I dipped into her seas searching for treasures. Her black hair was my sky, and her jasmine pearls were my stars, and her face was the moon. I pushed myself inside her, and she turned into a painful painting that slowly revealed its details. I went slow, but I got excited when she pulled me closer. It didn't last long. Moments later, we were panting in bed, embracing like two lovers who'd been together for years.

"Good night," she whispered. "I love you."

Hussam said that to me every night before bed. The thought of him felt like a stab. I whispered my good night back but kept my eyes on the window, wondering again if he was outside.

"It wasn't your fault."

I open my eyes. I'm on the kitchen floor. The clothes on my back are wet. Apparently, I managed to open the faucet earlier, enough to fill the kitchen sink, then flood over the edge. I look up at a greyish Kalila, who floats nearby. I anchor my palm on the wet floor and push my body out of the inch-deep pool of water.

"What are you talking about?" I ask.

"Your father catching you in bed with Hussam is not your

mistake," she says. "You think it's your mistake, but it's just the fault of circumstance."

The water has soaked through my shirt and now drips down my pants. "Are you reading my thoughts now?"

She slips through the wall to the living room, and I run after her, afraid she might disappear again. She grows legs and stands on them.

In the Quran, Allah called our nightly sleep the small death. I wonder if the worlds we visit in our dreams are a manifestation of the worlds within us. I wonder if we tell ourselves that dreams don't make sense because we cannot logically understand the world we're eventually heading to. Kalila must have been able to slip into my dreams like a drop of water soaking my clothes; she expanded within me and planted herself there, and I feel it. She brings me calmness and joy. Just having her there, sitting, gloomy as a day in March, is enough for me to celebrate, to take a deep breath.

"Hussam stayed with you like a ghost," she says. "He haunted you. You are not at fault for your failed marriage. You were forced into it." When she smiles, her lips turn red, her cheeks glow, her eyes brown, and her hair flickers like glitter.

"Stay with me, will you?" There is no begging in my voice anymore. "You balance me, and your presence allows me to tell—" I hesitate. "I think you like listening to my stories."

Her colours return in waves. The light of her face extends to the rest of her body, and I sigh in relief. But the light doesn't stop there. Soon the furniture that was once covered in dust snaps into its original glory: shining wood and glowing metallics. The radio stops its flickering and regains its lost dials, and the chandelier in the ceiling rebuilds itself, filling its missing pieces with reflecting light.

"Are you doing this?"

She doesn't answer. "I think you were doing what every lover does," she says. "You were allowing your body to lead you into the heart of your relationship."

"My love for him brought him down."

She holds eye contact with me. "I think you're carrying the sins of others. Sins you never committed."

My sin with Rima is different. She was promised a husband. She didn't know she was being shortchanged. She got a dysfunctional man, a man drenched with his love for another. She made me coffee every morning before I went to class, so that I could be alert as I searched for Hussam in the university's halls. She washed my shirts so that I could always look handsome and put together in case I ran into him. In the evenings she asked me about my day and kissed me goodnight in a bed I wished to share with him.

"I cheated her," I tell Kalila. "I am their hurt and their curse: Hussam, Rima, my father, and Mohammed Omar."

I learned that Hussam had moved in with a group of students from the upper regions of Syria. He'd asked if he could visit the newlyweds and offer his congratulations, promising to bring a gift, but my father informed him that we had all the gifts we might need. "No more space for anything, even a small silver spoon," my father said.

In the first months of my marriage, I felt monitored by my father. He kept a copy of my university schedule under the glass of his desk, and he called me constantly to ensure I kept my trips outside of school to a minimum.

As Rima's belly grew bigger, my chance meetings with Hussam became fewer. He stopped responding to my texts and picking up the phone when I called. Even when we randomly bumped into each other on lunch breaks, he'd merely nod in my direction and walk away.

Hussam always hung out at the same table with his roommates, in the basement cafeteria of the Language Centre, which had the best cheese sandwiches with garlic and pickles, warmed and pressed on a hot plate. He wore the same red-and-white scarf his roommates wore, and his voice got louder as he roared in laughter with them. He even began to emulate their heavier, harsher accents. I started frequenting the same cafeteria. I'd pretend I was studying or listening to music on my headphones, hoping that he would come over, that we'd talk like we talked before, and we would laugh like we laughed before, and we would kiss. He never did.

One day, I went to say hello to him at his table. I noticed that their usual loud conversation was subdued that day, and I thought that this might be the right time for me to introduce myself to his friends. I raised my hand in a quick hello, and the conversation they were having stopped.

One of his roommates examined me. "Do you know him, Hussam?"

"Yeah, I know him," he said. "We used to live together in his father's home."

I stood awkwardly, waiting to be introduced.

"Wassim, this is everyone." He gestured to his roommates. "Everyone, this is Wassim." His roommates nodded in my direction before going back to their whispering.

"Hussam, can I talk to you?" I wasn't even sure what I wanted to talk about.

"Why?" There was hostility in his voice.

"Let's talk alone?"

He sighed loudly, grabbed his sandwich, and squeezed between his seatmate and the poster-covered wall of the cafeteria. I followed him to a table in the corner. His demeanour had changed. He twirled the plastic seat around and saddled it, as if to use its back as a barrier between us. He kept looking back at his friends.

"So, I wanted to see how you are doing." I paused. "We haven't talked in almost a year."

"Since your wedding, I think," he stated. He didn't seem to care to hold eye contact with me. "How is the wife? Did she give birth yet?"

"Any day now," I said. "She just passed the nine-month mark." I was surprised at how cheerful I was talking about this. Rima had grown a little miracle that was half made by me. A clean slate of a human who would grow up to be a better man that I was, and who would become the true son to my father. I was a failed experiment—a disregarded body suitable only for reproduction. Mohammed Omar would be the right version of me, and he wouldn't disappoint his grandfather. He wouldn't cheat his mother.

"Joy." He didn't bother asking the baby's name or sex.

Silence filled the space between us. I wanted him to say that he missed me like I missed him, to tell me that he would always be mine, to remind me of the sweet kisses we exchanged. I wanted him to hold my hand or to play footsie under the narrow table. He seemed completely disengaged. I'd never felt this far away from him in my life, and he was so close I could touch his cheeks.

"So, what's this about?" he said.

The October sun shone through the window into his eyes, and they looked as brown as melted honey.

"I just wanted to talk to you." My voice came out scratched. "You seem to be mad at me."

He chuckled, as if I'd told an amusing joke, then spat on the floor. He had gained a darker tan over the past few months, and his arms and chest had grown larger. I knew that his roommates had found him a job at a construction site, where he assisted them in window installations and door frame measurements. He was thinner, with thicker thighs and a muscular back. I saw a picture on Facebook of him hanging out an unfinished window on a construction site, no safety net beneath him.

"I'm not mad at you," he finally said. "I'm avoiding you."

I felt as if he'd punched me in the gut.

"You simple-minded kid. You're my bad omen. You're my destruction." He paused, then lowered his voice. "I've known nothing but you," he said as if he had rehearsed it for days. "My father, your father, this country—this is all you."

"Me? What do you—"

"Just stay away from me." He stood up. "I want nothing to do with you anymore."

"But I promised to protect you." I almost shouted before remembering where I was. "I made that promise," I whispered, but he didn't look back.

That night, I had another attack.

My eyes opened wide, as if my eyelids were elastics pulled and then snapped back. I saw darkness on the ceiling. I wanted to wake Rima, but I couldn't move my arm. I felt her warmth next to me, her belly crowding me, her nails clutching the bedsheets. I tried to inhale deeply, but my lungs collapsed in my dreams and deflated in my rib cage. A drop of sweat trickled from my forehead down to my ear. The droplet whispered the murmurs of gossiping thousands. They all stared at me while covering their mouths and muttering to one another. They clucked their tongues and rolled their eyes.

I moaned. Rima tossed and turned in bed, but she didn't wake up. I heard the steps of someone outside the door. I whimpered again. My father's new wife popped her head in.

"In the name of Allah," she shouted, "what's wrong with you?"

Rima jumped up, startled, holding her belly. She wailed and called my name, shaking me by the shoulders. I couldn't tell her to calm down or shut up. I couldn't ask her to stop shaking me. Her nails dug into my skin. My teeth were clenched and my mouth was dry. She jumped out of bed, turned on the lights, and called my father.

In the hospital, they inserted a tube down my throat and into my lungs. They held my jaw open and placed a rubber barrier between my teeth. Doctors gathered and whispered. My father was calm at first, then he got louder as the night went on and my symptoms intensified. They finally brought in a specialist who inserted a needle in a vein near my elbow. My body relaxed like a rug unfolded. I was soon asleep.

That was the first public attack. I'd had my first one weeks after Rima told me she was pregnant. I stood in the corner of the living room faking a smile while my insides devoured themselves. I had another in the doctor's office when the technician told us it was a boy and asked me if we'd decided on a name.

I took the medicine; I went to the therapist. Rima suggested that someone might have placed a curse on us. My father believed her and hired a sheikh, who came into our home and brought an incense thurible. He swayed the burning ashes across our living room and bedroom, filling the house with an intense smell.

"No evil spirit will remain here," he said between the layers of fog. I agreed; even I wanted out of that place.

I called Hussam every now and then. Sometimes he declined the call. Other times he let the phone ring until I ended up at his full inbox. I saw him in the hallways of the university or walking with his roommates between buildings. I could always pinpoint him, as if there were a radar within me for that sole purpose. I smiled when I saw him laugh with his friends, frowned when I saw him angry or cursing. I snuck into the Language Centre to see his grades posted on the wall. He was doing well, and on his way to graduate.

Then I saw him at one of the protests.

Protesting inside the University of Damascus was dangerous. Plain-clothed secret police walked among students at all times. Older men with shaved heads and large moustaches. We saw them in our lecture halls not taking notes, in the food court not eating, or smoking next to our gatherings, positioned to listen to our conversations. Protests broke out every now and then and lasted for minutes. In the break between classes, when the halls were filled with students, protesters with covered faces shouted pro-revolution slogans, then scattered and merged into the crowds. The moustached men ran after them.

I instantly recognized Hussam with his red-and-white scarf covering his face. Only his eyes were visible, but I knew his body like the geography of my own neighbourhood and the hills surrounding Damascus. He was carried on the back of a masked man. He chanted, and a dozen students in similar scarves or surgical masks repeated the slogans. Students ran away, anticipating the coming wave of secret police. Within seconds, Hussam dissolved into the crowd, and all that was left behind was his scarf.

I called him that night to ask him not to do it again. He didn't pick up the phone.

I saw him again in another protest, and this time he was the one carrying the lead chanter. When the secret police stormed, he zigzagged his way through the crowd. I raced after him as he slipped into the first lecture hall he found. By the time they appeared at the entrance, he was already in a seat looking intently at an open book, his jacket turned inside out.

I walked down the stairs of the large lecture hall, entered the row he was sitting in, and sat next to him.

"What the fuck are you doing here?" He didn't lift his eyes off his book.

"What the fuck are *you* doing here?" I repeated. We locked eyes, then he pretended to read.

"You won't understand, you idiot." He flipped a page of the book so hard he almost ripped it off. "Now leave me alone before you get us both arrested."

"Hussam, you have to listen to me," I begged. "I can't sleep,

I can't eat. I can't do anything but think about you, and you're throwing your life to the wind with these roommates of yours."

He took a deep inhale. "Are you fucking kidding me?" he whispered. "These people took me in when your father kicked me out. They fed me and gave me a roof over my head."

I reached for his hand but he slapped my fingers away.

"You simple-minded fuck. You think your sleepless nights are important now?" He looked back at the secret police, then broke his gaze when one of them looked our way. "You'll get me arrested, you fucking asshole. Just leave me be."

"We can go to a different city like we always said we would. We can even go together to Beirut."

"You, me, and your wife and kid. Sure. One big happy family."

"I would—" I struggled. "I would leave her for you."

This time, he held my gaze. It felt as if he could dive into the black sea of my inner thoughts and pull out pearls and forgotten treasures. I wanted to kiss him.

"I love you," I whispered. I wanted to keep him for myself. I wanted him to sleep on my chest.

"Go back to your father and wife, Wassim," he said.

Before I could respond, a heavy palm hit Hussam's shoulder. "You, come with me!"

He didn't struggle. He stood up, pushing the book he'd pretended to read off the table. "I'm coming," he said. "You don't need to hold me like this."

I wanted to scream, to tell them that he wasn't protesting, to lie and plead and beg for his release. But what good would that do? We were criminals in the eyes of this city. We were the outcasts of our society. How would I explain the gravity that pulled me toward this man instead of to the wife and child at home? My father should have known that no matter how big a wedding he planned, or how large a bed he bought, his son would always be a louti, a faggot. Hussam didn't look back at me as he was dragged away. I stopped myself from running after him. Who could stop the secret police in Syria? The regime knew no mercy, and if I stood by him, I would join him in their dungeons.

"You protected yourself. There's no fault in that," Kalila says. She floats over and sits next to me. Chills spill down my spine like cubes of ice.

"I am his curse," I say. "I'm the reason he was arrested."

"Oh, child. The reason he was arrested was the world we lived in and the regime tightening its knots around our necks."

Kalila tells me that we treat our memories as if they're a clear vision of our past, but they never are. We paint our memories with our own guilt and shame. We enhance our roles in the misery of our past. We blame ourselves for things we could never change. We think of ourselves as the protagonists of our history, but we are merely background characters in the twists and turns of those with power.

"You were powerless," she says. "Nothing you could have done could save him."

But I remember: I remember his face when he felt that hand clamp on his shoulder. I remember the pity in the eyes of other students. I want to argue with Kalila, but the sun rises, and the morning breeze fills the house with a chill. "It's cold," I say.

"The sun is coming. You will feel warmth soon."

VANCOUVER

The fog is thick, but I walk farther. Arms extending, eyes shifting. I know I'm dreaming, but I'm fearful all the same. There's
a sewing needle in my mouth, ready to stitch what's left of the
root of my tongue. My severed tongue wiggles in my palm,
incapable of speech without the air of my lungs. The needle
sews the wound in my mouth with a thick thread. It pierces
from below, then it spikes back in from above, cinching tight.
The needle finishes its job and my tongue is now all stitched up.
I try to pull the thread off my skin, but it slips from between
my fingers. It slides between the hairs of my moustache and
tightens upon my upper lip. The thread knots as if the hand of
a wool-maker pulls on it. It finishes its job and my mouth is
sewn shut. The thread is long, and I hold its ends with each
hand; I want to snap it sharply, but the root of my tongue, with
my voice box and my lips, might come off my face. I moan, but
the fog swallows the sound. My severed tongue jumps out of my
palm onto the ground and slithers out of sight. I have to find it.
I fall on my knees and search frantically. I crawl on all fours and
yelp through locked lips, and there's nothing to find among the
rocks and stones on the ground. My knees and my palms bleed.

I want to cry, but my eyes melt on my face. I want to breathe, but my nose is blocked with tar and dust.

A loud long horn sounds, and it clears the fog as if sucking it out of the atmosphere.

I crawl on calm water surrounded by the reflection of a starry sky. I can't detach my palms and knees from the water's surface. I'm stuck in a praying position on all fours, and the threads from my mouth are wet and getting heavier; they pull my face toward the water and I tense my neck to keep from drowning. The water streams with momentum, taking me to a waterfall. I'm thrown off the edge, stranded between earth and sky. The loud horn comes back, and I look up to the clouds of fog. It's dotted with jets and they drop their bombs and I'm cornered and alone and stuck. I scream.

Ray shakes me. "Sam! Wake up! You're kicking me."

I jump out of bed, the echoes of the horn still ringing in my ears. "What's that noise?"

"You're speaking Arabic." We're in our dark bedroom, the heavy curtains closed. Ray is framed by the soft light of a fake candle he likes to keep on through the night. "Go back to sleep."

The long horn sound comes back. I imagine it to be the cry of a mourning monster approaching the seashore. It's followed by the squawks of seagulls.

"What's that noise?" I ask, this time in English. I go to the window and lift the curtains, look out at the dark skies and the trees around our building. Their branches are long fingers reaching for me, wanting to leave their marks on my skin. The buildings are blanketed in white fog that gets thicker the farther out I look.

"It's the foghorn." Ray sighs. "Did you take your sleeping pills?"

"What's a foghorn?"

The sound returns once more, louder this time.

"You have to remember to take your pills."

He's right. I always have nightmares when I don't take my pills. Sometimes I dream of my father, waiting for me at an imaginary border, a dotted line on a gigantic map. I try to avoid him; I jump across the dotted line back and forth as if it will hide me from him. He appears on all sides of the line, and his hand always holds me by the collar. Sometimes I dream of a rocking sea that I've never seen, or at least can't recall. Sometimes I am a boat, my wet wood pressured by the grip of the sea. The waves slap me, and I mourn my emptiness. I'm a hollow boat without an oar or a soul, and my journey is infinite. I'm a boat that won't sink. I can't sink. I'm a boat forgotten on a rocking sea until my wood is rotten and disintegrated into the salt.

"Ray, what's a foghorn?"

He pushes the covers away and sits up in bed. His eyes glow in the fake candlelight. "It's a signal, to warn ships of hazards like coastlines or other boats when they can't see in the fog."

I get back in bed, distancing my naked body from his. "You know," I whisper to Ray. Our backs are to each other. I hear him groan. "When I tried to escape Turkey to Europe the first time, before I talked to you on Facebook, I got on a rubber boat with other refugees and attempted to cross the Mediterranean to Greece."

I can vividly recall the day I stood outside the Syrian intelligence building, where I'd been detained for what felt like weeks. In fact it was only three days before I was informed that someone had paid my way out. I passed three different check-points. The first was on the floor I was imprisoned in, right outside the elevator, where two officers pulled me from a small cell I'd been kept in with forty-five other prisoners. I was told to stand by the elevator door, my back to its sliding metal, and was searched one last time. They handed me a piece of paper and escorted me into the elevator. I was pushed to face the mirror, which was darkened with photos and posters of the current president and his father and brother. Their stoic faces, shielded by large sunglasses, mocked me. I was forced to walk backward toward a second checkpoint at the doors of the building, tripping on legs of chairs and over people forced to lie face down in the hallways. They softly moaned when I bumped into them. The T-shirt I wore was dotted with a line of blood where the hot edge of a knife had left its mark. I was held by the shoulders and turned around to face the officer at the building's gate. He told me to walk down a fenced road toward the next gate, which I did alone. I didn't dare look up. At the final checkpoint, they looked at my papers and then pushed me outside. That was when I realized I was still barefoot.

I was told by my roommates that my name would forever appear on blacklists at every checkpoint in Damascus and across the country. The government took old computers from school labs and installed them at checkpoints for easy access to the list, which grew longer with every weekly update. My roommates told me I should leave the country before the next update, or else I'd be arrested again. One of them gave me the name of a distant relative in Istanbul and told me to get there as soon as I could.

The relative wasn't much help. He gave me a bed to sleep on, then demanded I pay rent with money he thought I had. Weeks later, I ran out of valuables, except for my phone and a gold necklace my mother had given me when she left Damascus to return to her village. I had a decision to make: stay in the uncertainty of Turkey or find my way across the sea.

Even though I'd kept the necklace on me for years, I sold it to a man in Istanbul. It was easy for me to let it go, just as it was easy for her to let me go when my father's body hit the ground and she couldn't afford the city on her own. "Stay with Wassim and his family," she told me before she packed her bags and left.

The money I made from the necklace was enough to pay for my one-way ticket across the sea. Leave everyone behind, I told myself. Leave them all to rot in that war and go find a place for yourself far away. Leave this city with its high buildings and small minds. Run before they change the laws and force you back to Syria, where you'll end up recruited into the army. Don't look back. Forget that Damascus ever existed. Let it go like you let go of the sand in your shoes after you cross the sea.

After an overnight bus ride from Istanbul, I walked up and down the port of Izmir, trying to determine which of many faces was the face of a smuggler.

"I walked for hours until someone pssted at me," I say to Ray. Is he listening? "He asked if I was interested in getting on a boat—as if he was offering a romantic trip across a lake."

I nervously said yes and was led through zigzagging alleyways to a makeshift office under the staircase of a two-storey building. A man with a big belly and a large moustache sat at a desk with coffee-stained papers on it. I knew he was Syrian even before he opened his mouth and spoke Arabic.

"Men with big bellies are seen as more desirable in my culture," I add, as Ray shuffles in bed. "They have better chances at getting married; they get better jobs. Their bellies are a sign that they've never gone hungry."

The man offered me a cup of Turkish coffee, but I pivoted the conversation to the matter at hand. He claimed to have a boat going the next morning to Greece, and I insisted that I wouldn't pay until I was on the boat. After some back-and-forth, we came to the agreement that I would pay half at the port when I boarded and the other half on the sands of Greece.

"Do you know how to swim?"

I nodded.

My father had taught me when I was seven, explaining that according to the Prophet, children should learn three things: swimming, archery, and horseback riding. "I can't afford a horse, and arrows are not a weapon anymore," he joked, "but I can teach you how to swim." He held me beneath my armpits and threw me to the deep end of a pool, then stood watching. I remember floating through the air before hitting the icy water. Then I flailed. I tried to move my arms and legs rhythmically but gave up and spread my limbs like a starfish looking up toward the surface, bubbles escaping my mouth. My father jumped in to lift me out.

"You silly thing," he said. The water barely reached his chest. "It's not that deep." His voice was so disappointed; the next time he pushed me into a pool, I swam just to avoid the embarrassment.

"I was asked to arrive at the port at midnight." I wonder if my voice is actually leaving my body as I tell Ray this story.

I arrived carrying a large bag. Psst Boy stood under a streetlight and whistled me over. He guided me through alleyways in makeshift refugee camps filled with flickering fluorescent lights and the whimpers of Syrian babies crying. I finally found myself standing by a small bus with a roaring engine and hushed passengers.

"Do you have the money?" the man asked.

"Where is the boat?" I replied.

Psst Boy insisted that I wouldn't be getting on the bus until I paid what we agreed upon, and after a moment of contemplation I pulled the crumpled ball of cash from my underwear and placed it in his open palm. He counted the money and slipped it into his pocket, then stepped away from the door to let me on. I was the last to board; the bus closed its doors, turned off its lights, and lurched forward. Its sudden jolt threw me into the first empty seat I found. Psst Boy sat across from me, leaving an empty seat between us. Faces of other passengers flashed in and out of focus as we rapidly drove through the beams of streetlights.

"There were at least four or five families," I whisper to Ray. The foghorn echoes, and this time it's smooth and reassuring. "Two dozen kids under the age of fourteen, a dozen women covered in hijabs, and two women sitting in the back seat alone without covers on their heads."

The two women were Christians, Psst Boy volunteered. I told him the sea knows no religion.

We drove on a well-lit road for hours, passing cars and traffic lights and bridges leading to dark paths. Two or three Turkish police cars with sky-blue arrows painted on their sides passed us. Then the bus took a turn onto an empty road, wobbling on the uneven surface. A child cried but was hushed by multiple nervous shushes. The sound of waves crashing on a rocky shore returned. The stars were edged off by the dark peaks of the mountains on my right, while the white tips of sea waves glimmered under the tranquil starlight on my left. Finally, the bus slowed to a halt and Psst Boy asked us to disembark.

Two men were waiting as we descended the hillside toward the sea. The sands felt shifty and uncertain. I heard a short sharp scream and felt the weight of a body slamming into the back of my knees—one of the Christian women. I almost lost my balance, but I managed to hold steady. Her friend helped her stand.

She didn't apologize.

The two smugglers stood by a pile of what looked like used garbage bags; we gathered around them silently, and they handed us each a bright orange life vest from the pile. They did not explain how to wear them. My vest was wet, as if freshly used. *Useless*, I whispered to myself, but I buckled it around my waist anyway. We were then asked to walk into the water to meet the boat a bit deeper in the sea. The two Christian women protested. They wanted the men to bring the boat to the shore, and they were afraid of the cold water and the mystical creatures of the sea. The smugglers walked away without responding. Slowly, we followed them. Fathers and mothers carried their children on their shoulders. The two Christian women held each other's hands and walked through the waves, screaming whenever a wave hit them. I took my shoes and socks off, bagged them in my backpack, and merged with the water. The two smugglers at the front directed us with their flashlights to the rubber boat. A third man stood on top of it and stage-whispered commands to those trying to board it. The water was up to my waist by then, but I was thankful for my preparation; I had placed my remaining money in a plastic bag and inserted it in my underwear. Was it August or October? I can't remember anymore. Was the water cold and refreshing, or was it icy and horrifying? I gripped the man's hand as I climbed up into the rubber boat and was welcomed with a used wet towel. In the dim starlight, I counted fifty-six people on the boat at that point and figured that another bus or two had arrived earlier. The two Christian women, with tears in their eyes, took a corner away from the dozens of confused children.

"Are you still listening?" I ask Ray. Was that a hmm? Or was it the distant sighing of a fridge or the flushing of a toilet somewhere in our building? My body is not in this bed. It floats over the West End and slips down Davie Street until I reach the statues of the laughing men. I breeze through their laughter and glide down the seawall. My body rests on one of the logs at English Bay. The fog thickens like a soup and covers the water. The ships in the bay disappear in the fog, unable to see the well-lit seashore or the forests on the tip of UBC's curve. One of the ships releases its foghorn, and the fog flutters with the sound and breaks for a moment before gathering again. With the second foghorn, the fog shimmers like a sky full of stars, and then returns to its thickness. The third foghorn, like a final call from an angry God, shatters the fog and releases the shore lights to be seen by every ship.

Ray turns toward me. "Why are you telling me this now? You need to sleep."

"I need to tell you this." The story within me aches like an untreated wound. It's unheard and I need to speak it. It roams my insides like a caged animal gasping for air. It trembles. "Please, just hear me out."

"In the morning, Sam."

"I don't know if I can wait."

He doesn't respond.

"Deep in the waters, the engine cut out," I go on. "Everyone on the boat could tell there was a problem."

The smugglers had led the boat until the lights on the shore disappeared. The small engine coughed twice before it stopped altogether, dimming what soft light we had. The smugglers conversed nervously, and hand gestures turned to pointing fingers. The passengers grew restless.

"What's happening?" a man asked. He held a baby in his arms. One of the smugglers motioned for him to sit down.

"Why are we not moving?" a woman asked, her voice breaking. "I can't see lights from any direction." It was a moonless night, and the stars barely gave enough light for us to see a ghoulish trace of one another. I could tell it was one of the Christian women who spoke; the others would have pushed their husbands to speak.

"What's happening?" the other Christian woman screamed. Now everyone asked questions and angrily blamed the smugglers for stopping the boat. Children cried, and a couple of women wailed. A man stood up and said that we should all use our palms as paddles and row through the sea, but others jeered him.

Another said that he fixed his father's old car and that maybe he could fix the boat engine. He approached it but was pushed back to his seat by one of the smugglers. I wanted to disappear. I imagined myself drowning, arms and legs extending in the sea like a starfish, bubbles escaping my mouth. I tightened the buckle of my life vest; this time my father wouldn't come to save me.

Ray sits up in bed and turns on his bedside lamp. "I'm sorry you went through this, but you're here now. You're safe and sound. You need to stop reliving this and move on."

He gets out of bed and pads to the bathroom.

"It's not like I left this story behind at the airport when I arrived!" I shout after him. I straighten up in bed and turn on my bedside lamp. "You said you'd be here for me."

"Not at four o'clock in the morning." He washes his hands.

My eyes begin to water, but I will not cry. My Syrian self is in pieces, and each piece becomes a spider that spins webs on my skin. They entrap me and tighten their silk around me. I'm mummified and unable to breathe. The children cried, the water was cold, and a gun barrel left a mark on my temple. My father's blood stained my hand, and the salty waters of the sea sloshed against my wounds. And Wassim. What I did to Wassim sends shivers through my body. There is no redemption for this, no happy ending. This is rooted in my skin like birthmarks.

Ray comes back with a glass of water. He opens the drawer on my bedside table, unscrews a medicine bottle, and shakes two pills into his palm. He offers me the water and pills with a tired smile. When I reject them, he sighs and grabs his pillow. "I'm going to sleep in the other room," he says. "You need rest, Sam. This isn't good for you."

When I say nothing, he walks out, softly latches the bedroom door closed.

Does the sea remember me? Was my name on a list of those destined for a watery prison and a cold final embrace? The memory feels like a wet life vest: strapped on my back, hooked over my shoulders, tightened. It foams salt water into my eyes and soaks my bedsheets. I try to take a deep breath but instead take in the salt of the sea. I look up and the ghost of my father hovers horizontally over my body, his blood dripping onto my forehead.

"I'm dead," he finally says. His calm voice seeps into the room like a breeze from a barely open window.

"I'm so sorry."

"Why didn't you save me?"

"I didn't know how."

He reaches down and squeezes my voice box between his fingers. Maybe I should let him suffocate me. Maybe it's time to let go. I deserve judgment, an ending. I can't live without the justice that should have been visited upon me. My father's ghost opens his mouth and spews seawater onto my face, leaving seaweed tangled in my hair. I hear the foghorn again and when I open my eyes my father's ghost is gone.

I fumble for my phone and hover over the Skype icon. No, I should let Arda be. I've burdened him enough with my stories. After all, I left him in Turkey and came here. He was the one who taught me how to find Ray, how to search Facebook for older white gay men, how to craft the perfect opening message. Maybe I *should* call him. He always knew what to do.

Arda picks up after a couple of rings. He holds the phone

under his chin; the sky is blue overhead, and the sun fills the screen with bright light. He's in his uniform and sunglasses.

"Hey, Hussam."

"I'm not okay, Arda." I see my own face in a small box in the corner. Puffy eyes, snotty nose, hair a mess. I sniff.

He takes his sunglasses off. "What's wrong, babe? What's going on?"

I hear the foghorn once more and the window vibrates with the sound.

"I think I'm going crazy." I hiccup on my words. "I want to come back to Turkey."

"Don't be ridiculous."

"Arda, you don't understand." My voice breaks. "I think I'm dying. This city is killing me."

He pauses. He lifts his phone up to his face as if examining me. He taps on the screen and flips his camera. The Gaziantep refugee camp stretches under the unforgiving sun of Turkey's valleys. It's crowded; men shout at one another, women hurry their steps, and boys on bikes zoom between the tents. The wind picks up dust and it flies into everyone's eyes. "You want to come back to this?" he asks.

"No," I whisper.

"Then what?"

"I thought I would find comfort here," I say.

"Stop being a child, Hussam." He flips the phone back to his face. "You got everything everyone here hopes for. Who kicks a blessing away?"

"I'm lonely."

"Then find some friends."

"No one here speaks Arabic."

"You speak English."

"You don't understand."

"No, you don't understand. You forgot what it means to live on this side of the world, kid."

We hold each other's gaze across continents. There is a pain in me that roars to be released. This bed is comfortless. I want to jump across the screen and sleep on Arda's single bed in his little office. I drop the phone on the covers and cup my face in my hands.

"Hey, hey. Don't cry." Arda's tone changes. "It's okay. Just tell me what's going on."

"I have so much weight on me. I'm so tired, Arda. I want to put it down, and I don't know how."

I don't think he understands. He gets pixelated, then freezes. "I am tr— break my— but it's—"

"Arda, I'm losing you."

"Furthest corner of the— Go to sleep, Huss— talk in the morn—"

I nod and tell him I miss him before the call abruptly ends.

From the boat, I was arrested by the Turkish Coast Guard and placed on the first bus to Gaziantep to join other Syrian refugees. I'd asked them to leave me in Istanbul. I repeated myself: *Istanbul, Istanbul, Istanbul, Istanbul.* No one listened. The bus was packed with other refugees, mostly men. It smelled of sweat, and those who had cigarettes smoked them in the back. The trip lasted over sixteen hours, and my metal seat dug into my bones. The windowpanes were scalding to the touch. Hours into the drive, I needed to pee. We were told there would be no stops until we were at the camp, and some of the men in the back pissed into empty water bottles. The bus filled with the stink. I had no bottles. I asked the driver to stop so that I could pee at the side of the road. He ignored me, and the guard sitting next to him spoke harshly to me in a language I don't speak.

"I need to pee." I imitated unbuttoning my trousers. This somehow got him even angrier. He shouted at me and pushed me back. I switched to English. "Pee! I need to piss, you dimwit." But he still shouted at me in Turkish. I finally gave up and returned to my seat.

Twenty minutes later, one of the guards came to me, sent the man sitting next to me to the back of the bus, and offered me an empty bottle. "Here, you can use this," he said.

"You speak Arabic?"

He shushed me and pointed to the others. "I don't want people to know, they beg me in Arabic to release them and I can't do shit about that." He explained that he was born in Sanjak of Alexandretta, a territory that continued to be disputed between Syria and Turkey, both countries believing it belonged to them. People born there speak Arabic and Turkish. He turned his back while I pissed into the bottle, then threw it out of the window.

He extended his hand. "I'm Arda."

"Hussam."

"That's a good name."

There were around seven thousand Syrians living in Gaziantep's refugee camp, Arda told me, and most were not allowed to leave the hastily built camp nestled in a bare valley. "Try to find yourself a job at the school," he said. "Build yourself a friendship with the UNHCR officers. They'll be able to give you permission to leave the camp, and maybe you'll end up working as a translator."

When we arrived, I was placed in a large tent with bunk beds for single men. I awoke every morning to the shouting of Syrian men and women selling vegetables or repairing shoes. Stuck here and unable to leave, we turned the tent village into a town with souks and cafés and schools.

My English helped. I assisted an American teaching children basic English in the school tent and made money on the side. Every week, supplies were carted in on large trucks that stood outside the high gates of the camp waiting for orders. People gathered there in anticipation, and a staring contest would ensue between the bored Turkish driver and the Syrian men. Fights broke out about who'd come first and who most deserved a spot in the front of the line.

I always waited for the commotion to be over before picking up my own bag of supplies. Sometimes it contained olive oil and rice, other times hotel bottles of shampoo and shower gel to use in the public showers. Sometimes the bread was dry and the bananas were mouldy, but I learned to dip the bread in hot tea to soften it and to skin the mouldy bananas without them falling apart.

Arda was the first man I touched since Wassim. Being with Wassim had been like holding fire with closed palms. My heart caught fire, too, and after him it blew away like dust. A metal cage had taken its place. I put every man I touched after Wassim in that cage and locked the door. I draped a curtain over it and they slept there like wounded birds. Arda was the first bird, and he never minded the darkness. He came to my bunk in the middle of the night and woke me up, asked if I'd like to join him on a walk. We ended up in his office, where he locked the door so that no one would stumble upon us, and we kissed and jerked each other off in his small metal bed. I slept on his chest. After that we began to meet up once or twice a week.

"You should find someone on the other side of the world to get you out of here," Arda said one night. He explained that his previous Syrian fuck buddy, also a resident of the camp, had actively searched for an American man online. It wasn't long before the order came to release him on his merry way to the US. Arda showed me pictures of him on Facebook, selfies taken with an older white man in front of Lady Liberty and outside of Broadway shows.

"Aren't you mad he left you?" I asked.

"This part of the world is not made for people like us." There was a brokenness to his voice. "I'd rather he were alive there than dead here."

I relaxed on his chest and rested my head on his shoulder.

"Each of us needs to decide," he whispered as he softly caressed my hair, "to live and die here, or find our way west."

The next day, I used all my savings to buy a used smartphone. I downloaded Facebook and Facebook Messenger and started the search that led me to this very bedroom.

It's now 4:11 a.m. I haven't heard the foghorn in a while. I open Instagram and search Dawood's name. His photos are of landscapes and meals he enjoyed. I have to scroll for ages to even find one picture of him. No wonder he only has two hundred followers. I click the message icon.

"U up?"

The message is sent.

The message is read—4:21 a.m.

I stare at the screen for one minute. Two minutes. Three minutes. Four minutes. Five minutes. Six minutes. Seven minutes.

DAMASCUS

Kalila asks me to tell her what happened next. She insists. I escape her gaze and return to my room, but she waits by my bed. I open a curtain and find her gazing at me through the glass. I run upstairs, and she emerges through the floor like a white dove, her dress hovering around her in waves. I go downstairs to the kitchen and open the faucet, and I see her face reflected in the inch-deep water that pools in the sink.

"I don't want to talk about this anymore," I tell her reflection.

"You're the one who conjured me here, kid." She's replicated in every door frame. "You brought me here to talk." Her many forms speak at once. "So, talk."

"I don't want to talk about leaving Damascus." I pass through her standing by the gate of the house. I fling it open and her ghost dissipates.

"I'll be here for you to finish that story," I hear over the creak of the door.

I didn't bring a jacket, but the spring weather is getting warmer. I climb the fence, minding the gaps and anchoring each foot. I need to find a place of quiet in a city filled with the noise of war. I jump to the other side, startling a man passing by.

"In the name of Allah!" he shouts, pulling his headphones out. "What's wrong with you?"

I continue on. He curses at me, calls me crazy, simple-minded. I don't look back. I stamp my feet on the uneven sidewalks, kicking dirt and pebbles. I avoid holes that were meant to be fixed and others that were forgotten. I march down the Qassa'a street, following the same path Kalila did when her father walked her to the hanging of Eli Cohen. I pass the Bab Sharqi gate; its large doors, almost as high as a small building, are shut, but a side door, so low I have to bend my back and tilt my head to clear it, is open. I avoid people's eyes. My hair hasn't been cut in months, my beard is so long it reaches my collar, and my shoes are dirty and full of holes. Women evade my path, and children follow me, curious. The Straight Street is emptied of white foreigners praying and touching its stones. The shops on each side still display their fabric bags and T-shirts with broken English slogans. *I visited Damascus and all I got was this lousy T-shirt.* The handprint of a saint on one of the walls is not crowded; its palm-shaped indent collects dust after years of oiled hands touching for blessings.

My forehead is already sweating, and my feet ache, so I stop outside the Assad Basha Khan, under its arched copper dome. It's on an old street paved with cobblestones from the time of my great-grandparents. Some stones are missing, and the vacant spaces trap water; the farmers lead their carriages around them. They keep an eye on the daily produce they bring from nearby farms to sell in the souks of Damascus. They whip their sickly horses that neigh in weak protest. Sounds echo here. The snorts of pained horses and the sighs of tired farmers. The hustle of the street vendor fills the dome with intertwined voices trying to catch the attention of bored women. An old man with a broom sweeps outside his shop selling lanterns and backgammon sets. He eyes me from afar.

"Shoo. Keep moving." He brushes the ground in my direction, as if I were made of dust.

I walk through the khan's gate. The caravanserai was built in the late seventeenth century: a wonder of its time and the biggest inn ever built in the old souks of Damascus. A chill runs down my neck when I pass by the two columns framing its ornamented wooden gate. Its walls are built in layers; black and white bricks alternate as the circular ceiling twirls into many minor domes, conjoined to create a massive dome in its centre with a glass top. They look like dancing dervishes sending their prayers upwards. The light shines through the mosaic of the glass top and creates waves of sparkles on the waters of the fountain beneath it. I sit on the edge of the fountain. The breeze comes from an opened window in a corner and carries with it droplets of mist. They smell of jasmine and old letters. I dip my fingers into the water and close my eyes. The city moves around me. Its people walk by, cross my path, avoid my corner, whisper. My body tingles as I carry the weight of the years this khan has witnessed. The travellers from Baghdad and Mosul and Aleppo and Beirut who stayed in this inn to run a trade or visit a long-lost loved one, their stories crawl on my skin like ants.

"You're not supposed to be here."

A young man in military uniform stands over me. He must be nineteen or twenty. He's one of the lucky ones, appointed to guard a historic site in the safe heart of Old Damascus away from all the fighting on the outskirts of the city.

"I'm sorry. I'm just tired." I stand.

He examines me and offers a crooked smile. He steps out of my way as I walk toward the exit.

"Wait," he calls from behind. "You can sit with me by my post if you like."

He points to a small kiosk at the gate of the khan. There are two wooden chairs and a small table outside it, standing imbalanced on the uneven stones. On the table, an old electric heater boils a pot of water. The man looks unthreatening even in his official garb. The uniform is ugly but clean. His green shirt is pressed, and his buttons look as if they've been washed with a glass cleaner. I hesitate, but he smiles and presents both hands, palms facing the ceiling.

He pulls a rusty spoon from inside the kiosk and turns his attention to the boiling water. His kiosk is narrow, with only enough room for him to sit down or stand up alone. It has no door and two holes in its wooden walls for windows. It won't protect him from a chilling cold or a stray bullet. He drops generous amounts of sugar into the boiling water. I like my coffee light on sugar, but I won't complain. We sit down, watching the coffee as it slowly rises.

He offers me a cigarette from his opened pack. I'm not a smoker, but these days I'm not in the habit of refusing free things. I place the cigarette awkwardly in my mouth, and he lights it. After my first inhale I cough so hard I worry my voice box might come out in my hands. He laughs. The coffee is about to overflow, so he takes it off the heater. We watch in anticipation as the top layer of the coffee mushrooms to the rim of the pot, then sigh in relief when it retreats without spilling.

"Are you from Damascus?" he asks as he pours the coffee into two dirty glasses. I nod. His accent is Damascene, which makes sense. Only big Damascus families would be able to afford putting their children in safe posts during the mandatory military service, while the sons of the poor and working class are taken away and thrown into the war. He wears a gold crucifix around his neck that seems too effeminate for a young man. Probably it's his mother's, passed on to him for a spell of protection.

"You're not a big talker, are you?" He offers me the coffee. I take it by the rim of the glass and sip. The hot liquid burns my tongue, and I hiss in pain.

"Easy there. The coffee won't run away." He laughs at his own joke.

"Why?" My voice croaks.

"Huh?"

"Why are you offering me this?"

He shrugs. "You look like you needed a cup of coffee."

He has a petite mouth and a small nose, which stand in contrast to his large eyes, which are blue like mine. Under his green military hat, his head must be bald. All military personnel are required to shave their heads to prevent the spread of lice. His eyebrows are blond, indicative of blond hair he inherited from the French invasion.

We drink our coffees in silence. I don't want to offend him by killing the cigarette too soon, but it burns my lungs with every breath. He throws his into a nearby puddle, and I do the same.

"Thank you." I take another sip of coffee.

"Don't worry about it, man. You remind me of my brother," he says. "He's your age." He points to my face. "He also liked to grow his beard."

The brother, the guard tells me, had been arrested by the regime forces, mistaken for an Islamic extremist because of the size of his beard. His mother had cried, blaming herself for not insisting he shave.

"We're Christians," the guard adds, as if to defend his own religion. "We had nothing to do with the extremists."

The brother was gone for most of the summer months and all of the rainy fall days before appearing outside their door on a chilly winter morning, wearing the clothes he'd worn the day of his arrest. The mother held on to her son, refusing to let him go for a rest or a shower. He rarely spoke about what he saw in prison, but his thinning waist and his refusal to let anyone see him in short sleeves left the small family with a vague under-standing. The government officials had realized their mistake and released him. Only weeks later, the brother was called up for his mandatory service.

His parents wailed. They begged and pleaded with contacts and relatives to help them find a way to delay the appointment.

"One day," the guard says, "we heard a scream from his bedroom." The young guard laughs in a way that starts out genuine and gradually turns nervous.

His brother stood in the middle of the room, looking dizzy. He held his own severed big toe in one hand and a kitchen knife in the other. Blood streamed from the wound in his foot. "Now they won't be able to take me," he announced to his family, before falling to his knees.

"He thought that if he was missing his big toe, he wouldn't be enlisted," the guard says. He laughs. "It worked. They agreed to let him stay home, citing his mental health as an issue."

The young guard says that when it was his turn to join the army, his father sold his farm at a loss and with the proceeds paid a high-ranking officer to ensure he got this post. He gestures to his kiosk, painted ages ago in the colours of the Syrian flag. It needed a fresh coat.

He opens his pack of cigarettes and pulls himself a new one. I notice his trembling fingers. He offers me one but I shake my head. He lights up.

"I wonder sometimes if I should have cut off my own toe."

He seems smaller. His body barely fills the uniform he was given. The blue in his eyes becomes misty. I hesitate, but then I pat his knee twice before I retreat.

He smiles. "Where is your home?"

"I don't have one," I say. My home with Kalila is as imbalanced as the cobblestones of this road. It's not built on any foundation other than my own damnation. It is my prison, my hiding place, and my exile, as permanent as the rainy days of Damascus. It might end without the gargle of thunder. I might return to find it taken by another Damascene traveller or to find that it never was there to begin with. My father's home is not mine either. I forfeited it the day I decided to follow Hussam, leaving behind my father, my wife, and my child. I had to cut all my ties with Damascus to be with Hussam. What a selfish thing to do. I am the catalyst of all the pain of the people around me. I forced Hussam into a lie all those years ago, and it grew bigger and bigger. Even that trip chasing him was fruitless. I shouldn't have touched the guard who brought me comfort and coffee. I don't want to stain him with my curse.

"I've got to go." I stand.

"But you didn't finish your coffee yet."

"I've got to go," I repeat. I walk away.

"Brother. Wait. Brother," he calls. "Wait. I don't even know your name."

I take the first turn I find and keep walking.

I am not meant to find friendship anymore. I am meant to keep my diseased body and corrupt soul away from the innocent people of Damascus. My ears are not to hear their stories. My mouth is not to kiss their pain away. I am the green moss on the trunk of my family's tree. I sap the life out of its bark and burn the leaves off its branches. I strangle its blossoms. I should have withered like a sickly flower in the direct rays of the sun, leaving space for other, brighter roses to raise their petals up and seek the warmth.

Instead, I married a woman and produced a child. I cursed them with my infected self and left them empty. I am their phantom limb. I chased a man after I killed his father and caused his arrest. I should have been the one falling off the rooftop.

I am on the outskirts of Old Damascus, on a busy main road outside the citadel's gate, by a traffic light. A bus with a never-closing door gains speed near me. I run parallel to it and jump aboard.

"Hey. What the fuck?" the driver shouts.

I mumble something unintelligible so that he thinks I'm crazy and lets me through without paying fees. I take the first empty seat and rest my forehead on the dusty window. It's a jammed afternoon only worsened by checkpoints on every major road. The bus heats up under the direct sun. Women fan their faces and men sweat into their shirts, leaving stains under their armpits. I jump off the bus to the slow-moving traffic near the Yousef Al-Azmeh Roundabout and walk by the dessert shops and boutiques.

I end up on the corner of Al-Hamra and Al-Shaalan. Hussam and I used to come here all the time. In the early evening we'd walk together to Al-Medfaa Park at the end of Al-Shaalan Street market. We bought shawarma from a famed shop on the corner. I used to buy my Nintendo 64 cartridges from a shop that now sells gift boxes and birthday cards.

Al-Medfaa Park had been a forbidden place for us until we dared to visit it once, frightened of being discovered. It's where all the gays of Damascus congregate, an open secret in the city. Every evening they gathered in twos and threes, talking and smoking and exchanging phone numbers. Hussam and I watched them from afar. Sometimes we did so from across the street, under the bright lights of the United Colors of Benetton. Sometimes we walked by, eavesdropping.

"I think they're speaking a made-up language," Hussam had whispered to me once. He wrote down the random words we heard and sat at his desk trying to decipher the rules of that language. They moved syllables around and added an *esh* sound at the end of every word. We never dared to talk to any of them, and none of them talked to us. They talked *about* us. They waved us over with smiles, but we never joined. They wore colourful T-shirts and tight jeans and sunglasses perched atop their foreheads, gathering their chemically straightened hair.

We heard them laugh. We heard them gossip, or call one another across the street by female names. At that, we recoiled.

Now I look back and wonder if I should have been dipping my toe in. Maybe if I had, I'd have diluted my sinful soul with theirs. Maybe I would have found myself someone older to tell me how they dealt with their family's pressures, how they found love in Damascus, and how they avoided the eyes of the onlookers when they exchanged loving whispers. They always stood tall and huddled together like a pride of lions. Maybe I would have learned to stand as tall as they did.

No one gathered at Al-Medfaa Park today. Maybe the boys were fearful of the war.

"Hey." I hear the call from behind me. "Yes, you. Hey." The voice comes from a car. A man leans out his window and ushers me his way. "Yeah. You. Come here."

I don't move.

"I won't bite. I want to talk."

The man looks much older than me. Probably in his late fifties. He has a long nose and piercing eyes. His thinning hairline has a couple of stray hairs remaining on his forehead, which he lets grow longer. He smiles and waves me closer. When I still don't move, he parks his car. I peer at him through the passenger window.

"Get in. Let's talk."

He waits as if his offer is enough. It's a fancy silver Honda with sleek doors and a sunroof. If I'd been good to my father, I think he would have bought me a similar car. The man gets anxious and waves me in again.

"What do you want?" I ask, point-blank.

"Well. I know the kind of men who hang out here," he admits. "Just get in the car. I can guarantee you a hot shower and a good meal."

My stomach growls in response, and my skin itches for a hot bath. The man seems peaceful and sweet.

"You look like you could use a friend," he says.

Maybe I can start anew with this man. He might own a home of his own. He wouldn't offer a hot shower otherwise. What would happen if I never returned to Kalila's home? If I disappeared into this man's car and was lost in a new layer of Damascus? I highly doubt this man navigates the same roads Rima does. Or my father. Maybe he can be my new escape. He's a fellow escapee, another cursed one. Maybe our curses would cancel each other out.

"Are you coming?"

I reach for the door handle.

"What's going on here?" A harsh voice comes from across the street. A man my age examines us both. The driver slams his gas pedal and the car roars off. The man across the street still eyes me. I turn my back and walk away.

"Wait," he calls after me. His accent is confusing. It's not Damascene. "Wassim! Wait."

I turn on my heels. He rushes after me. I know his face, but I can't place him.

"You are Wassim, aren't you?" he says. "It's been ages, man."

The accent, short and snappy with a heavy pronunciation of the throaty letters, brings back memories of high school. Final exams with another student sharing my table. A card game with a flush of cards hiding a sun-kissed face. A ball flying off into the corner of a football net. The fogginess of the face clears: it's the Iraqi boy who brought porn pictures to school and shared them with me and Hussam.

"You're that Iraqi boy," I say.

He laughs. "Well, I'm not a boy anymore. It's Jamal."

He wears a trendy T-shirt and a white scarf under a light red jacket. He smiles warmly. I grab his hand in a handshake. He squeezes it and gets closer for a hug, then second-guesses himself and keeps his distance.

"Your father is looking for you," he says. "We all heard that you were back in Damascus."

I recoil at the mention of my father. "I know. I don't want to go back home."

"We all thought you went after Hussam," he states so casually. It feels like he stepped on my toes.

"No." I take a step back. Silence covers us like a black curtain. The sun sets in the distance, and everything around us glows.

"I hope he's okay," he says. "He blocked me on social media. I think he blocked everyone from Damascus." He pauses. "I honestly thought the two of you got to Canada together. I know you were close." He locks his eyes on me. "Where are you staying?" He inspects my clothes, dirty, old, and rumpled, my untidy beard and long hair.

"Nearby."

He nods. He walks and I walk beside him. We head down Al-Shaalan Street in silence. He keeps looking over at me as if he's about to say something, but he retreats before the words escape his mouth.

"You know," he finally says, "times are changing." He looks

around and lowers his voice. "Spring is almost over, and summer is coming. Maybe this summer will bring warmth for people like you."

"People like me?" I ask, avoiding his eyes.

"Well, people who live outside in the cold," he says. His voice is clear enough for me to hear, but guarded enough for the people around us to miss. "People rejected by the world around them."

I'm confused. He examines me for a second. "I have been a refugee here for ten years," he says, "and you—" He smiles. "And you are who you are."

I'm shivering. I wish I'd brought a jacket with me. I miss home. I miss the warmth of my little spot in the corner of the room I call my own. I miss the dusty smell and the creaking doors. I should go home to Kalila. We reach the corner of Hamra and Al-Shaalan streets.

"People like us live on the outskirts," he says. We stop at the corner and face each other. "I'm not running away anymore. I want to bring what I want to me instead of seeking it elsewhere."

His eyes scan the windows of the shops around us. He feels right in this city: as if he belongs. Even with the heavier accent and the sun-kissed skin and the thick mane over his head. He fits so perfectly in Damascus. He is everything I am not, and it makes me retreat within myself a bit. He extends his hand once more, and we shake.

"Come here, you." He pulls me in and gives me a bear hug. At first I'm anxious to be so close to another human, but then my body relaxes. I revel in the warmth of his chest against mine and the tingle of his cheek on my face. He squeezes me and I hear cracks from my spine. I shouldn't be touching this man. I don't want to stain him. I try to wriggle out of his embrace.

"My clothes are dirty," I whisper, and he squeezes me in closer.

"You're fine the way you are."

I smile before I realize I'm smiling.

"Man, I have a little gift shop right there." He points to the shop where I used to buy my Nintendo cartridges. "If you ever need anything, come to me." He pauses, then looks me in the eye. "It will be our little secret. I won't mention it to your family if I ever run into them."

With a warm wave goodbye, he heads into his shop.

As I walk away, I'm puzzled by Jamal's warmth and friendliness. Is he also gay? He didn't ask me for anything, nor did he touch me in any way other than a friend would. He didn't need to tell me tales of broken hearts or distressed brothers. He just opened the space for me to be myself for a moment. It felt good. Necessary. I wish he had hugged me longer—not in the way I wished for that from Hussam, but in a way that made me think I could talk to him about my life, and drink coffee with him, and he would listen. In a way that made me think we could watch a Syrian melodrama on television and make fun of the overacting. Still in my reverie, I arrive at the gates of Old Damascus. Jamal and I could talk shit while smoking argileh on the side of a road, near the Tomb of the Unknown Soldier or down on the Airport Highway. We could crack sunflower seeds together. Soon I'm outside the Assad Basha Khan, but the young guard is not there anymore; he's been replaced by one with dark eyes and a dirty uniform. An old song that Hussam used to listen to pops into my head. Its lyrics are about finding a place for us, somewhere peaceful and quiet with open air. I whistle the tune. I'm at Bab Sharqi, and the large gate is opened, both wings of it are spread. The evening chill covers the city like a blanket and the skies turn dark blue, as if a whale rested its belly on the dome of the sky. The streetlights around me turn on as if with a snap. They overglow for a moment, then balance back to a warm, orange radiance. I turn to look: the street behind me morphs from darkness into light, like an orange tree blossoming in the early days of spring. People, so many people, walk in and out of the Bab Sharqi gate, and I hear a distant street performer singing a husky song accompanied by the strings of an oud. The night brings the sounds of war to calmness and suddenly Damascus is back, and I'm back with it. I want to stay outside and witness its return, like a child witnessing a carnival arriving in town, but the cold drills into my bones and I shiver. I am light in my step as I walk down the road and through the metal gate. I crack the door open and it slides so easily. Kalila awaits.

"Welcome home."

VANCOUVER

I wake up to the smell of eggs frying. My eyelids feel like steel gates that have rusted shut. I shield my face with the back of my hand. When I finally manage to focus my vision, I realize I'm not at home. There's a desk in the corner, a small TV mounted on the wall, and a mirror on the closet's sliding doors. Oh god. I promised Ray. Just the two of us, he said. It took me a month to get him off my back after that night at Junction. I finally managed to go out with Michael and Brian last night. Just to Pumpjack. Then Brian gave me that pill. We must have had a rowdy night.

"Oh, you're awake." The door cracks open and a guy walks in with a steaming mug in his hand.

"Hey, you." I'm naked in his bed. My headache is like a cricket in my head, and it chirps.

"Hey, sleepyhead."

Where's my bag? Fuck. My phone is in that bag. Did I leave it in the coat check? I'm fucked.

"I'm making eggs." The Host sits on the side of the bed and hands me the coffee. "Last night was great." He wears baggy shorts and has freckles all over his cheeks and shoulders. "Do you want to have a shower or something?"

"Yeah. I think I better leave soon."

"I thought we'd have breakfast."

"Nah. I think I better go."

He shrugs.

"Maybe I can wash my face?"

He fetches a towel from his closet and explains that the bathroom is shared, but his roommate is probably still asleep. He asks me to be quiet. I tie the towel around my waist and walk down the hall. This place is familiar. Ah. I fucked his roommate months ago. If only I could remember the guy's name. Jason? Jackson? Jacob? It's definitely a Jay.

I wash my face with soap and cold water and steal some gel I find on a little shelf to do my hair. When I return to the Host's room, my clothes are neatly gathered on the made-up bed. I quickly dress. I search around and confirm that I must have forgotten my phone somewhere yesterday. I need to come up with a good lie about where I spent the night.

"Sam?" Fuck, it's Just Jay. He walks out of his bedroom and finds me in the hall. "What are you doing here?"

"I'm just leaving." I rush out the door.

On Georgia Street, the buses drive fast and the traffic lights take their time before switching to the walking white man. Ray and I have been shaky at best over the past weeks. He'd slept in the spare bedroom a couple times since that night, before I managed to persuade him to come back to our bed. I apologized and told him that my sleeping meds made me groggy. I blamed bad dreams and dramatic pasts. He can't stay angry at me. He likes to read while resting on my chest, to bite my ear and tickle me. The day after I apologized, he gifted me an Apple Watch, as if I were a dog he was training with positive reinforcement.

I cross the street to the Shangri-La. There are people cleaning tables at the restaurant; they look up, and each one is a copy of my father, grinning. I look the other way to see a mural depicting a map of the world. Each region is connected to another with coloured threads. The map lights up at night, I've seen it before. But at the moment it's dimmed, the threads trembling in the morning breeze. Some threads, I notice, are only attached to one side of the map. They fall off and gather on the ground with no purpose. There's not a single thread connecting Syria to anywhere. The little country on the mouth of Asia Minor sits alone. To Vancouver, there are at least a dozen threads coming from all over the world: Australia, Europe, even Mexico and Egypt.

I wish I had a ladder. I wish I could just climb the wall, grab one of these threads, and connect it to Damascus, then extend it all the way to Vancouver.

I scratch the dried cum caught in my arm hair, and it flakes off like dead skin. Ray will kill me. I promised him monogamy, and I doubt anything I say would convince him I didn't fuck around last night. I finally reach our building and realize, as I stand outside the glass door of our lobby, that I lost my keychain as well. I sigh. I have to wake Ray up to let me in. I won't hear the end of his rant. I punch in the code and the intercom rings three times before I hear Ray's sleepy voice.

"Hello?"

"Hey, sorry, I lost my keys."

"Of course you did."

I hear the familiar buzz, and moments later I'm at our apartment's door. It's left open. I sneak into the apartment like a burglar. I remove my boots by the welcome mat. My feet are dirty. I tiptoe to the bedroom, bracing myself for the inevitable fight.

It's dark, but the light comes in softly through a gap in the curtains. There are two men in my bed. Ray and a younger man: the twink dancer from that night at Junction. At least we clearly both had our fun. Ray scrolls his phone, his reading glasses low on his nose.

I slip into the bathroom and close the door behind me. God, I look like a fucking zombie. I start the shower and step in just as someone enters the bathroom, lifts the toilet seat, and pees. The stream is steady and powerful—must be the Dancer. He leaves without washing his hands.

By the time I'm dried off, Ray has opened the curtains. The Dancer looks confused that I'm there. Ray, on the other hand, is just naked in bed on his phone.

"Welcome home, stranger."

"Do you want coffee?" I ask.

Ray just looks at me over the rims of his glasses.

I open the closet and let the towel fall from my waist. I'm buck naked in front of the Dancer, but I don't care. I put on a pair of shorts and a tank top.

"Sure," the Dancer says, "I'll have coffee."

"Sure. Coffee, Ray?" All I get is his judgmental look.

"I'm Tommy, by the way," the Dancer says.

"I truly don't care."

I head for the kitchen and whistle while I make coffee. Ray and I both have our cards on the table. We are both losers.

There's no right or wrong anymore. There are no negotiations. For the first time, I think of us as equals. Ray is no longer towering over me. I feel fine. This is fine. In fact, this is the best thing that ever happened to me.

"Your coffee." I offer the tray to our guest, and turn it toward Ray, too. I lift the covers and climb in. The Dancer squeezes closer to Ray. He's now stuck between us.

"You're cheerful this morning," Ray continues to scroll through his Instagram feed, liking photos of shirtless boys. "For someone who was supposed to be home hours ago."

This coffee is good. The Dancer's leg slowly inches closer to mine. "Maybe we can all get along this morning?" He rests his leg against my thigh.

"I called you dozens of times, Sam."

"I lost my phone."

"Were you mugged?" This time he lifts his eyes off his screen. In between us, the Dancer sips his coffee, pretending he's not there.

"No." I graze the Dancer's skin with my toes. He cracks a smile.

"Care to elaborate?" Ray's tone is getting higher.

"Nope."

The Dancer giggles, which doesn't go over well with Ray. He puffs his chest and straightens up in bed. He mumbles something and puts his coffee mug on the nightstand.

"Did you give it up for drugs?"

I laugh in a short burst. "No, you idiot." I smile. "Brian paid for the drugs last night."

Ray spends the next twenty minutes lecturing me. I zone

out the more he talks. "I bought you that phone three months ago," he says. "Your credit card bill is basically a list of every gay bar in the city."

The Dancer sinks deeper under the covers, his whispered maybe-I-should-gos drowned out by Ray's wave of anger. Ray, at the other end of the bed, doesn't take his eyes off of me. His upper body tenses. His ears are perky like a wolf's, and his white chest hair is trimmed to a sharp shortness.

"Is this how you repay me for all the kindness I showed you? Is this how you show you're grateful that I brought you here to Canada?"

"Grateful? Stop lying to yourself, Ray. You didn't sponsor me out of the goodness of your heart. It made you look good and charitable. You basically bought a Syrian husband online. Let's not kid ourselves, sweetheart."

The Dancer eyes both of us now. I'm sure he'll talk about this to his friends over boozy brunches for the rest of his life.

"Don't talk to me like that!"

"I'm sorry your toy is talking back at you. Maybe check the return policy?"

"I'm not joking, Sam."

"I'm not laughing, Ray."

The blanket waves with our breathing.

"Sam. I just want this to be easy," he says, in a calmer voice. "This is not easy. This has never been easy. I understand that you had a difficult life back in Syria, but you're here now. Why can't you just let it go and be happy here?"

"Fuck you and your happiness."

The Dancer cowers at my burst.

"Sam, just listen."

I jump out of bed. "My name is Hussam. *Hussam*. Push the air out of your lungs to the top of your mouth, then squeeze your lips to produce that *haa*. How hard is that?" I walk to my closet and begin to stuff a backpack with clothes.

"What are you doing?" Ray sits up in bed. The Dancer jumps out of bed too and puts his clothes on.

"I'm fucking leaving."

"No you're not. Are you insane? Where would you go?" Ray finally gets out of bed and pulls his silk robe from its hanger. "You're acting crazy."

I head to the den. I put my laptop in the bag, then drop to my knees to gather its cords. I hear Ray's footsteps.

"I bought you that laptop. You can't take it."

I stand up and look him in the eye. "If you come close to me, or try to take this laptop, I swear to god I will scream so loud your neighbours will call the police."

He hesitates, shifting his eyes. "Sam. Just calm down. You probably had too much last night," he says.

"You just can't imagine me angry at you, can you?" I pack the cords, my phone charger, and my tablet too. The Bose headphones he got me for my birthday. My Ray-Ban sunglasses and their box. "You suffocate me. You fucking kill me every single day I'm with you."

I look over my shoulder and see his face crumble with pain. I've hurt his feelings. We both hear the door slam behind the Dancer.

"You don't want me, Ray." I'm almost whispering now. "You want this perfect Ken doll that you bought with your money.

You want me to empty myself and be a shell for you to fill with whatever you want me to be."

"That's not true. I just want the best for you."

I zip the bag and pull it over my shoulders. I pull a sweater off of my office chair. "I can't be what you want me to be. I can't—"

"I just want you to be mine."

It feels like the first time I truly see him: There is a stunted child underneath the facade. A child who carries an unattainable image of what a relationship should be, who believed the lies Disney told him about forever love and magical first kisses. A man who was told he was wrong for being gay, who was put down by the world for so long before the world finally relented. That twisted experience made him harder: it made him incapable of seeing anything other than his own truth. If the world lied to him for the majority of his life, and he had to keep believing in himself against all odds, there's no way for him to let go and admit he was wrong about anything ever again. I suddenly pity him. The damage is done; there's no fixing him. In addition to his warped sense of his own righteousness, he comes from a generation of queer men who will forever carry the bitterness of knowing how horrible the world could be.

"I'm sorry." I pass him toward the door.

"Wait," Ray calls after me as I press the elevator button. He steps into the hall and pulls money out of his wallet. "Take this. You clearly don't have your credit cards on you."

We face each other in silence. The elevator dings, and I hold the sliding door open.

"No." I say.

"Just take it, dammit."

I give in and swipe the bills out of his hand. Our fingers touch. For the first time, his fingers are not made of ice. With my palm, I tap twice on his cheek, and he sniffles and releases a short chuckle. The elevator door beeps for being held open too long, and I get in. Ray says something, but I can't hear it over the noise.

Out on the street, I am alone. My heart beats fast. My legs shake. What have I done? Where will I go now? This is madness. My only home in Canada is upstairs. I have nowhere else. Michael lives with roommates, and Brian's place is two shades away from being an opium den. My fingers tremble and I feel like vomiting. Maybe I should go upstairs and talk my way back to being with Ray. A cold breeze lifts my shirt, and tremors slide up and down my spine. I hesitate by the door, then walk away. I should leave Ray on his own for a bit. He'll find a way to get in touch, I'm sure of it. He'll beg me to return and I'll act all hard to get at first. He'll call. I know it.

I drag one of the pink chairs at Jim Deva Plaza to a sunny spot and I sit. Right beneath the No Smoking sign. I search through my bag. Winner, winner! I retrieve a baggie containing two joints and a lighter.

The sativa is strong; I'm filled with energy again, even though I must have slept for what? Three hours? Maybe even two? I sit there for what feels like hours. The joint ashes away, and I use its last embers to light the next one.

I see a van pull up at the corner. The first passenger to get out is a man in a brown wolf costume. Am I high or is this real? He must be sweating his balls off under there. On top of the fur are various leather items: chaps, a vest, and a spiked collar. Who released the crazies? Two other people in furry costumes jump out of the van. One is a fox wearing a fitted cowboy getup, its pointy ears sticking out of two holes cut into the hat. Another is a bear, covered in black fur, moving slowly as if just out of hibernation.

I saw a YouTube video about this once: It's VancouFur. A self-proclaimed journalist in the video explained that furries are a subcategory of the queer fetish community who dress up as animal-inspired characters. They have sex in those outfits?

Another van pulls up and two more furries spill out. This time it's a unicorn in a dress and a second wolf, more menacing than the first, with big, sharp teeth. They head off toward the Sandman Hotel around the corner.

"We need to stop running into each other this way."

I turn around to see a smiling face, teeth shining in the sunlight. He wears cute linen shorts and a tank top.

"Hey, Dawood!" I say, joint still between my teeth. "Or should I call you Rachel?" I cough and wheeze.

"Isn't it a bit early for a joint?"

"Nah. It's Mexico somewhere."

He laughs. "That's racist."

"I'm brown—I can't be racist."

"Lateral racism exists, love."

What does that even mean? "What are you doing here?"

He lifts his arms to show two bags of groceries. "What about you? What are you up to?" He smirks. "Other than getting high on a Sunday morning."

I take a deep inhale and gather in my head all the things I want to tell him. My fight with Ray. My overstuffed bag. My lost phone. I want to tell him that I don't know why I don't remember people's names.

"Oh, look," he says before I get to answer.

Metres away from the gathering furries, another van arrives. This time it isn't furries who disembark. A man in his late twenties helps a woman in a hijab off the bus, and two children pile out after her. They see the furries, and they scream in excitement. They're not conversing in English. This is Arabic.

"Are those Syrians?" I ask Dawood, but I know the answer.

Dawood explains that the Sandman is being used as a hub for newly arrived Syrians.

Children rush out of the bus toward the furries, while their parents and grandparents call after them to calm down.

"There must have been a flight from Lebanon or Turkey this morning," Dawood says.

The parents busy themselves ferrying bags into the hotel while the children swarm around the furries. They caress the costumes, jump up to stroke the ears. The unicorn princess is on her knees surrounded by six Syrian girls. She raises her hoof to her mouth and jiggles her shoulders, imitating laughter. The girls speak to her in Arabic. One of them, no older than four, grabs her arm. The unicorn lifts her up and they hug.

"Maybe we should tell the parents that these are gay people," I say.

Dawood gives me a sharp look.

"But these men have sex in those costumes," I say.

"For someone who spends most of his night looking for sex, you sure have some negative thoughts about it."

Many of the furries lead the Syrian children into the hotel. The parents, dragging their oversized bags, walk in step with them. A teenaged Syrian pulls her phone out and films it.

Soon the busy street returns to its normal traffic, and the buses drive away.

"It was nice to run into you," Dawood says. "I'll be going now."

I ask him if I can come over.

"Hussam." He inhales sharply. "I'm not up for fooling around."

"I need a place to stay."

He eyes my backpack with bits of clothes spilling out of it. "I see," he says. He hesitates, then hands me one of the grocery bags. "Just for a bit, until you figure things out."

"Thank you!" We walk down Davie, and I wonder if he'd let me hold his free hand.

DAMASCUS

I wrap gifts at Jamal's shop now. I sit in the back room, away from customers' eyes, surrounded by sheets of patterned paper and colourful ribbons hanging on rods. Jamal pops his head in every now and then and hands me a box to wrap.

"Wrapping paper is a delightful thing." He slides a pair of scissors through a crisp sheet, and I lean over his shoulder to see. "You have to cut it swiftly, as delicate as de-thorning a flower."

I don't have a schedule; Jamal never asked for one. I show up whenever I like and go home as I please. He pays me for my day's work. I told him he doesn't have to, but he insisted.

"This is for the sweat on your forehead." He presses the money into my palm.

He buys us lunch every time I come in: deliciously fried chicken wings, shawarma sandwiches with extra garlic dip, savoury pastries with cheese melted on top. He locks the shop door and brings the food to the back room. Sometimes we talk. Sometimes we eat in silence while he scrolls his phone.

I'd bought cleaning supplies with my recent pay and spent two days on my knees at home scrubbing the floor with soapy water. I sprayed windows with an off-brand Windex until they were crystal clear. Kalila bossed me around, commenting on my cleaning.

"Is he good-looking?" she asked.

"Who?"

"Jamal. Is he good-looking?"

I pictured Jamal's tanned skin and deep-set eyes, crowned with long eyelashes. His thick hair, well groomed and styled.

"I think he's straight."

"That's not what I asked."

"I don't want to think of him that way," I told Kalila, and she dropped the topic.

This morning, his face brightens when I push the glass door open.

"I brought you something." He takes my hand and leads me to the back room, giddy with excitement. He unzips a backpack and pulls out a package of new underwear, as well as T-shirts and pants that he spreads neatly on the table for me to examine. "I was going through my closet. I thought you might want them." He stands there proud of himself, like a kid who finally mastered riding a bike.

"I can't take those," I mutter. They'd be too big and would drape on my frame like old curtains.

"Don't be an idiot." He insists I try them on. He picks a yellow T-shirt garnished with pink flamingos and palm fronds. It smells recently washed. I give him my back and start to remove my hoodie.

"Are you okay?" he says behind me.

"What do you mean?"

He points to my side, where the black-and-blue tint still looks painful. "What happened?"

"A police officer kicked me while I was sleeping under a park bench." I insert my head into the T-shirt. I feel the silence behind me while I smooth the fabric and turn around. His lips are knitted together. "What do you think?"

"Great. You look great, man." His voice breaks. He turns me toward a mirror hanging on the back of the door. "Look at you. What great taste in clothes you have."

We both laugh. His palm rests on my shoulder. I was right, the T-shirt is a size too big for me, but it actually looks good. The colour feels warm, like a sunny afternoon.

The little bell on the glass door jingles. "Customers!" he announces, and rushes out to the front.

On my way home I decide to buy a bottle of shampoo and an Aleppo soap bar. I'm excited at the thought of the hard soap made from olive oil and lye; I can already smell the laurel oil on my hands. I stop by a small supermarket and the clerk keeps his eyes on me as I walk around.

"What?" I finally ask.

"Are you going to pay for these?" He eyes the items in my hands: the soap, the shampoo, and a Kit Kat.

I pull the money out of my pocket and place it on the counter. I unwrap the Kit Kat and leave the wrapper on the counter.

Outside, I decide I want to surprise Kalila with a treat; I'll buy coffee like I used to. It's not on my way home, and it would add a good hour of walking to my day, but I don't mind. The bombs in the air are distant, and people are out and about enjoying the late afternoon breeze. I trek in the direction of the old man coffee shop. He knows my father, but I don't care. With my long hair and big beard, he probably won't recognize me.

Streetlights glow, and the shop's neon sign is on. The old man stands outside the shop by his old-fashioned coffee grinder. The grinder gurgles, and coffee powder pours out of its mouth like a brown spring of sparkling mud. It smells so good; I want to fill my palms with it and slap it into my face. I walk up to the old man and offer him what money I have left.

His eyes examine me. "You sure you don't want to buy some bread with that, kid?"

"I'm sure."

He walks in, ignoring me.

"Wait, I want to buy coffee," I insist.

"Child, this won't buy you enough coffee to make one cup."

The soft coffee pours out of the machine into a small tank placed under it. I take a couple steps away but find myself dragged back by the smell. I stand outside looking in. At first he ignores me, but eventually he lifts his eyes. He relents. "C'mon in, child."

Inside his dark shop, old bags of Arabian coffee lean against one another on the shelves. A plate filled with coffee beans rests on the counter, surrounded by petite white coffee cups decorated with flowers. The man opens a tank similar to the one outside, takes a large spoon hanging by a thread next to it, and fills a paper bag with coffee.

"Here, no one should be denied coffee."

I raise my hand with the money, and he waves it away.

"Child, don't be stupid."

Even closed, the bag smells of freshly ground beans.

"Can you add some cardamom?" I ask.

The man smirks. He takes the bag back and spoons two small scoops of yellow powder in. He hesitates, sighs, then adds a third. "A beggar and a chooser." He closes the bag and shakes it well, then hands it to me. "When will Allah send me a paying customer?"

I grab it with both hands and rush out. I stop at the door and look back to see him sitting on a wooden chair reading his Holy Book of Quran.

"Thank you," I say.

He waves me out and goes back to his reading.

At home, I unwrap the soap and take a cold shower. The weather has been warmer, so the icy water is much more tolerable. I scrape at my body and hair with the soap, which opens up like a blossoming flower and fills the bathroom with its scent. Kalila waits outside the bathroom, her back against the door.

"Hurry up. I want you to make coffee. I'll read your fortune in the cups, like my mother taught me."

I use scissors I borrowed from Jamal's shop to cut my hair shorter, and then I tighten it back into a bun with a thin ribbon. I trim my beard short too. I unpack a pair of underwear from Jamal's backpack and put them on. I find a belt and use it to tighten his pants around my waist. I also find a pair of running shoes and some brand-new socks, and I put those on too. I step out of the bathroom.

Kalila whistles. "Damn, Wassim. You clean up nice!"

I feel myself blush. "It's not my best look."

"Stop talking shit to yourself." She is stern. "The voice in your head should be the nicest voice you hear."

"It was just one comment."

"No. I'm serious. You are the only person who can build you up or break you down. Treat your thoughts like hurt children. They haven't learned yet how to handle pain. They need comfort and reassurance." She looks me up and down. "You look great. This is the best I've ever seen you."

"I look great," I repeat, half convinced. "Now, can we make coffee?"

I've tried before to get the stove working but with no success. I try again and still no luck. Kalila, smiling, snaps her fingers. A lively flame springs up.

"You mean to tell me I could have had a hot shower or a warm meal all this time?" I sigh and fill the old coffee pot with water. Together, we stare at it on the burner, as if our attention alone could cause it to boil.

"You know, things are about to change," she whispers. "I think I'll see a future for you in the coffee cups."

The water boils and I carefully open the paper bag. With a rusty spoon, I add in three scoops, careful not to spill any outside the pot. "You don't mix the water and the coffee yet," I explain. "Turkish coffee needs to melt slowly into the pot. You need to allow it time to integrate into the water."

I hold the pot by its handle and bring it closer to the flame. When the coffee rises, I remove it from the heat. I repeat that a few times until the centre of the rising water, layered with coffee, breaks. "You need to let the coffee flip on its own inside the water."

She smirks, and tells me she knows well how to make Turkish coffee.

She points to a higher cabinet. I climb onto the counter and find two cups tucked away, covered in a layer of dust as thick as a cloth. I clean them and pour us equal amounts of coffee. I take both cups to the newly cleaned window overlooking the dark garden, and we sit on two chairs facing each other. I sip on the coffee as I watch her ignore hers. When all that's left in my cup is the dark layer of grounds, she asks me to flip the cup upside down onto an empty dish.

"Make sure not to let a single drop seep out," she instructs.

She gazes into my flipped cup and explains that her mother taught her how to read the cups when she was twelve. She'd told Kalila that she saw her for the first time in a coffee cup in 1944. Her mother could see that she would have a beautiful baby with dark walnut hair and black eyes. Cuddling her belly, she thought it would be a boy, but then Kalila was born.

"It was a time of change in Syria," her mother told her. "I just assumed the change also seeped into my belly and made you a girl." Kalila felt loved by her mother regardless of coffee cups and their prophesies. While Syrians were revolting against the French occupation outside, sending the blue-eyed soldiers and commanders back to Europe, her mother held her baby shower with neighbours, celebrating with dessert and black tea.

"I called you Kalila, like the talkative fox in the folk tale," she told her. Kalila was born murmuring, and her mother spent many a night awake beside her as she mumbled in her sleep.

The last French troops left Syria around the time of Kalila's first birthday. She was too young to remember them leaving, but their language stayed behind. People stopped calling pants by their Arabic name and instead called them *pantalons*, and called shirts *chemises* and hats *chapeaux*, even when the origins of all these French words were Arabic. The French influence also extended to architecture; new buildings in downtown Damascus had tilted rooftops and long, large windows that allowed too much sun into warm homes during summer months. French words were integrated into the Syrian dialect alongside ones that had stuck around from the earlier Ottoman occupation, like *tuz* for salt and *afendi* for master.

Kalila learned about her period around the same time the Syrian government announced a unity with the Egyptian government, turning the two countries into one. Jamal Abdul-Nasser convinced Syrians to be the first to join Egypt under his ruling. He hoped to convince Iraq, Lebanon, Jordan, and Sudan as well.

Kalila's parents went out to a party with her extended family, telling her she was old enough to stay home alone. She sat by her window looking out onto the lights of Damascus. The city was alive and electrified with the celebrations of unity. She heard chanting, which usually ended with loud laughter, as if those singing were suddenly aware of the ridiculousness of their songs. She got bored and turned on the old black-and-white television and watched the late shows. Syrian national television played endless speeches by Jamal Abdul-Nasser demanding respect for the Arab nations.

The tall Egyptian, with his straight nose and grey hair, appeared almost godlike on the podium in Cairo as he told the thousands gathered that he'd accomplished the impossible, uniting two countries that didn't even share borders. Later that year, Abdul-Nasser would visit Damascus. Syrian people were so mesmerized by him that they gathered around his car and carried it on their shoulders across the streets of the capital that was no longer a capital.

Kalila started to doze off in front of the television. The face of Abdul-Nasser was replaced by a famous Syrian singer performing a song about lovers touching for the first time. Somehow these two melted together in Kalila's mind. She finally fell asleep dreaming of Abdul-Nasser and his singing voice.

The celebrations were echoed in 1961, when Egypt and Syria broke their unity after only three years. Abdul-Nasser had focused all his attention on Egyptians, burning bridges with the Syrian elite, who felt left behind. He sent young, inexperienced Egyptian military officers to become leaders of well-trained Syrian generals. Kalila, by then fifteen, witnessed almost identical festivities: the chants were repeated, followed by the same laughs.

Her husband slapped her across the face for the first time in 1971, the same year that Hafez al-Assad led a third military coup and overturned the semi-democratic system in Syria, becoming president for the rest of his life. They had been married for six years, and she kept having miscarriages. The first time she miscarried, they were sitting in bed having coffee. He joked that she should look in her mug to see if she would have a boy or a girl. Next thing she knew there was wetness between her legs. Her water had broken too early. Her husband rushed her to the hospital, held her head in his lap in the back of a taxi, massaged her forehead, and asked her to hold on to his child. By the time they arrived at the hospital, she'd given birth to a baby the size of a peach.

By the sixth time, she knew the drill, and he did too. She called him calmly, telling him that her water broke again despite the many medications her doctors gave her and the many calming teas her mother bought her from Souk Al-Attareen. He told her he was busy, that a military coup was sweeping the country.

"They happen every other day. Can't you just come and take me to the hospital?" she asked, almost bored with the whole routine, and he insisted, angered, that she should go by herself. In the evening, he arrived home to find her still sitting in her water. She hadn't felt like going to the hospital, so she used the sewing scissors to cut the cord herself.

"I'm tired. I don't want to do this anymore," she told him, and he asked if she meant going to the hospital. "No, getting pregnant. I don't want to get pregnant anymore."

He had patience for only one dramatic turn of events that day, and he slapped her to bring some sense into her mind.

"Are you going to read my cup for me?" I flip the cup. Curves and shapes have stained the inside of its rim and gathered in its bottom, revealing stories I don't have the language to interpret.

"The Assad government called that last coup the Corrective Movement," she says instead. "From then on, things were never called by their real names. Coups were called corrective movements, dictators were called fathers, and abusers were called husbands."

I search the coffee stains for a familiar shape. Some of the blackness forms the waves of a sea, and within it, I see a foundering boat. A man jumps over the side into the mud of the coffee beneath it.

"Why did you do it, Kalila? Why did you . . ."

She smiles. "I'm sorry I burden you with my stories." She takes my coffee mug. "I told you." She looks at the bottom of the mug. "There's change in the air for you. I see two stars in the sky. You are one of these two stars, and your happiness is another."

"That's sad," I say.

"Why?"

"Up there in the dome of the sky, no two stars are ever meant to meet without a disaster."

"But you are not a ball of gas millions of light years away, Wassim. You are a human with words in your mouth and ears on the sides of your head. You can reach out and build connections with others. You have done so already with Jamal."

I look her in the eyes. "Every time I'm around another human, I bring them disaster."

"This world is a mess," she says. "We walk knee-deep in the mud of our times, and we don't make it through unless we hold on to one another."

I look away into the dark garden. A misguided bird flies through. Or is it a bat?

"Wassim." She lulls me back. "You don't need to infuse yourself into the people around you. You can build bridges between you."

We hold our silence for a while. It feels thick, like the mud at the bottom of our coffee cups. "Stop drowning into people."

"Maybe you should teach me how to read your cup." I overturn her cup and look inside, but it's filled with spiderwebs.

VANCOUVER

"Excuse the mess," Dawood says, opening the door to his apartment. It's a one-bedroom. A small bathroom to the side, a little kitchenette. From the living room, I see the foot of his unmade bed.

He points to an old sofa in the corner. "You can sleep there tonight, if you like." He points to the bedroom. "That's my room."

I follow him in. It's spacious, with a large walk-in closet. Half of the closet is filled with ironed shirts and handsome suits, and the other half is women's clothing: bodysuits adorned with rhinestones, expensive-looking gowns, a feather boa the colours of the rainbow, and multiple mannequin heads bearing large, elaborate wigs.

"This is where Rachel is born and where Dawood hides," he says theatrically.

The room is filled with a warm late morning light coming through a window overlooking Davie Street. A peekaboo view of the ocean appears between the many tall buildings around it.

"I've got to get ready for my gig this afternoon." He opens large metal boxes resting on a vanity. "You're welcome to come with me if you like." He pulls out large brushes, coloured palettes, and an assortment of plastic bottles, tubes, and tubs. I sit on a round cushion next to an old sewing machine.

"Do you sew?"

"Yeah." He points to the drag outfits. "I also sew for other queens," he adds, "but only for the ones I like."

He radiates warmth. Our eyes meet in the mirror, and I stand up, lean over him, and wrap my arms around him from behind. I print kisses on the back of his neck.

"What are you doing?" He eyes my reflection in the mirror.

"I'm kissing you."

He closes his eyes in pleasure and I slip my fingers under his tank top. He snaps out of my arms and stands up.

"You have a boyfriend."

"Not anymore."

He turns to face me. "I'm sorry to hear." He puts his palm on my chest and pushes me back. "Now stay there," he says.

I take a couple steps back. It feels as if I've had my hand slapped for trying to take a cookie from the jar. In the mirror, my father's ghost stands in the middle of the room, spewing black ooze. A scream echoes within the cavity of his empty body and snaps out of his mouth into my ears.

"I think I better leave," I say.

"Oh, don't be silly, Hussam," he says. "Stay, sit down. Just keep your hands to yourself."

I stay and watch Dawood's meticulous preparation. Every bottle has its place. Every small colourful palette is opened with an angle and intent. He slaps brushes on his palm until all the dust from past sessions floats away. "You have no idea," he says, "but this is such a drag queen noise."

I question him with my eyes.

"It brings me comfort, you know." He sits facing the mirror. "Sometimes we need to learn what brings us comfort from within. Find what's within us that makes us happy." He looks at me. "What's the thing that brings you comfort, Hussam?"

Comfort. What even is that? My insides vibrate at all times. I spin so fast while everyone around me stands still. *Comfort.* He said it with such ease.

"I don't know," I answer with conviction.

"Well, that's a great place to start," he says. "That means you have all the options in the world to try and find out."

"You sound like an inspirational Instagram meme."

He laughs and wipes his face clear with a scented tissue. "That doesn't mean I'm not right," he replies. He takes off his tank top and puts on a T-shirt with a large neck hole and smudges of paint and colour all over it. "This is my painting garment. You like?" he asks.

I nod. It's short, like a crop top, and I can see the trail of hair on his flat stomach. He brushes his black hair and ties it back. He selects a headcap, like those that people wear for swimming, and tightens it. "You gotta look smooth." He smacks his lips as he cuts a piece of tape and expertly plasters it on the side of his forehead, anchoring the cap. Next, he pours liquid foundation into his palms. "It was hard to find a foundation in the colour I need," he says. "Most colours here are made for white people." He slathers it on his face, minding his eyebrows, then pulls a special brush from his drawer and layers it evenly. By the time he's done, a good twenty minutes later, his face glows.

"Are you finished?" I ask.

"Child, we haven't even started yet."

"Why?" I ask.

"Why what?"

"Why are you a drag queen? Why do you want to be a woman?"

He pauses, then bursts into laughter. "I don't want to be a woman." He points to a photo of Rachel stuck in the corner of his mirror. "She's not a woman. That's an illusion. A larger-than-life play on femininity. I'm a man who participates in the art form of drag. My gender doesn't change according to the clothes I'm wearing."

"But you look like a woman, you refer to yourself as a she, and you wear women's clothing," I say.

"Pharaohs wore high heels, Arabian men wore eyeliner and kohl in the early days of Islam, French noblemen wore layers of foundation. At the time, those were considered manly things." He looks back and points the tip of his brush at me. "Look at yourself," he says. "You're wearing tight jean shorts, a shirt that shows your muscular arms. You have a heavy, well-groomed beard and a buzzcut. You are in drag, my friend. You're expressing an identity through the clothes you wear and the facial features you enhance. You're in hyper-masculine drag right now."

I examine myself in his mirror. I look at the body hair that I groom meticulously, the T-shirt that enhances all the right parts.

"When I put Rachel Minority on, I'm unstoppable," he says. "She makes me feel like I'm more than a man. I'm capable of entertaining, of bringing a smile to people's faces, but also, I'm free from the norms of society. When I'm Rachel, I'm celebrated for all of what I am."

"You're putting makeup on," I say, "not leading the Syrian revolution."

He doesn't reply, instead dabs foundation onto his light beard with a sponge. Slowly, the soft hairs disappear.

"Can I use your wi-fi?" I pull my laptop out of my bag. He points to the password on a Post-it note taped to the mirror. After shading the top of his forehead to make it less pronounced, he colours his cheekbones, then rounds and smooths them, all while completely ignoring me.

I connect, and my Facebook buzzes with new notifications. There are over twenty new messages and a couple of pings from group chats. Brian has already posted photos from last night and tagged me in six. I don't remember any of it. Ray sent me a quick "hey" an hour ago. A notification appears from Michael.

"Sam u online? Where r u? Ray texted me."

I ignore him. Dawood applies black eye shadow, studying his reflection with one eye. He admires his handiwork. Another layer of foundation. Another layer of paint. Within moments, he has his eyebrows curved on his forehead.

"What are you doing?" I ask.

"Leading the Syrian revolution." He sighs loudly. "Sorry. That was passive-aggressive."

"You look weird. Your face is grey."

"I'm not even halfway done, darling." He pops his tongue. Rachel slowly arrives, and Dawood, with his calm and steady voice, leaves the room. She opens a small box of highlighters and dips a new sponge in. Her body language loses its gentleness, and instead, she becomes animated.

Michael messages me again. "Brian found ur bag in his car. Ur phone is dead. Where r u?"

I type a long message, including all the details of my fight with Ray and my run-in with Dawood. And then I delete it.

"I'm at a hookup's house. What did Ray tell you?"

"He said u left home. He said u were weird. Wanna come over?"

"Let me text you later. Busy."

"Busy, eh?"

He sends me a gif of two men fucking. I smirk and go back to watching Rachel. She's drawing a dark, glimmering line at the edge of her eyelid.

"The eyelashes need a moment to dry." She snaps a fan open and fans herself.

"How do you remove them?" I ask.

"With difficulty."

There's something about this man. About this woman. This creature. There's something beautiful and sensual about him sitting there in his shorts, with his old crop top covered in makeup. This shouldn't be sexy to me; I like men. I love their beards, their hairy chests. I love men who forget to shave, men who call me names. I love men who make me fear for my life. But this man makes me feel a way I've never felt before. He mixes his brown skin with the colours of his put-on persona, and somehow, they fit. How can he so easily be gay and Syrian at the same time? How did he reconcile those two identities?

He walks over to the closet, swaying his hips, and pulls one of his wigs off the shelf. I creep up behind him and start kissing his shoulders.

"Hey!" He struggles to get away from me.

I hold him. My hands go up his crop top to his chest.

"Stop," he demands, and he pushes me back with his body weight. "Have you lost your fucking mind?"

"Why are you being so uptight?" I say. My father's ghost hangs from the ceiling, watching the exchange.

"Dude, you have to learn to get some self-value from something other than your dick."

"I'm sorry, okay?"

"I think you better go."

I gather my things. "I really am sorry," I say. "I thought I could—"

He raises a palm up to stop me and begins touching up his face. I walk out and close the door softly behind me.

Stupid, I utter to myself at the elevator. *Stupid fucking idiot.* When did I learn that love is a forceful grab instead of a welcomed touch? Dawood was the only person in all of Vancouver who treated me as more than whatever preconceived notion they had of what a Syrian man is, or what a gay man is. Dawood saw me for the man I am today but also for the man I was before, and he didn't shy away. He didn't reject me, or discard me after a night of fun. *I'm so stupid.*

"Hussam." His voice is calmer, as if speaking to a child who has misbehaved. "You forgot your bag."

"I really am sorry, Dawood," I say. "I just need to feel—" I hesitate. "You're a safe man to be around," I finally admit. "I just need to feel safe. I don't know if I've ever felt safe." I dry my eyes with the back of my wrist.

"Come back in, Hussam," he says.

"I don't want to bother you anymore."

"Just come back in, you idiot."

I let the elevator door close and walk back inside his apartment.

"No more funny business," he warns. "Promise?"

"I promise." I squeeze my lips between my teeth. I won't let my eyes betray me. I will not cry.

He examines me. "You should cry," he says.

"Huh?"

"Cry. I feel it in your body. You should just let go."

"It's okay."

"No, it's not," he says. "There's nothing wrong with a man crying."

I'm angry at the tears forcing themselves out. I groan as if I'm carrying a weight I can't stand. I shiver and cup my face with my hands. I cry.

"That's it. That feels good, doesn't it?"

My weeping comes in waves, like a salty sea. Dawood holds me, and I cry on his shoulder. Eventually I try to wriggle loose, but he squeezes me tighter. I give in and rest a little longer in his warm arms.

"Let's clean you up, yeah?" He leads me to the bathroom and stands there while I wash my face, then hands me a small towel. I rub my face dry, blow my nose in it, and hand it back to him. He chuckles and tells me to keep it.

Back in the living room he says, "Let's talk." He sits on the sofa and signals me to sit next to him. "What's going on?"

"I don't want you to be late for your gig."

"Blair will cover for me. Don't worry." He pulls out his phone and uses his front camera as a mirror, then reaches for a bag of baby wipes on a side table and starts removing his makeup. "Just tell me, what's going on, Hussam."

Today is the day I tell him everything.

I tell him about my father and Wassim and Arda. I tell him about the days I slept on the streets after Wassim's father kicked me out, the nights I slept on the cold unpaved prison cell floor, the dirty apartment in Istanbul, and the bunk beds in the refugee camp. I tell him about the day I got on the boat. The sun peers upon us from the windows and Dawood gets me a glass of water. When I started telling, I was guarded. By the time I tell him about the dead boat in the middle of the Mediterranean, telling feels like a flood I can no longer control.

"We were alone on the sea," I say. "Shouting accusations at one another. Afraid of drowning. Then someone pulled a gun."

Psst Boy had sat quietly while the other smugglers conversed about the dead engine. He pulled the gun out from under his useless life vest and shouted at everyone to shut the fuck up. He scanned the boat twice, and everyone fell into a complete silence. "I will kill you all," he said.

The waves murmured as they hit the side of the boat. I rocked back and forth with their gentle nudges. Psst Boy pointed the gun at my face, and the boat cradled me. My vision narrowed, and all I could see was the tip of the gun, its metal sweating droplets of water. My eyes followed the gun's barrel as it dipped with every wave. The smuggler's hand shook, and his fingers tightened. My teeth chattered. I wrapped my arms around the wet vest and felt it foaming with salty water, drenching my clothes.

"We need to lose some weight for the engine to kick back in," he said. His eyes shifted among our dimmed faces. "Come on, everyone, you need to toss your bags overboard." We didn't know that the rubber boats were usually followed by men working with the smugglers to collect the floating bags from the water and search them for goods.

At first people resisted; they stood by their luggage and their baskets and their plastic bags. The two Christian women searched through their bags, one hurrying the other. Finally they found a little plastic bag that one of them tucked into her bra. Maybe it was their purse of money, maybe it was a necklace given to them by their mother.

The smuggler pointed his gun at me, ushering me to the side of the boat. I stood and looked at the sea. I dug my nails into the bag I had beside me. It felt alive between my hands, like the back of a person who ached under my forceful grip. "Goodbye," I whispered as I pushed it off the boat. It plunged deep into the water before surfacing again, waving at me to the gentle rhythm of the sea. A departing ex-lover. A clinging past. The sea slowly lured it away toward darker horizons.

"All the bags are in the water," one of the smugglers confirmed. Men and women looked on with wide eyes, their pupils large, like sheep too slow to escape an attacking wolf. Psst Boy tucked his gun away.

The men gathered at the end of the boat, by the engine, and pulled on its long cord. On first pull it roared briefly before the sound was muffled by the waves. They cursed and pulled a second time, but it didn't respond. By the third attempt, there were whispers around the boat that the engine would not start.

"What are we waiting for?" one of the Christian women said.

"Try again," Psst Boy insisted, and the men worked the ropes of the boat's engine, which coughed some fumes, announcing its death. The boat shook with a heavier wave, surrendering to the currents to guide as they pleased.

My pants, wet from walking in the water, were now freezing, and the drenched life vest felt heavy on my chest. We sat in silence for hours, not sure what to do next. The smugglers gave up on the boat's engine. They sat with us, and somehow I couldn't pinpoint them anymore.

I searched the horizon. I tried to distinguish between sea and sky, but darkness engulfed us. Looking in the direction I assumed to be east, I prayed for the sun. I wondered if I would survive the cold or if I would be found the next morning covered in a layer of ice, the ghost of my body embracing me like a shell. I crouched in my seat and hugged my knees. If I didn't gather my body around me, I felt it might erupt; my arms detaching, my core liquefying, my hips melting into the rubber of the boat. I couldn't look at the water anymore. The crashing of waves got louder and intensified. I couldn't look at my fellow travellers. I blocked my ears with my hands, but the noise still filled my brain. I wanted to scream, but I was afraid of a bullet.

"Here we walk on the roads to our treasure. We walk together, and our hopes are our guiding map."

The voice of a child singing came out of nowhere, soft and heady like a siren's lullaby. Muffled at first, then clearer when I uncovered my ears.

I knew the words. It was an old song all Syrians knew by heart, a song closer to our veins than the national anthem, more meaningful than the thousand songs petitioned by the Syrian regime to glorify our presidents. We grew up with this song, and everyone's ears perked up when we heard it. It was the end credits song of the dubbed *Treasure Island* cartoon we all watched when we were young.

The four smugglers emerged from among the passengers and located the child. Psst Boy pulled his gun again and kept it relaxed in his hand. He ordered the other men to shush the little kid, and they stood around him and lifted their index fingers to their lips.

The boy stopped singing.

I realized, that very moment, that the four men must have been my age, if not younger. Psst Boy with his gun could be nineteen, maybe twenty.

"None other than us would follow this dangerous route to this Treasure Island."

The singing returned from another child on the other side of the boat. As the words left his mouth, another child joined in. *"It's a strange land, but our treasure is there. The maps to it are unreadable, but we are committed to reach it."*

All the children on the boat joined the song. *"We fear the dangerous challenges; they are aplenty"*—the sea waves carried the song—*"but we're together, and we're on the road to the treasure."* Adults sang too, and the two Christian women joined in. All sixty-one souls on the boat sang—a choir of refugees.

"We are all together; and we're on the road to our treasure," I sang with all my might.

A light came from afar and grew. The four smugglers looked upon it as the voices grew louder and they, too, began to sing the old song. Psst Boy, perhaps figuring he could masquerade as a refugee, dropped his gun into the water and sang next to me in a throaty voice.

Those children were our foghorn. It was the Turkish Coast Guard who heard them and came looking for our boat in the dead of the dark night. The guards didn't believe their ears at first and thought that the rumours were true: that the souls of refugee children who drowned at sea returned to sing a final song. They came anyway, looking for the source of the song, and found the hopelessly lost boat. They arrested the four smugglers, pulled the boat behind them, and returned us to the city of Izmir.

"They kept us prisoner for days before releasing us back to the refugee camps," I tell Dawood.

I get up from the sofa and look out the window at the peek-aboo view of the ocean. There are many layers of buildings between me and the seashore, but I see it. It's the most beautiful sunset I've ever seen, clouds of purple crowning an orange sun like a mandarin, and a shimmering path of light waves in the waters. I must have seen better sunsets before, ones that glowed with gold or turned the sea into a mirror, ones that whipped mist like a cream. But today's, this beautiful sliver of light hitting my face right here in the messy living room of a drag queen, is the most beautiful I've ever seen.

I feel Dawood's hand on my shoulder. My rib cage has opened like theatre curtains and jasmine roses blossom within.

"Thank you for sharing that with me," Dawood says.

"Thank you for listening." I'm blinded by the light, but I don't want to blink.

He asks if I want to eat something, and I nod.

"Sushi?" he asks.

"I hate sushi."

"Oh thank god! Me too!"

I feel giddy as we walk down Denman to get shawarma. I'm not holding Dawood's hand, but I feel his warmth beside me. We stand outside the shop and watch as the man puts too many different kinds of vegetables in the wrap. "We don't do it like this in Syria," I tell Dawood, and he smirks. He orders a re-do and instructs the chef on exactly how to do it: a much larger dip of garlic, lots of pickles, some tahini, and the right amount of hot sauce.

Dawood hands me the sandwich. "Happy now?" I nod. Garlic sauce drips on my lips. We return to his apartment and sit together on the sofa.

"So, I have a phone number of a counsellor who I think you'd find really helpful," Dawood says after we finish eating. "She's a queer woman of colour who has experience working with refugees. You'll love her."

I instantly tense. "I'm not crazy."

"Don't be silly, we're all crazy one way or another."

"No. I'm not crazy." Walls of cement build up within me.

"Okay. You're not crazy." He raises both palms. "But everyone needs to talk to someone, Hussam. You carry so much on your shoulders, and you can put that weight down. You can't solve everything with drugs, sex, and alcohol."

"Why are you talking to me like this?"

He sounds surprised. "Like what?"

"Like you know what's best for me."

"I don't mean it that way, Hussam. But you can't be expected to live a fulfilling life until you untangle that heavy past you shared with me."

"I don't want to talk to anyone." I feel cornered. I get up and walk backward to the door. "This is my private life. My private story. I shared it with you because I trusted you. Don't make me regret that."

"Calm down, friend. I'm just—"

"I am fucking calm!" I shout.

"Okay. You're calm. But why don't you want to talk to anyone? It's totally normal to—"

"Because I pushed him!"

"Pushed who? Your father? You just told me Wassim is the one who did."

"No. Not my father." I grab my bag and rush to the door. "I pushed Wassim."

I slam the door behind me.

DAMASCUS

I read somewhere that sixteen Syrian men and women were on board the *Titanic* when it sank. Only two Syrian women were among the survivors. Did they still remember they were Syrian years later? Did they tell their grandchildren of the tragedy they once witnessed, or did they bury the truth within them and move on, their stories unheard?

"I got on a boat once with Hussam," I tell Kalila.

She floats next to me and I lean toward her. "This story has no happy ending." I take a deep breath. "It's wasting away inside me."

I'd heard that Hussam had been released from prison a couple of weeks after he was arrested. My father had helped in his release, calling his friends in high places. He cursed Hussam on the phone, said that the child of his dead friend only brought him misery. Finally, one friend promised to ensure Hussam's release if my father bought him a cup of tea. "That was one hell of an expensive cup of tea," my father muttered under his breath. He paid the man enough money to buy a camel, and the next day Hussam was released.

We waited for his return home all day. Rima baked sweets and prepared a bath. She brought out some of my clean clothes for him to wear. When the evening came and he didn't, we called to confirm that he'd been released and we were told he had. We waited until the wee morning hours. We knew he'd been kicked out of the apartment he rented with his roommates and had nowhere else to go. But he never came.

The next day, I found one of his roommates on campus. When I asked him about Hussam, he walked away. I grabbed him by the elbow but he snatched his arm back and swivelled around, ready to punch me.

"I'm just worried," I told the man, and he relaxed his fists.

"He left for Turkey. Hussam is done with this land. This country was done with Hussam a long time ago anyways."

One week later, I packed my bags in the middle of the night and prepared to leave my father's home. Rima awoke and turned on her bedside lamp. She'd forgotten to remove her mascara the night before and had black smears around her long lashes. The baby babbled in his crib, then went right back to sleep.

"What are you doing?" she asked. She patted my side of the bed, as if to make sure I wasn't there. "Where are you going? Are you having one of those attacks?"

I ignored her, taking T-shirts out of the closet, which Rima routinely folded tightly and perfectly. I unfolded each one, balled it in my hand, and shoved it into my bag.

"Wassim, come back to bed." Her voice was calm, almost soft. It was the voice of a mother lulling her baby to sleep.

"I've got to go, Rima." I avoided eye contact. In my bag, winter sweaters were stuffed with summer shirts and a useless hat. I pushed my shoes, with their mud-caked soles, on top of all the clothes. "I have to leave here."

"You've finally gone insane." She rested her head on her pillow and turned off the light. "Just be quiet while you pack," she said. "At least let me have one good night's sleep."

I left with my dirty bag and whatever money I had. As I tiptoed across the living room, I heard the heavy snoring of my father. Outside, I gingerly closed the gate behind me. I stepped softly down the first flight of stairs, but by the second I gathered speed, taking steps in twos and threes.

I can't remember if I took a cab or a bus, or if I ran all the way to the bus loop. Buses to Aleppo used to run once an hour back in the day, but since the civil war started, they only left in the early morning, attempting to make the trip in daylight. By then, the four-hour trip took twelve or fourteen, depending on how many checkpoints were on the road and how many fights broke in the small villages bordering the highway.

"I took the first bus to Aleppo that morning," I tell Kalila. "I arrived there almost twenty-four hours later. I took a taxi to cross the border to Turkey within the hour."

"Did you think of those you left behind?" she asks.

"All I could think of is how much better their lives would be without me."

Rima would be able to sleep through the night, without my panic attacks. I cast a shadow on her like a stone statue. Never a real man. Never the man she was promised to marry. My father would finally be able to forget his first marriage; I was the shrine of my mother, a constant reminder of her death and a broken image of her. Even without his discovery of Hussam and me, I was a painful clock ticking off-beat. Mohammed Omar, the child I never wanted, would grow up not hearing the rumours about his father. He would be better off without me. They all would. I did the right thing by leaving them, and they would understand that one day.

The taxi driver asked if I was escaping military service, and I told him that I was an only child. "You're a lucky one," he said. "You're the only one who won't be called up in these times."

"You never know," I said from the back seat.

"You never know," he repeated.

There were three of us in the car: myself, the driver, and his friend in the front. They told me the trip wouldn't be long, and especially since I was legally leaving Syria with my passport, there wouldn't be any trouble at the border. We passed the windy streets of Aleppo quickly, leaving behind the heavy shelling noise in eastern neighbourhoods. With every explosion, I jumped in the back seat, while both the driver and his friend nonchalantly continued their conversation. On our way out of the city, we were saluted by its dimly lit citadel. The fortress, made of stones too large for a dozen men to carry, had survived two thousand years and hundreds of wars. It looked abandoned, save for a large Syrian flag and a tower-tall picture of Bashar al-Assad.

Hours later, we neared the Turkish border. We parked in the long line of cars leaving the country, some empty except for a passenger or two, others packed to the roof with luggage. The line stretched for miles ahead of us, and the driver and his friend left the car to smoke. I heard a ringtone coming from inside the car. I lowered the window and told the driver that his phone was ringing. He flashed me his phone in his hand, and before I could say more, the ringing stopped.

By the time we reached the border check, the sun had already risen, and dryness filled my mouth. The driver's friend had fallen asleep, while the driver smoked yet another cigarette, puffing the smoke through his opened window. He elbowed his friend awake and they handed their documents to the officer to leaf through.

"Where is Malek?" the driver asked. "I thought this was his shift."

"Malek is sick today," the officer responded. He looked at me through the window, and I handed him my passport. He looked at it and then at my face. He lifted the passport up to examine it in the direct sunlight, then he bent it. I thought he might bite it next to ensure its authenticity, but he finally handed it back. The driver was about to start the engine again, but the officer asked him to open the trunk.

"Malek never asks us to open the trunk." His voice was steady.

"I'm not Malek. Now open the trunk."

The driver exchanged a look with his friend before he pulled a lever by his side and the trunk unlocked.

"What's going on?" I whispered to them.

The driver hushed me while following the officer with his eyes. "We're fucked." His friend nodded in agreement. It finally dawned on me that someone was hiding in the trunk; that's where the ringtone had come from. The officer pulled the trunk open. Seconds passed. My fingers trembled, and I felt a tightness in my stomach.

"You brought this on me," I said to the driver and his friend, and they shushed me in unison. A few more seconds passed, then the officer closed the trunk, tapped on it twice, and ordered us to drive away.

The driver, not believing his ears, hit the road fast, leaving a cloud of dust behind. I wanted to look back, but he shouted at me to keep my face forward. We drove for ten minutes in silence, until the border disappeared behind us, and then he parked on the side of the road and the three of us jumped out of the car. Together, we opened the trunk.

Inside was the smuggled man. He was drunk.

The driver explained to me that the man was due to join military service to fight on the front lines. Not wanting to be part of the war and knowing well that his name was on the no-travel list, he had no option but to be smuggled.

The man broke into fits of laughter and stank of whiskey. He told us that using the flashlight on his phone, he had found a box containing four bottles of whiskey stashed back there. "I had nothing else to do but drink." The man shielded his eyes from the harsh sun. He'd guzzled the alcohol on an empty stomach and had passed out until the officer opened the trunk. "We both froze," he told us. Without thinking, he had handed a full whiskey bottle to the officer. The officer looked at the bottle and back at the man, then snatched the bottle and closed the trunk. "The funny part is," the man said slowly, "I can't tell if I gave him the bottle filled with alcohol or the one I drank then filled with my own piss."

All four of us broke into loud laughter.

Kalila breaks into laughter, too. Our giggles echo back to us, and gleeful tears gather in our eyes.

Finally, she calms down and asks me if I found Hussam.

"I asked about him at the refugee camp," I tell her.

They never allowed me in. It was a place for refugee

claimants who were processed by the United Nations High Commissioner for Refugees, and they were already overwhelmed with the huge number of refugees crossing the borders both legally and illegally. I stood outside the camp, head and arms poking through the fence, and I asked. They searched their databases on an old computer and told me Hussam was not there. I left disappointed and headed next to Gaziantep.

From a distance the city was an ant colony peppered with journalists and their fixers and translators. White people scurrying around, on the cusp of landing the story of their lives. Each of them was trailed by a Syrian man. The Syrians translated for the journalists, put them in touch with contacts, asked questions on their behalf in every interview, drove them to distant houses of leaders of the Free Syrian Army, and taught them how to sit respectfully on the ground while drinking tea and to cover their hair before meeting religious leaders. The journalists then wrote their stories from their air-conditioned hotel rooms and shared them on Facebook and Twitter.

A small river split the city into two, and I walked it up and down searching for Hussam's face in the crowds. There were cafés offering argileh and tea right next to bars offering beer and wine, cornered with shawarma places. I asked every owner of every shop if they had seen Hussam. I showed them photos on my phone, and no one recognized him. Defeated, I returned to my cheap motel and slept through my alarm the next morning.

I got out of bed and went to the lobby to look for a cup of coffee and a new lead. A fixer for a journalist noticed me and said hello.

He nodded when I showed him Hussam's photo. "He worked as a translator for a journalist for a couple days," he said. "He needed the money to go to Istanbul."

"How would I find him in Istanbul?" I asked the fixer, who shrugged. He paused at the door and told me that Hussam still had the marks of the Syrian government police on his body.

"I told him he needs to go to a doctor, but he just wanted to get to Istanbul as soon as possible."

So I followed him to Istanbul.

I arrived on a freezing cold day. I had on all the clothes I could possibly wear, layering two T-shirts under a dirty sweater and my jacket. The bus from Gaziantep dropped me on the outskirts of the city. I was told that it was a long walk to Istiklal Street, the centre of downtown Istanbul, but I walked anyway, guided by Google Maps.

It was my first time walking in a city where I didn't speak the language. People's faces were familiar, like pictures of distant relatives. Some of the men had big curly moustaches like those I'd seen only on the faces of old men in Damascus. The mosques were surrounded by gardens and repeated the same prayers, but the sounds of "Allahu akbar" from their minarets sounded different, accented, as if spoken by someone who had no training in producing the heavy Arabian *haa* or the deep, chested *qaf*. My eyes teared, and I kept on walking. I didn't know where I was going, but I knew I was meant to be with Hussam. I was sure I would find him.

I was freezing when I reached the Hagia Sophia mosque in the early morning hours. The clean streets glimmered in the morning light, and the sun dropped its warm blanket on me. I tried to enter the mosque but was told it was only open for tourists at this hour and escorted out.

I sat down on a bench outside the mosque, and a fluffy cat jumped up and sat next to me. Street cats in Damascus were fearful and never approached strangers. This cat was loving. It walked without fear and dropped into my lap like an old friend. I fell asleep on that bench, cuddling a street cat. When I woke, Hussam was sitting next to me.

"Your father called me." He looked at the mosque, avoiding my eyes. "You shouldn't have come." He fidgeted with his fingers, and I heard his knuckles crack. "I know your Find My Phone password," he said before I could ask. "I've been following you ever since he called."

"You and my dad are on talking terms?"

"He paid me to leave Syria." His dark brown hair glowed in the sunlight, and he had dark circles under his eyes. "He got me out of jail and asked me never to come back."

"Why didn't you tell me?" My voice was hoarse.

"Why would I tell you?"

"Why are you treating me like the enemy?" The cat was gone, having left a phantom warmth where her body had been. "Why didn't you just talk to me?"

He sat there, elbows resting on knees, leaning forward, fingers seesawing in one big fist. Tourists walked around us, gazing at the mosque as it glistened in the light.

"Did you know that my father left his family once?" Hussam said. The mention of his father stabbed me in the chest like a spear. "He fell in love with my mother and decided to leave his family, who rejected her, to build a new home for them elsewhere."

"I'm sorry, I didn't mean to—"

"Shush."

Dreary clouds appeared at the corners of the sky and slowly sieged the sun between them. I felt a drop of rain on my nose.

"Do you think it would have been different if he didn't leave his family for a fantastical concept like love?" he asked. "Maybe he would have been alive now. Maybe I would be a different man."

The look in his eyes kept me silent. We sat in the dying sun until it rained on us. He insisted that I go back home, but I wouldn't listen. He asked me to call my father, but I refused. He threatened to call my father himself, and I begged him not to. "For our old times together"—I had tears on my face mingling with the rain—"please don't do that."

His shoulders slumped and his head hung low. He told me to follow him, and he walked under the heavy rain toward Istiklal Street.

That night, we stayed in his room, which he paid for at a daily rate. He told me I could sleep on the bed and that he would sleep on the floor.

"You're only here for the night. Tomorrow I'm sending you home."

I did not argue.

He turned on the television and sat on the floor with his back to me. I spent hours looking at him while he sat there. I prayed he would catch me watching him. I wished for our eyes to meet and for the old spark to ignite. Hours later, he spread a small blanket on the floor and turned off the lights, rolling himself inside the blanket like a tortilla.

"Good night," he said.

"Hussam?"

"Hmmm?"

"Remember that flavoured milk ad we used to see on TV?"

"Okay?" He sounded annoyed.

"The one with the hot dude who works out shirtless at the gym, claiming that his muscles are all due to the great taste of Karam Milk?"

"Yeah. I remember the hot dude."

"The jingle is stuck in my head."

Distant sirens and chatter seeped into the room from the busy street outside.

"*Look at those large muscles, touch this big chest,*" I hummed. "*One, two, stay strong. Three, four, hit it hard.*"

I heard Hussam's giggle. "Best part," he said, "is the hot dude training a younger man while singing that you need milky protein to be strong."

I laughed and continued with the jingle. "*Let's all drink this milk. What a taste. What a pleasure.*"

"That shit was homoerotic." He chuckled. Silence returned to the room, and we both sighed.

"I'm sorry," I said.

"For what?"

I didn't speak. We were silent for a long while. I thought he'd fallen asleep.

"I'm angry at you. I'm burning with anger," he suddenly said. "I never saw a good day with you. It's not worth it. This is not worth it."

"Don't say that," I told him. "I love you."

He sniffed. "Love is a silly thing we call our sex drive. It's meaningless. If anything, it's a burden. This is our burden, and I'm trying to let go of it."

I slipped out of bed and onto the floor. I placed my hand on his cheek. He didn't push me away. "I love you. Love is the reason I did everything I did for us both. Loving you has been the hardest thing and the easiest thing I've ever done." I felt tears rolling down his cheeks. "Don't cry. I'm here for you."

"Please go back home, Wassim," he said. "Please leave me alone. I don't want to be with you anymore. I want to be free of this."

I printed kisses on his cheeks and nose, and he held on tight as I tried to unroll him from his blanket. "We can go to Europe together, Hussam," I said. "I'll find a job, and you'll decorate our little apartment. We will have our happy ever after, I promise you."

"Just please leave me alone."

"I would never let you go."

I finally managed to unwrap the blanket and pull him closer to me, and we embraced. He felt soft and breakable in my arms, shaking against my chest.

"We'll go to Izmir and find a boat to take us to Europe tomorrow," I said. He nodded. That night, he fell asleep in my arms on the cold floor of his room in Istanbul. It was the first time we'd ever slept together until morning.

The next day we took a bus to Izmir and arrived by evening. We searched for a boat for two days until we finally ran into a smuggler on the harbour. Hussam negotiated to pay the second half of our fare once we made it to the European shore.

On the night of our crossing, Hussam and I sat next to each other on the bus. I placed my hand on his. He snatched his away and gave me a dirty look, gesturing toward the smuggler who was watching us from across the aisle.

I told Hussam that the two women in the back must be Christians. They were the only ones without hijabs.

"The sea knows no religion," Hussam said.

After a long drive on well-lit roads, we finally arrived at an unpaved path down to the beach. Minutes later, we gathered outside the bus and were instructed to walk down a sandy hill toward the water.

"I don't know if I can do that, Hussam." He shushed me, and we went down the hill one after another. I lost my footing at one point. He heard me scream and turned to catch me before I fell on my face. I thanked him, but he just sighed and asked me to watch my step.

On the boat, wearing our useless life vests and cradling our bags, we sat down on our wet seats. Hussam told me that when we got to Europe, we each should walk in a different direction. "This is the end of our road together, Wassim." His hand was wet and cold. "You take an eastern road, and I'll take a western one. We part as friends."

"No. Hussam. We are staying together."

"I need you to let me go."

I hummed in protest, but he shushed me.

Then when the boat stopped working, all hell broke loose.

I deserved it. I deserved his hands pressing against my chest. I deserved the imbalance as I lost my footing and fell back into the water, surrounded by the bags and baskets of others. I'd known it since the day his father fell off that rooftop that I would be punished for it. I knew that it was my true sentence for killing his father all those years before. Like the sixteen Syrians on the *Titanic*, I was welcomed by the water and invited to its depth. I screamed to the people on the boat, but my screams were lost in the fight that broke out on board. I waved to Hussam. He pointed at his life vest and imitated the act of inflating it. I quickly did.

"Hussam!" I called his name one last time, but he turned his back to me. I tried to shout again but a wave filled my mouth with salty water. A moment later, the boat was too far for anyone to hear my cries.

There's a moment when you're fighting for your life from drowning. A moment when you calculate your chances. I wonder if the sixteen Syrians on the *Titanic* calculated their chances too. I wonder if they fought until their pain was too much for them to handle and decided that drowning, after all, doesn't seem that bad compared to living. I closed my eyes and surrendered my body to the waves.

"I woke up the next day on a shore coughing water," I tell Kalila. I didn't know if I was on the Turkish side or the European. I was alone, surrounded by the bags of people I didn't know. I opened a few of them and found some clothes.

"I began to walk."

VANCOUVER

I am seduced by the night lights. I leave Michael's, my system filled to the brim with whatever he had in his apartment. He's probably flying over the Rockies by now. I'm glowing in the depth of darkness, and I'm dancing. The lights around me flicker, and I stand still. I raise my arms like a crucified man. I watch from outside of myself. I stand in a circle of dancing men at an after-hours club, and the lights dim until they're gone. The last thing I see is my smile; it's automatic, it's drawn there, it slips into the darkness, and I'm alone.

A hot man on Grindr asks if I'm up to party and play. He says there are eight of them and all have been tested. He already bought the Molly and removed the fire alarm. He sends me pictures of him in a jockstrap, spit-roasted between two men. The app tells me I'm a hundred metres away.

I'm buzzed in without questions. I take the elevator alone. I knock on the door, and it opens. The living room is dark, but the windows are not curtained. The view is of the beach. The night sky is blanketed with stars, and the moon leaves a trail of silver shimmer on the waves of the sea. There are ships in the distance gathering in a long line, protecting the bay like boulders. I ask Grindr Man whose apartment it is. "It's an Airbnb." He leads me into the room, shirtless, wearing the same jockstrap he had on in the photo.

There are seven other men. A tall man with a tattoo on his shoulder sits on the sofa. His legs are wide open, and another younger man is cradled there, sucking him off. Two naked men stand in a corner, drinking and chit-chatting. Three others cuddle on a sofa in front of the TV, where porn is being played. There is a sex swing assembled in the middle of the room. It must be somebody's pride and joy. The swing has cuffs on its chains, and its leather bed hangs midair like a stage set for a performance.

"The party hasn't started yet, obviously." Grindr Man hands me a drink from over the counter and asks if I want some coke. I snort a line and ask if he has more.

"Easy now, tiger." He laughs. He brings me to sit next to the tattooed man on the sofa.

"Hey," Shoulder Tattoo says. The guy between his thighs slurps.

"Hey," I reply.

Just another hit. Just another one of those and I'll be fine. One more bump and my life will look rosy again. The spinning will stop, and I'll banish the ghost. Just one more high and I can handle the low. One more cloud and I'll be standing free in the sun. Just an umbrella for me to stand beneath. Just a boat for me to sail upon. One last hit and I'll be fine. Just one fucking hit.

I fill my nose with powder. I fill my mouth with a cock. There's an empty space inside of me, and the drug is planting roses there. I feel like laughing. I laugh. I feel like screaming. I scream. I feel like kissing all of these boys. I feel like a god worshipped by them. They lift me up. They put me down. Their hands on my skin are cold, like sea waves. Their faces are blurry, like echoes of themselves. Their hunger for me makes me happy. Just one last hit and I'll stand tall. One more hit and my father's ghost will surely dissolve. I am a lover on a rooftop kissing his dear boy crush. I am a man standing tall on the edge of a boat, pushing away my worries to be swallowed by the sea. I don't know why I did it. I don't know why I pushed him. There was a gun in my face. My heart was beating like a drum. He was safe in the waters, better than on that boat. I was free on the boat, better than a forever with him. I'm not the one who pushed him; the ghost of my father did. He kicked him in the face, a reversal of what happened on that rooftop back when we thought the world was small. I'm the one who pushed him, my fingers digging into his chest, my nails marking his skin. I don't know why I did it. Because of all of this. Because of none of it.

I am naked. When did I become naked? The boys are ghouls putting on their bibs to eat me raw. They gather around me on the swing. The cuffs are tightened around my legs. I love this. I hate this. I love this. I don't know how I feel about this. Shoulder Tattoo inserts himself into me. I feel him pushing himself all the way in. This hurts. This heals.

"Happy Pride!" Grindr Man stands by the head of the swing. Everyone laughs.

My eyes burn. My mouth is dry. My fingertips are cold. My fingers are popsicles melting away. I can see my bones. They're called phalanges. The bones in my fingers crackle as they fall off my hand one after another. How do I know they're called phalanges? My body swings back and forth to the rhythm of Shoulder Tattoo's thrusts. I'm pulsing with pain at every push. He digs his nails into my calves and pulls me in. My head hits the chest of the man behind me when he pushes me away. Someone cups my chest in both hands then slams my face with his cock. I open my mouth and take him in.

There is a vindication in this pain. The slit of a scalpel cutting away the tumours of my past. This pain is a deliverance, atonement; I'm on my knees praying, I'm on my back taking the whips of my sins. Every dig into my body is a stone upon my barricades. Use my body as if it were meant for conquering. Break into it with a sledgehammer, destroy it, and plant a white-and-red flag on the pile of what remains. This joy is my prize and the price I pay. His nails breaking blood, his dick shattering me, and the drugs are my absolution. This is why my father died, why I was arrested, why I pushed Wassim and left Arda and slithered to Ray.

The darkness comes upon me. In the corner of my eye, I see the faces of those who shouldn't be here. My father, Wassim, Arda, and Ray, gathered for my final goodbye. They sit on the sofa watching, exchanging pleasantries, commenting on the performance of Shoulder Tattoo. I don't feel my body. I don't feel my soul. As I slip into nothing I wonder: Is this comfort?

Is this comfort?

Is this comfort?

Is this comfort?

Is this comfort?

Is this comfort?

A choir of eyeless children carry me on their shoulders singing. I merge into a sea of muck. I descend. I close my eyes, and when I open them, moths fly out. I emerge from the water for a deep breath, but the air is made of shattered glass. I shiver, and my skin crawls with dead bugs. I'm metamorphosing into an animal unworthy of sacrifice. My limbs shrink. My body decays. I am nothing.

Is this comfort?

Is this comfort?

Is this comfort?

Is this comfort?

Is this comfort?

Is this comfort or is this the back end of a slap? The burn on my face as I retreat inward. Is this comfort or is comfort not meant for me? An unattainable concept beyond my own ability to experience? Is this comfort or is comfort a black hole on the other end of the universe? Sending beeps and signals to me since birth, warning me that I would never reach it. Telling me to not even try.

I'm in a bed. The sheets are harsh beneath me. My limbs ache. Spots of light dance around my retinas. I try to open my eyes. All I see is whiteness. A flashing light hovers over my eyelids. I hear words being exchanged, but they're muffled as if coming from underwater. My nose is scorched. I try to take a deep breath, but it hurts more. I cough. "Try to take in air slowly," I finally hear.

It feels as if someone's sitting on my chest. An incubus, perhaps, feeding off my bad dreams. "Here you go, easy does it," I hear a woman say. I see a nurse in blue scrubs at the foot of the bed, a whiteboard on the wall behind her.

White male. Mid-20s. Overdose.

I try to gather my words, but coughs emerge in place of sentences. She gets a paper cup of water from a bedside table and directs the metal straw at my mouth. "Here, drink," she says.

"I'm not," I grunt at her.

"Huh?"

"I'm not white." My voice is hoarse. It feels as if I haven't spoken in months.

She looks confused at first, then realizes and goes to the board and erases the word. "What are you, then?" Her accent is Irish.

I ignore the question and try to sit up with difficulty. The light flickers and a beeping machine emits a high-pitched note across the room. "Can you turn that off?" I say.

She shakes her head. "Anyone you want us to call?" she says.

In the corner, the ghost of my father sits on a chair. Blood pours out of his mouth and pools on the floor.

"No. No one to call." Ray's number is the only one I know by heart. I just want to go to sleep.

"First name?" she asks.

"Hussam."

"Hisham?"

"No. Hussam. Hoouuusssaaaammm."

"Got it. Hisham, let me call a friend or a family member. We have your phone." She steps outside, leaving me alone with my father's ghost.

"Are you going to haunt me forever?" I ask. His ghost doesn't move.

The nurse returns with my phone, fully charged, and hands it to me. "It arrived with you," she explains.

I'm greeted by missed calls from Ray and Michael.

"Can I have a bit more water?" I ask.

"I'll be right back."

I go to Instagram and open my conversation with Dawood. I look at the last message I sent him, at four in the morning those many nights ago, still left on read. I click on his story. There's a video of him performing the same Warda song I loved so much. It's followed by a video of him with friends at a late-night spot, with argilehs all around and a table full of Arabian food, shawarma and hummus and the like. In the next, one friend is happily belly dancing, popping his hips to the beat; a white boy attempts to mimic the move and fails, to the laughter of his friends. Last is a photo of Dawood in drag makeup but boy clothes, surrounded by his friends, all looking up at the camera.

I stare at the photo. I keep reopening it every time it expires. One of the friends' faces becomes Wassim's, waving goodbye.

I click the Message button.

"I have something I need to tell you."

DAMASCUS

We hear the chants from outside. They're getting louder. We rush from window to window and peek from behind the curtains, waiting for glimpses of faces between the cracks of the fence. We separate to check different windows for a better view. My footsteps echo, bare feet on wood floor. We run into each other in the hallways. We giggle.

"Here they come," Kalila says.

Shouts and screams. Their anger makes us shout too. We chant with them against a regime we've never understood.

"We should open the curtains," she says.

"But wouldn't they see us?"

"Maybe it's time for us to be seen."

I open every curtain. Suddenly the dust from the house is sucked out the windows as if by vacuum. Kalila begins to shine with colour, and the house shines around her. The furniture is restored to its former glory, and the sheets that used to cloak it float away like children dressed as ghosts for Halloween. They take with them the spiderwebs and dust bunnies, and they land on trees outside. The birds chirp in protest.

We sit on the floor under one of the waving curtains. I tell her that I went to see Rima and Mohammed Omar this morning.

Jamal had told me that Rima wanted to meet. She'd seen me through the shop window and waited till I'd left to ask him about me.

"The woman deserves to know," he said. "She deserves to move on with her child."

"I don't know what to say to her."

We were in the back room, surrounded by colourful ribbons and wrapping paper. "The world is changing around us, Wassim." Jamal steadied the scissors as they slit the paper. "She's more understanding than you think."

She would return in a couple of days, he told me, and he promised to let me know. "Look at you." Jamal signalled me to place my finger on top of the ribbon so that he could tie a beautiful knot. "You're a much better man than the one I knew from school. A much better man than the one I ran into in the park all these months ago."

He tightened the knot and used the blade of the scissors to fluff the ribbons' ends.

"Jamal is right, Wassim," Kalila says. We sit crossed-legged on the floor facing each other. "You have come a long way."

I nod and smile shyly.

Rima waited for me outside the shop. She brought Mohammed Omar with her. I hadn't seen my child in two years, and he'd grown so big. She kept his hair short, but locks of it fell on his forehead and hid his eyes. When he looked up to greet me, he extended his hand as if I were a stranger.

"Say hi to my friend, Omar," she instructed the child. Then

I could see that his eyes were bright blue, like mine. I smiled and shook his hand.

"He grew up fast," I told Rima.

"Children tend to do that."

We walked together down the street to Al-Medfaa Park. We bought ice cream for the boy and he giggled happily with the cone in his hand. "Don't spill any on your clothes. I just washed them," Rima said. We found a bench in the park and sat down.

"I've slept on this bench," I told Rima.

"I brought these with me." She pulled a folder of papers out of her purse. "I need you to sign them."

Divorce documents. My information was already filled in, and she had a copy of my ID card as well. She placed the documents in my lap and handed me a pen. I looked at the papers while Rima kept her eyes on Omar, who had finished his treat and now ran around the park between benches.

"How is he at school?" I asked her.

"He hasn't started school yet. He's only four."

"I'm sorry."

"Don't be sorry."

"But I am."

"I'm not stupid, Wassim. I know why you followed Hussam to Turkey. I know why you left and you never returned. I know why you had those panic attacks."

Blood rushed to my face. I felt my heart beating so fast it echoed in my ears. I took a deep breath and held on to my seat.

"You knew all along?"

"We were both forced into this marriage." Her voice was angry. I thought she might slap me or call me a faggot. Instead, she sighed. "Let's not bring up the past anymore." She looked at the papers. "I just need you to let me go."

I signed my name on each page. She examined the papers quickly, then placed them back in her bag.

"What will you do now?" I thought about taking her hand, but she was not my wife anymore. I had no right to touch her.

"We'll be fine. Your father said he would take care of us." She called Omar's name and he came running.

"Would you please at least tell him I'm dead?" I said.

"You silly thing." She smiled. "We already told him that."

She held Omar's hand, and they walked a few metres before he turned around and waved at me. "Goodbye, Uncle."

I waved as I watched them disappear.

"How did that make you feel?" Kalila asks. The chants from outside demanding freedom echo throughout the room.

"Honestly? It was okay."

I tell Kalila that it felt like it was the right thing to do. Rima wanted to be released from my past mistakes, and I gave her that. I didn't want to repeat my experience with Hussam. She deserves to be free from me, and my son deserves that too. In a way, I feel free of them as well. I'm no longer the anchor holding them down to a burning city. "I felt released," I say.

"You allowed them a free pass into the world we live in," Kalila says. "You are not the shame of your family. You should have never been."

"I brought them harm," I say.

"You were generous to offer them a door to be accepted into Damascus, and it is their choice to take it," she insists. "But a world where people are ashamed of who they love is not a world I want to live in."

The chants continue to fill the house. I go to the front gate and watch them marching outside. The men cover their faces with surgical masks, and the women hide their features with veils. "Come down and join the protest," they chant to the men and women watching them from the windows of nearby buildings. Some open their windows wide, others close them shut.

"Aren't they afraid of the police?" I ask.

"Maybe the time of fear is over." Kalila holds the gate open. "Maybe you should join them."

Anxiety fills my heart. I try to gather my nerve; I take one step forward, then two steps back. "I can't." I hold on to the doorknob.

"It is time." Kalila's face glows like a star. "Maybe we both paid enough for our pasts." She looks out at the protesters through the fence. Their faces are angry, yet they also sparkle with joy. There is a beauty to their gathering; it fills them with pride. They're afraid, but they feel protected among their own. "They accepted their fate for too long, and now they're filling the streets with their anger."

"Would you come with me?"

She flickers like a flashlight running out of battery, and the whole house flickers with her. "I'm not meant to leave this home."

Then, before my eyes, she transforms back into the older woman she was when I first met her, the woman she was when she died. Faint lines appear on her forehead, and her eyes lose the spark of innocence.

I hold on to her, afraid she'll disappear. "You don't need to tell me why you did it if you don't want to."

"I didn't kill myself," she says.

Kalila's last day in Damascus was in March of 1986. She was forty-one. Her husband hadn't been home in days; he had a habit of disappearing on nights they fought and returning a week or two later. She knew he had another home he lived in. She knew he had clothes that someone else was washing and ironing. Over the years she watched him gain favour with the ruling party, getting closer to the officials and ministers. She knew he spent his money throwing them gatherings and parties. She knew his business was booming.

She accepted her fate of living in the shadows of his life. She tolerated his casual visits to her home and her bed. She lay down in the middle of the bed while he lay on top of her like a starfish. He filled her bedroom with the smell of his cigarettes.

Kalila told her mother she felt abandoned by her husband, and her mother insisted that the man of the house was always right. She suggested different perfumes for Kalila to wear in his presence, stuffing to put in her bra to uplift her breasts, and nightdresses that revealed her legs and echoed the colour of her eyes. She half-heartedly tried all of these tricks, and they all failed for lack of conviction on his part and hers.

Her father, whose voice used to fill the house with orders throughout the day just as his pipe filled it with smoke throughout the night, got quieter over the years. Until one night he didn't wake up. He died days before the protests broke out in Hama, where his great-grandparents came from. Led by the Sunni majority, protestors demanded an end of the Syrian regime in Hama after multiple central neighbourhoods were emptied of their original owners and given to the Alawite families coming from seashore villages. Over the years, the Sunnis felt pushed to the outskirts of their own city. While protestors were demanding change in Syria, Kalila and her mother were living normal, almost uninterrupted lives, visiting each other once a week, commiserating about the absence of their significant others, completely unaware of the war happening in the old city.

Their first indication came weeks after the protests started. Her mother received an overseas phone call from a distant relative asking if they were all right in Damascus. "I tried to buy tomatoes yesterday," she answered, "but the market had none."

"I mean, we hear that things are happening in that other city. Are you safe?"

"What's happening in what other city?" Kalila's mother asked, and silence fell upon the phone. The relative coughed twice and changed the subject.

Then, on March 13, 1986, the conflict flared up in Damascus.

It was a cold morning, and many people wore extra layers to work. Buses gathered in the main bus loop under the Presidential Bridge. Aisle upon aisle of buses waited to bring people from their homes and send them on their usual routes to their workplaces.

Kalila heard the explosion all the way from home and ran to the second floor to look out the window. She saw a column of smoke rising from downtown and people running in the street. A man dropped his bags of groceries on the ground and rushed to find shelter. A woman with her child opened the first door she found and cowered behind it.

Kalila kept trying to call her husband, but the phone never connected. At first she got a busy signal, and eventually she could no longer get the phone to dial. She turned on the radio but all she heard were nationalistic songs that sounded like military chants.

Later that day, she'd hear from neighbours who had friends who knew people who'd seen the explosion. A bus, filled with people, had exploded downtown. It was meant to explode under the Presidential Bridge and cause it to collapse, but the timing was off. The bus became a ball of fire that shattered its glass and melted its wheels. The hands of men and women trying to escape extended out the broken windows. The fire rushed with loud screeches toward the sky. One man caught on fire and ran screaming toward others for help. People ran away from him as if he were the devil.

She learned that sixty people died on that bus, and that over a hundred more were injured.

The streets were silent that day. The people of Damascus swallowed their sins and sat at home digesting them slowly.

Rumours were whispered to one another behind closed doors. Some believed that this was an attack by the Muslim Brotherhood terrorists. These people cheered when news segments added theatrics to their reporting: bloodied terrorists, surgical military operations, epic Syrian fighters. They looked the other way when the city of Hama was completely destroyed overnight by shelling tanks.

Others believed the story told by the protesters: the regime had plotted the explosion to gain sympathy from its people. It wanted to paint the protesters as terrorists so it sacrificed the lives of sixty people for the chance to remain in power. These people's voices got quieter and quieter, until they disappeared.

Rumours would also later emerge about Kalila's death. Some said that she killed herself in shame, carrying the wayward child of another man. Others said she went insane living alone in that home all by herself. Her mother believed that her daughter slipped and fell off the railing, and mourned her in agony until the end of her own days.

What actually happened, she tells me, is that her husband came home drunk that evening. It took him hours to find a way home with all the streets closed with checkpoints. He drank a bottle of vodka that he'd hidden in his car. Officers on every corner harassed him with questions.

"I called you a million times," she said.

He waved her off and walked upstairs. "I need to take a shower. Make me something to eat."

"Come down and talk to me," she said. "The world is burning and you can't pick up the phone to call your wife."

She didn't know why she was angry. Was it the explosion shaking her own sense of her city? The fact that she couldn't get her mother on the phone or go visit her to make sure she was safe? Was it because he never called? Did she feel alone and abandoned? Did she feel the city was a stranger strangling her?

"I won't make you dinner!" she shouted. "Go back to your mistress and let her feed you."

He stopped climbing the stairs and turned to her. "What did you just say?" he shouted.

"I know you. I know what you are!" she shouted back.

"I keep you despite you being barren, and this is what I hear from you?"

He rushed to her room, and she followed. He rampaged through like a rhino, breaking everything in his path. She stood silently, waiting for his rage to subside.

"You are not a good woman!" he screamed at her. The mirror across from her reflected the burning men and women inside a bus.

"I'm leaving you," she finally said. She sat down at her vanity and ignored him while he broke vases and kicked furniture behind her. She did her makeup and tightened her hijab over her head. "I'm going back to my mother's."

She left the room and soon after felt a rush of air at her back. As she turned, she saw him charging toward her, belt in hand, ready to strike.

She stepped out of his way and lost her balance by the railing, slipping down the stairs. She felt a gasp of air stuck in her lungs as the back of her head slammed into the floor. The last she saw was her husband's face, looking down at her from the railing.

The regime officials accused her husband of working with the Hama terrorists, and he disappeared into the halls of Syrian dungeons, never to be heard from again. Rumours circulated for a while that he wasn't involved at all but that a close relative of the president wanted to end a market competition between them and asked the right people for the right favour. That rumour soon was forgotten, like the protests in Hama, like the sixty people who died in that bus, like Kalila and her mother. Like this house.

"Don't be forgotten, Wassim," she says. She becomes a fog that engulfs me. "Don't swallow your sins." Her voice echoes in my head. My own face reflects in hers. I hug her mist closer to me. For the first time, I can feel her in my arms, warm like a cup of coffee in my hands on a cold morning. Her arms cross behind me, and she squeezes.

"I'll miss you," I say.

"You'll meet me again soon enough, kid." She glimmers one last time, and fades away.

I look around the house as it's drained of its colour. The dust returns to its windows, and the white sheets float like ghosts and settle on the furniture. I smile at the sight of decay. It leaves me with joy knowing that this home welcomed me with warmth.

I leave my shadows behind me and walk out of the house. Each step is an echo. When I reach the gate I glance back. The house looks as though it hasn't been lived in for years. Vines climbing its walls, their leaves dried on its windows, curtains shielding its secrets.

I pass through the rusty gate that never closed properly and join the crowd. Their clothes are colourful, like a river reflecting a sunset. A woman with a veil covering her face hands me a shawl and tells me to cover up. I smell jasmine and mothballs as I tighten it around my face. I walk with them, shoulder to shoulder. We hear the distant sirens, but we march forward. Chins up to the sky, voices filled with pride, eyes tearing. The man next to me trips, and I grab him before he falls and lift him up.

"It's a beautiful day to revolt," he says. I nod. I raise my fist to the sky.

2017

If either of them had been asked, both Hussam and Wassim would say that they were the one to initiate contact after all these years.

Hussam was riding a bus on Hastings, heading to East Van for his weekly therapy session. He scrolled listlessly on his phone while listening to Tracy Chapman on his headphones. Between targeted ads and Chapman's plaintive vibrato, he stumbled upon a photo posted by Jamal. Hussam, who'd blocked most of his Syrian contacts when he got to Canada, had unblocked Jamal on Facebook a couple of months earlier but had yet to interact with him. It was a typical group pose for a birthday party in an old Damascene café in Bab Touma. Jamal was in the middle, his arm resting on the shoulder of a beautiful brown-haired woman. Paper hats on their heads, party horns in the hands of those around them, an elaborate Black Forest cake on the table. Hussam almost paid the photo no mind, mumbling along to lyrics he only half knew. But instead of scrolling past, he lingered on the image.

He realized Wassim was in the background.

Hussam zoomed in on the face obscured behind the others. Wassim looked content with his beer, uninterested in joining the group photo. He sat on a couch with two other men. His hair was thinner and shorter, and he'd grown his beard long enough to get him random security checks at airports. The blue eyes were impossible to forget, though. Hussam would recognize them anywhere. He tapped the photo, to see if Wassim's Facebook profile was tagged, but it wasn't.

Hussam scrolled the comments, his heartbeat louder than the bus's frequent announcements, but he didn't see Wassim's name there either. He combed through the many profiles in Jamal's long list of friends until he finally found an account with Wassim's name written in Arabic. The account lacked any physical evidence of Wassim: the profile photo was a beautifully decorated gift box with colourful ribbons tied up around it like early summer flowers. A pair of scissors rested artfully beside it. He scrolled up and down the profile, but it was completely empty. No photos to be seen, no public posts to be read, no links to funny YouTube videos of puppies or kittens.

He realized he'd missed his stop. He jumped out the back door and ran under the heavy Vancouver rain, knowing damn well that Wassim would feature extensively in today's therapy session.

Wassim, on the opposite end of the world, was naked in bed in the home he shared with four gay men in Bab Sharqi. It was almost two in the morning, and he should have been asleep for hours, as it was his shift to open up shop tomorrow. But Jamal's birthday party lasted until the unofficial curfew at eleven, and Wassim's boyfriend had to spend the night. They made love to the background of war noise coming from the nearby rebel neighbourhoods of Jubar and Jaramana, the smacks of their lips louder than explosions and blitz.

Wassim had been dating Asmar for almost a year by then, after mutual friends elbowed them together into a blind date. Wassim showed up to their first date anxious, feet dragging. Asmar showed up freshly shaven with a shy smile. They discussed the war, hushed by the looks of people around them, as well as a soap opera Wassim had never heard of and their mutual appreciation of the Lebanese singer Fairouz. A stray orange cat cozied up to Asmar in the café, and he absentmindedly stroked her back while intently listening to Wassim. The softness in his eyes, and the way the cat arched her back to enjoy the tips of Asmar's fingers, endeared him to Wassim almost instantly.

Jamal's birthday party music still reverberated in Wassim's ears, keeping him up. He tossed and turned, lulled by the soft snoring of his man, until it was clear his mind needed a distraction. He turned on his phone and searched the internet for fun and cheap ways to celebrate his approaching one-year anniversary with Asmar.

A candlelit dinner would be dangerous in this city where they pretended to be close friends. Maybe instead he would borrow a dinner table from one of his roommates, buy some candles with his employee discount at the gift shop, and cook a meal for Asmar at home. Roll him some rice and ground meat in grape leaves, or even bake him a cake. How hard could it be?

Finally, sleep pulled on Wassim's eyelids. He was about to call it a night when a Facebook notification appeared on his cracked screen. He clicked on the icon repeatedly, promising to buy himself a new phone with his next paycheque. He saw it was just an algorithmically generated People You Might Know notification. He huffed in annoyance. He was about to turn off his phone when he realized the profile was Hussam's.

His name appeared in English, followed by the Arabic version in parentheses. The profile photo showed him in a puffy parka with a fur-lined hood, hands in his pockets, a wool cap covering his hair and ears. He was smiling shyly at the camera.

Wassim quietly pushed himself up in bed, trying not to wake Asmar. He spent the next half hour poring through post after post in English commenting on Canadian immigration policies, the weather in Vancouver, or tagging friends in funny videos that Wassim avoiding clicking on, fearing he might wake Asmar. He found a photo of Hussam sunbathing on a sandy bay with logs lining its shore, laughing in another beside a drag queen who towered over him, and one from a year ago with Hussam in a busy hall adorned with Canadian flags, wearing a fancy suit and holding a citizenship certificate proudly, eyes red with tears.

Asmar mumbled in his sleep and rolled onto his side to avoid the light coming from Wassim's phone. Wassim smiled, turned off his phone, and softly caressed his boyfriend's shoulder. Moments later, he pulled his phone back out, aware that it was almost four in the morning. He reopened Facebook, requested Hussam's friendship, and went back to sleep.

The friend request sat unanswered for a bit over a year. Every once in a while, Hussam would go through his notifications and find the request, then visit the private profile of Wassim, empty of any indication that someone was monitoring it. Every few weeks, Wassim would visit Hussam's profile, creeping on public photos and reading posts about places he'd never heard of. Many times he gazed at the deserted request and considered deleting it. Neither of them dared to answer the faint line of communication, but they didn't dare sever it either.

The friend request remained a topic of conversation in the weekly sessions between Hussam and his therapist, who one day advised him that maybe it was time for him to make a decision.

"There's no right answer here," the therapist said, while Hussam combed the small sandbox on her desk with a tiny wooden fork. "You can decide to accept the friend request, or delete it, or keep it there until the end of days. You just have to be comfortable with what you decide."

The therapist was the one Dawood had suggested back in 2014, and they'd been steadily seeing each other ever since. She was there when he bawled his eyes out talking about his father's death, and she helped him prepare for his conversation with Michael and Brian about his need to slow down. She named his post-traumatic stress disorder and helped him iron out his triggers. "Therapy is not miracle work," she told him. "There's no way for us to anticipate triggers. We can only prepare you to know how to handle them with care for yourself and others."

Almost sixteen months after the friend request was made, Hussam sat in a corner booth at Junction watching the finale of *RuPaul's Drag Race* projected onto a wall. He was surrounded by his circle of friends, many he'd made through Dawood, including a couple of other drag queens who weren't performing that night. Next to him, Michael and his new boyfriend cheered the loudest for Rachel Minority's hosting skills. Ray was there, too, sitting on the other side of the stage with two friends. Hussam caught his eye, and Ray nodded, smiled, then looked away.

That night, Rachel pulled Hussam onstage. "This man has been Canadian for two years," she announced. "Give him some love on his Canaversary." She pulled him in for a side hug.

"I can give him love tonight, if he wants," someone quipped, and the audience laughed. Hussam locked eyes with the tall white man, a bit older than him, and chuckled bashfully.

"How about we sing him 'Happy Birthday'?" Rachel asked the audience.

"It's not my birthday," Hussam protested, but the audience launched into the song nonetheless. They sang off-key, and he retreated into Rachel's embrace, avoiding eye contact with the handsome tall man.

"Wishing you the most peaceful year ahead, habibi," Rachel whispered away from the mic. Hussam air-kissed her, knowing by now not to ruin her makeup. By the time he returned to the booth, he'd already pulled out his phone and accepted Wassim's friend request.

On the other side of the world, Wassim's still-cracked screen silently lit up with the notification, but he was sleeping.

With the tangerine light of dawn sneaking through the curtains of his bedroom window, Wassim nuzzled up to Asmar. They'd been together for over two years by then, and Asmar had moved out of his parents' home, despite their objections, and moved in with Wassim. Asmar was studying to be a dentist but dreaded the end of his university years and even intentionally failed some of his courses. He knew that when he finished his studies, the regime would send him to the front line to fight the rebels and the terrorists. "You're lucky you're an only child," Asmar had once said to Wassim, sitting in the back room of the gift shop. "No one can force you to come back to the army."

"The government thinks I'm dead, anyway," Wassim said.

"You look pretty much alive to me."

Wassim smirked and focused on the gift in his hands.

Jamal had suggested they try to smuggle themselves into Lebanon to avoid service, but Wassim was reluctant. "You remember what happened last time I crossed the Syrian border, yeah?" His voice broke as if he'd just swallowed a gallon of salt water.

"That was then, this is now," Asmar said.

"Not everything you do will end up in a disaster," Jamal added.

Wassim shook his head and changed the subject.

Even with the friendship now established on Facebook, a year passed with only some indirect communication between Hussam and Wassim.

Hussam, finally able to see Wassim's private profile, was disappointed that nothing much was revealed to him. Wassim kept his posts to a minimum. His friend list tallied a meagre eight people: Jamal, Asmar, his four roommates, Jamal's fiancée, and now Hussam. There was a photo with Asmar, and another with Jamal; neither had a caption. The large cover photo was one Wassim had taken of an abandoned villa in Damascus's old district, and there were a few spiritual posts honouring the soul of a Syrian woman who had died in the 1980s, though Wassim's connection to her was unclear.

When Hussam shared his dilemma with Dawood, he couldn't explain why he couldn't just pick up the phone and call Wassim. They were out for a walk in the alleys of the West End, March's purple blossoms raining on them in the breeze.

"Did you know that monarch butterflies immigrate, too?" Dawood said. "Every year, they escape the cold weather and head down south for warmer days. They take the exact same route genetically mapped within their existence."

Hussam listened with uncertainty while Dawood explained that scientists had discovered that butterflies travel in straight lines, except for in one exact spot, the same spot every year, where they take a huge half-circle detour, avoiding a specific area.

"The scientists were baffled," Dawood said. "Why would they avoid flying over that one spot? Why would they add days to their trip despite their short lifespan?" The scientists, Dawood said, finally figured it out: millennia ago, a mountain stood tall where that flat land now was, and the butterflies used to travel around it. The world changed, earthquakes shook the land, and the mountain fell to rubble, but the butterflies continued on the route embedded in their minds since the dawn of their history. "The butterflies avoided the hardship for so long, they couldn't imagine it not being there anymore." A lavender petal landed on Dawood's forehead.

"Where are we going with this?" Hussam asked.

Dawood laughed. "There will come a time when you'll figure that out by yourself."

Wassim considered calling Hussam over Facebook Messenger many times but never mustered the courage to do so. Instead, he spent the year sporadically liking Hussam's posts and photos, offering a quick congratulations when Hussam changed his status to In a Relationship with a handsome white man, then a series of purple heart emojis when, six months later, the status returned to Single.

"You should call him," Asmar told him one evening as they walked down Hamra Street to get shawarma after Wassim's shift. It was early summer, and the breeze zigzagging through the mountains whispered soft late-night songs in their ears. Wassim was wearing his favourite T-shirt, a yellow one with pink flamingos and palm fronds. It used to be too big on him, but over the years he'd begun to fill it out.

"And say what?" Wassim said. "Hi, hey, yeah. I'm the guy who accidentally killed your father. How's the weather in Vancouver?"

"Don't be an idiot." Asmar elbowed him playfully. "Also, get yourself a new phone. That screen has been broken for two years."

"It works!"

"It's a miracle you can still see anything on it. Call him before this phone explodes in your hand."

They arrived at the shawarma place and waited for the chef to finish with the customers ahead of them.

"Honestly, my love," Asmar whispered after ordering, "you both fucked up so bad that there's no place for blame anymore."

Wassim hummed in agreement but didn't reply. They waited silently until the chef handed them each a sandwich.

"Hey, do I know you?" he asked. Wassim smiled and waved goodbye before walking away with Asmar, arm in arm.

Mending his broken heart took Hussam a couple of months. He wallowed, and blamed himself for the breakup, despite his friends' assurances that it wasn't his fault. He missed five therapy sessions and stopped going to Rachel Minority's weekly shows. He left his small rented apartment only for shifts at the Welcome Centre, translating between newly arriving Syrian refugees and doctors, dentists, and bank clerks. He loved it when Syrian women made him Damascene dishes as their way of saying thanks, or kissed his forehead and wished him a good wife and strong offspring.

"You are very handsome," a recent arrival whispered to Hussam in broken English. The man was younger than Hussam, with long eyelashes and skin still kissed by the sun back home. They were alone in the Welcome Centre hallway, waiting for the elevator.

"I speak Arabic," Hussam said in his mother tongue.

"I should have known." The boy eyed Hussam's name tag, with its little rainbow flag in the corner. "My name is Gabe."

Hussam chuckled. "Is it, though?"

The boy reddened. He jammed his fists into his pockets and swayed like a boat. "No," he said. "It's Ghassan, but no one can say it correctly here, so . . ."

"Friend." Hussam tapped the young man's shoulder. "Let them learn."

Ghassan smiled. "Now's about the time when my curfew at the refugee camp back in Jordan used to be," he said. "Us gays wouldn't spend the night outside our tents. You never knew who might be watching."

Hussam cocked his head, examining the boy. His shoulders were getting tenser, his fists dug deeper inside his pockets, and his features stretched on his face as if someone were pulling the skin by his temples.

"Once I was jumped by three other refugees and a Jordanian guard."

The elevator dinged, and Ghassan stepped in. "Are you coming?" he asked.

Ghassan's hair bounced joyfully when he turned around, his jawline anchored with fuzzy clusters of beard hair, his smile too mature for his age. The heavy jacket he wore in June was endearing and reminded Hussam of his early days in Canada. He could feel the boy between his arms. *Hard nipples, soft skin, parted lips*. Their clash would be glorious, he thought. Who cares that it might leave both of them shattered on the ground? Who cares if it agitated their skin and awakened their wounds? In the elevator, the ghost of his father appeared alongside Ghassan. He wasn't bloodied like he used to be, but a smile still revealed some missing and crooked teeth.

"I— I think— I better take the stairs." Hussam waved a quick goodbye. The elevator doors began to slide shut. "Take care of yourself, Ghassan."

As he walked down the stairs, Hussam texted his therapist, apologized, and confirmed his next session.

It took Wassim four more months to finally pick up his cracked phone and call Hussam.

He'd dropped Asmar that very morning at the bus station. Jamal had secured a counterfeit Syrian ID for him so he could cross the border to Beirut without being arrested for deserting his military service. For weeks the lovers had argued: Asmar wanted Wassim to use his years-old forged ID from Jamal to cross with him to Lebanon, but Wassim was adamant that he wanted to stay.

"I love you," Wassim finally said, tired of the endless conversation. He pulled Asmar in for a hug, and they rested back on the bed they'd shared for over three years.

"Why would you break us up?" Asmar said, his voice unsteady.

"Habibi." Asmar's heartbeat knocked against his rib cage. "I'm not doing this to us, my love. I'm doing this for me."

Wassim felt Asmar's body relaxing in his arms. He tightened his embrace around him, and Asmar let out a tearful sigh.

"I love you more than I have ever loved anyone in my whole life," Wassim said. "But this is my place. This is my home. I have to let you go for your own good. I have to stay for mine."

They embraced at the bus station, aware of the eyes of the bus drivers and passengers. They held hands for a moment too long, and Jamal in the background forced a cough to break their gaze. Wassim picked up Asmar's lone suitcase and helped him tie it up on the roof rack. They quickly embraced once more, and Asmar boarded the bus.

In Jamal's car, Wassim cried. He cried and cursed and shouted. He cussed the civil war that wouldn't give him a moment of peace, the regime throwing the children of Syria into the war oven, and the impossible life he led.

"War has its hands in everything, Jamal," Wassim shouted through tears. "It's in my morning commute and in my evening stroll. It's in the food I eat and the coffee I drink. War has infused every aspect of my life. The conversations with friends, the place I call home. It's in the jets dotting the night sky and the call for prayer interrupted by an explosion."

Jamal nodded and drove.

"All I want is to be in this place I call home, and to be with the man I love. Is that too much to ask? Is it too big of a sin?"

"You could have left with him," Jamal said quietly.

"Why do I have to abandon my land? Why do I have to go into exile for my life to make sense?"

Jamal tapped his thigh, then returned his hand to the wheel. He took a deep inhale. "We're about to reach the checkpoint." He handed Wassim a tissue.

Wassim blew his nose and checked his eyes in the little mirror on the back of the sunshield. Soon they were faking smiles for the bored teenage soldier checking their IDs.

Jamal wanted to give Wassim the day off, but he insisted on working, saying that if he went home to his empty room he'd go insane with mourning. In the evening he walked the old alleyways of Bab Sharqi alone before going home. His room-mates weren't home yet, so he climbed the stairs to the rooftop, which they'd turned into a small garden. The view was obstructed by the tall buildings that had been built in the past few decades, crowding around their traditional Damascene home. Clotheslines intertwined in one corner, and the leaves of various plants tangled in another, surrounding a rocking chair and a large wooden sofa they'd salvaged from a garbage dump. Wassim sat on the rocking chair, which creaked under his weight. He rarely smoked, but one of his roommates had left a pack with one last cigarette by the ashtray on the table. He pulled it out, examined it between his fingers, then lit it. He coughed and watched the cloud of smoke he exhaled rise up into the night sky.

Wassim held his phone for a moment, examining Hussam's latest profile photo. He then aggressively stumped his finger on the cracked screen until the app responded, and he saw the screen turn blue and heard the ring.

It was five in the afternoon on a Sunday in July when Hussam's phone rang.

He'd volunteered to drive Rachel Minority to the East Van Family Pride event she was hosting and performing at. Hussam spent the afternoon sitting on the grass in front of the stage, watching queer, trans, and two-spirit artists perform.

Afterwards he sat in Dawood's living room making plans to meet friends to watch the sunset on English Bay with well-concealed sparkling wine and snacks. The boys were already on their way to the beach, but he wanted to wait for Rachel, who was transforming back into Dawood in the shower. He was asking in the group chat if he should bring Settlers of Catan for yet another game when his phone rang.

Wassim stared at his screen. The pulsing blue, indicating that the phone was ringing, continued for an eternity. He wondered if Hussam would pick up, then began to calculate the time difference in his head to ensure he was calling at a decent hour. Before he could finish his calculations, the screen changed, and Hussam's voice came from the other end.

"Hello?" Hussam said, then switched to Arabic. "Umm, marhaba?"

"Is this . . . is this a good time?" Wassim stumbled on his words. He heard the whizzing of an airplane overhead, but when he looked up, it wasn't visible in the night sky.

"I don't know," Hussam said. He felt a tightness in his chest, as if a whole walnut was stuck in his windpipe. He jolted to stand and forced his right leg to stop shaking. "How are you?" he asked.

Silence fell on them. Hussam lifted the phone from his ear to make sure he hadn't lost the connection. He could hear Wassim's breathing on the other end.

Wassim dipped the cigarette in the muddy leftover coffee in his little cup and heard it fizz in the liquid. "I can see the smoke," he said.

"Huh?"

"There's a blitz on a nearby neighbourhood. I can see the columns of smoke rushing through the sky."

Hussam felt cold sweat on his fingers; he worried his phone might slip out of his hand. Through Dawood's window, he could see pigeons flying in the early evening sun, gliding the winds through the buildings, finding power in numbers when a black crow attempted to break their circles. He thought he should mention this to his childhood friend, but then thought better of it.

"Are you okay?" he asked instead.

"I'm all right." Wassim paused, coughed, and then rested his back on the rocking chair. "I'm good. I am. Are you okay?"

"I think so," Hussam replied.

Silence returned. Hussam could hear the air strikes echoing in the background. They sounded like the ticking of a clock's second hand: soft and repetitive, almost eternal. He held on to the windowpane.

"Okay, this was fun," Wassim finally said. "We should do it more often."

Hussam could hear the playfulness in his voice. He chuckled. "Yeah. I can't wait to share more awkward silence with you."

"Don't be a jerk," Wassim said. They laughed, tears gathering in their eyes. By the end of their laughter, they both sighed.

"I thought you were dead," Hussam said, his voice low and quiet. "I'm— I'm sorry."

Wassim held his breath. He thought of the dark waters swallowing him, the waves that hit his face mercilessly as he attempted to get back to the boat, and the salt he coughed up on the shore. He thought of Kalila standing in the window of her home, curtains waving at him as she smiled, her colours slowly fading away. He thought of Jamal's tenderness when he passed him his first change of clothes, and of Asmar's face in the bus, tears guarded in his eyes as he waved goodbye.

"I honestly think it was better that way for both of us," Wassim said.

"Ready to go?" Dawood appeared out of the shower, drying his hair with a hand towel. Hussam turned around, eyes red with tears, and showed Dawood who was on the phone.

"Is that your boyfriend?" Wassim asked.

Hussam felt Wassim's arms around him, as if they were back on the floor of the room in Istanbul. He felt Arda's warm palm on his neck, the chill of Ray's apartment, the pressure of the leather swing against his back. "No. Dawood is my good friend." He felt Dawood's arms embracing him.

Just then Wassim's roommates returned home, calling his name and bearing fried chicken leftovers from the restaurant one of them worked at. Wassim rushed to the rooftop's perimeter wall and gestured that he'd be right down. "I'm sorry," he said. "I honestly don't know why I called. I just . . ."

"It's okay. I'm happy to hear your voice."

"I guess I— I want to apologize."

"You don't have to."

"I'm sorry I didn't let go of you all those years ago."

Hussam felt Dawood's hands guiding him to sit on the

couch. He didn't realize how tense his body was until he felt Dawood massage his upper back. "I don't understand," he said.

"I should never have followed you to Turkey." Wassim felt his body shake, but didn't bother to gather himself anymore. "I shouldn't have forced myself into your life over and over again."

"Honestly, friend," Hussam said, "if we're going to count mistakes and collect apologies, we'll be here all night."

Silence returned once more, but this time it felt easy and soft. They smiled at the same time, divided by continents and oceans.

"We should do this more often," Wassim said again.

"Yeah," Hussam replied.

The conversation meandered into pleasantries; they dried their eyes and laughed at each other's jokes from the heart. They hung up promising to call each other again soon. Wassim's cracked phone finally gave in, and with his final touch to end the call, its screen sparked, then darkened. He rushed down the stairs to catch his share of fried chicken. Hussam's phone brought him back to his group chat and Catan. He leaned on Dawood and closed his eyes. Soon, he fell asleep, as if he needed to catch up on comfort he'd been denied for the longest time.

ACKNOWLEDGMENTS

It takes a village to finish a novel, and to my community of friends, writers, advisors, and lovers, I am eternally thankful.

To my mentor John Vigna, who opened his office door and welcomed me when I was burdened with fears and self-doubt. He learned about my culture and heritage, empathized with my lived experience, and was truly instrumental in turning this vision we scribbled together one day on a whiteboard into an actual living and breathing novel.

If I am the artist shouting poetics in the village's public square, Rachel Letofsky is the architect who keeps the village running. I am truly thankful for the hard work, the commitment, and the endless support Rachel offered. I couldn't ask for a better agent (or friend!). So much appreciation to her and to everyone at CookeMcDermid.

When I was asked who is my dream editor to work with, David Ross's name topped the list. I am beyond grateful for the care and attention to details he brought to this book. Queer joy is so rare in this world, and I felt it working with him every step of the way. Much love to him, and to everyone at Penguin Canada, for believing in my work.

Thank you to Canongate UK's Ellah Wakatama Allfrey for believing in my novel across oceans, loving it from the moment she heard of it, and offering me the space to thrive with it.

Thank you to my best friend, Cee Rouhana, for being the keeper of my sanity, to Tash McAdams for believing in me, to Samantha MacDonald for being my first reader, to Andrew McDonnell for walking me through my many drafts, and to Bradley Babcock for his endless support.

To my writing community at the University of British Columbia, namely Annabel Lyon, Alix Ohlin, Sharon McGowan, and Emily Pohl-Weary, as well as my friends Erin Kirsh, Napatsi Folger, Jaz Papadopoulos, and Anaïsa Visser. I couldn't have done this without you.

I also want to thank all the different organizations that supported me during the process of writing this book. Thank you to the Canada Council for the Arts and the BC Arts Council. Also, a huge thank you to the Saskatoon Public Library for allowing me to be their virtual writer in residence for the 2020-21 season.

I arrived in Canada as a refugee in 2014, and I was so alone it hurt, then I found the drag community in Vancouver and my life changed for the better. Thank you to Jaylene Tyme, Kendall Gender, Maiden China, Gloria Hole, Carmella Barr, Raye Sunshine, Alma Bitches, and all the other wonderful folks in the drag community who helped me find a home here.

Finally, to my husband, Matthew Ramadan, who had the good sense to leave me to my writing, and took on much of the stresses of planning our wedding, our move to a new home, and ordering my favourite wines. For every cup of coffee he brought me without asking, and every time he draped a blanket over my shoulders in the chilly morning hours, I am thankful. Above all, for truly, authentically, and generously believing in me, I am thankful.

The Foghorn Echoes is set in Monotype Van Dijck, a face originally designed by Christoffel van Dijck, a Dutch typefounder (and sometime goldsmith) of the seventeenth century. While the roman font may not have been cut by van Dijck himself; the italic, for which original punches survive, is almost certainly his work. The face first made its appearance circa 1606. It was re-cut for modern use in 1937.